Sarah stood out on the lawn, watching David's big yellow Cadillac move slowly down the drive. She grew angry thinking about David's plans to separate her from Martin — and as she did, her eyes began to shine.

Inside the car, David felt a resistance from the wheel. He tried unsuccessfully to turn it the other way. Suddenly his foot moved to the gas petal, increasing the speed to sixty, seventy, eighty.

Now Sarah was insisde the car with them. She could see their faces twisted with fright; she could hear their screams.

"God, no! Help us!"

"No one can help you," she told them.

They hit a tree and the huge car crumpled like a cheap tin can. David was killed instantly, but Monica was not: glass from the windshield went straight to her face, cutting it severely. She was alive, but her face was a bleeding lump of pulpy flesh. And one large, jagged piece of glass was sticking out where an eye had been.

Sarah had seen it all and smiled as the ambulances approached to remove the human wreckage . . .

READ THESE HORRIFYING BEST SELLERS!

Cherron

By Sharon Combes

ZEBRA BOOKS

KENSINGTON PUBLISHING CORP.

ZEBRA BOOKS

are published by

KENSINGTON PUBLISHING CORP.
21 East 40th Street
New York, N.Y. 10016

Printed in the United States of America

*To my mother and father, without whose love
and help this book would not have
been written*

Prologue

The large silver-gray fish made their way smoothly through the clear blue water. There were almost fifty of them. They all looked the same, with large, blunt heads and flattened bodies about two to three feet long. But it was the mouths that distinguished them, the strong, triangular jaws and the sharp, pointed white teeth.

The two oldest fish were the source of all the rest. This male and female had traveled a long way from the warmth of their native Amazon River. It had not been a voluntary journey. They and their brothers and sisters had been taken by a man and carried far away. The man had given them to some children. The other fish had disappeared then, so that for a long time only they two remained, alone together.

The boy child and the girl child had placed them here in this green stone-lined pool. Now they were surrounded by their progeny. The pool was so large that it never seemed crowded, and several times each day the boy and girl—grown to a man and woman now—would come to feed them.

The older fish stared at each other now, silently communicating their restlessness. It had been too long since they had had the challenge of a live victim. Things had been quiet in the house. All that the man and woman had brought them was raw meat.

But not today.

Sensing a disturbance, they listened carefully. Soon they could hear screams outside the pool. The fish began to thrash about, leaping above the surface of the water for a glimpse of what was going on. The man and woman were arguing with another woman. They were standing by the edge of the pool, shouting.

The fish assured each other that it would not be long.

The woman moved to leave, but the man grabbed her arm, scratching her so that her arm began to bleed. Then she was in the pool.

The old male fish saw her first, as her long, slim legs began treading water, searching for the bottom of the pool. He signaled the others but they needed no signal. The scent of blood had already sent them into a frenzy.

Fifty silver-gray fish moved swiftly towards the thrashing, splashing woman. Their mouths were pulled back, baring sharp white teeth.

The old male made the first bite, his strong jaws tearing into her rich, salty flesh. It had been so long since he had tasted the exquisite flavor of human flesh. Too long. And this was female flesh, soft and plump. The flesh of men was too often tough and muscular.

The others closed in, tearing away the rest of the screaming woman. In a few minutes it was all over, and all that remained were the whitened bones slowly sinking to the bottom of the pool. Gradually the dark, turbulent water became clear and calm once more.

Sated, the fish moved slowly through the blue-green water, swimming contentedly amongst the clean bones. All was peaceful.

Until the next time.

Chapter One

It was early spring in Gadsden County, and the sun glistened on the tall trees as if reflecting millions of tiny diamonds. Sarah Bankroft stood on the verandah of Cherron watching as her cousin Martin hoisted the large cases of Coca Cola and lemonade into the dusty Dodge pickup truck parked in the circular driveway in front of the house. Skip and Jubal, the two great black Labradors, stood by panting, obviously hoping that he would take them along for a ride.

Cherron overlooked one thousand acres of north Florida's richest tobacco country and seemed much as it had when it was built by Miss Sarah's great-great-grandfather in 1850. Hurricanes, family tragedies and even civil war had left little mark on Cherron. And now it all belonged to her.

The house was a grand building in the Greek Revival style. It was two stories high, but it seemed taller because the ceilings inside were eighteen-feet high. The roof of the verandah extended over the east and west wings, supported by four Corinthean columns in front and three on each side. It sheltered a marble floor that ran the length of the front of the house. There was a huge front door of mahogany and stained glass, and French doors at each side led to the two wings of the house.

Cherron had recently been given a fresh coat of white paint, but the crisp look was softened by the abundance of trees and flowers around the house. Fragrant jasmine vines climbed up the walls, and much of the house was shaded by pecan and magnolia trees.

A few yards from the house stood the stables and the tennis court, and beyond them, surrounded by a simple iron fence, was the Bankroft family graveyard. To the east was the great pine forest, to the west the old swamp. North was Route 39 and south lay the rich tobacco fields, source of much of the Bankroft family fortune.

Sarah Bankroft was rightfully proud of Cherron. At twenty-five she ran it as skillfully as any of the previous Bankrofts had, if not better. With the help of her cousin Martin she supervised the planting, curing, and selling of their valuable crop of Sumatra tobacco. Some people thought it was funny that a beautiful and feminine woman raised cigar-wrapper tobacco, but they didn't laugh when her leaves fetched top dollar at the Gadsden County auction every fall.

Martin Bankroft smiled when he realized that she was watching him. She was a beautiful young woman. Her long blond hair was pinned back from her face, revealing a magnolia-white complexion, an upturned nose, and eyes the haunting blue of the Florida waters. She was wearing a simple pink cotton dress that showed her perfect figure, and to Martin she seemed as delicate as a tiny bird.

He himself would have been a handsome man were it not for his taut jaw and for the lines of pain prematurely etched in his brow. His hair was thick and black, his eyes soft and brown. He was about six-feet tall, and his face had turned a nut-brown from the long hours spent supervising the Cherron workers in the tobacco fields. He wore a light-weight plain shirt and tan Levis. Only field hands wore blue jeans, and the Bankrofts were not field hands.

He watched as his cousin stepped down the marble steps.

"Martin," she called to him, "I just want to check my roses!"

She walked to the rose garden where roses of every size and color — red, yellow, pink, white, even purple, lush American Beauties, and delicate Royal Highnesses — abounded. Climbing roses almost obscured the white picket fence that surrounded them.

How she loves those roses! he thought.

Miss Sarah's garden was the envy of every woman in Gadsden County. They all wanted to know how Miss Sarah could grow them so large, so wondrous, year after year.

"What was her secret?" they all asked him. "*What did she* use?"

13

If only they knew.

He watched her as she picked a pink rose and pinned it in her hair. Then she walked towards him, just as he placed the last carton of Dixie cups beside the Cokes. He let the dogs jump in beside the boxes and slammed the back of the pick up shut.

"Everything ready, Martin?" she said.

"Yes, everything."

"Good, shall we go?"

As he helped her up and inside the truck she tugged at her dress so as not to catch it in the door.

"You'll ruin that dress," he warned her.

"Never mind me. The men are waiting."

He smiled. That was so like Sarah, more concerned about the people who worked for her than about her own comfort. The rest of the Bankrofts never gave a damn about their workers. They cared about no one but themselves. It was different now that Miss Sarah was mistress of Cherron.

From her upstairs room, Jessica Bankroft Morrow watched her niece and nephew as they drove in the pickup truck down the long, tree-lined drive. She was a tall, stately woman, but she looked old beyond her years. Her steel-gray hair was pulled back in a bun and her eyes were sad and troubled. She was alone in the house now, except for her son, who stood listlessly beside her. Devon was fifteen years old, but for all the interest he showed in life he might have been dead.

Still, she was alone in the house and that was something. Perhaps she would make her move now. She would take a look at the room and find out what was down there.

Martin and Sarah had warned her often enough to stay out of there, but it was her house too. After all, she was a Bankroft, she had been born here. She had every right to enter any room she chose.

She decided that as soon as Devon dozed off she would take a look at that basement room.

The road was dry and dust flew up from the wheels of the old vehicle as they made their way past the curing barns and down towards the tobacco fields. It was a short drive from the great house to the fields, but no other Bankrofts had ever seen fit to make it.

"Remember," her father used to tell her. "You are a Bankroft. You are superior to those field hands. You are to have nothing to do with them. Those are my orders."

No, the others would never approve. But they were not here to frown on her kindnesses. They could see, but they could no longer express their disapproval.

"What were you thinking about?" Martin asked her.

"About when I was a child. Do you remember how ugly I was as a child, Martin?"

"You were never ugly."

She studied his face as he concentrated on the road. "No, you never thought so, did you?"

"Never. You were always beautiful to me."

Dear, dear Martin. He always stood up for her as a child. Always on her side. She touched his leathery cheek, and he smiled back at her.

As they drew closer to the field, she watched as five tractor-like machines each pulled two men along on seats close to the ground, while the men inserted the tobacco seedlings into freshly dug holes.

In the nearby fields, where the planting had already been completed, other men were erecting cheesecloth shelters to shade and protect the tobacco leaves.

Martin stopped the truck in the shade of a live oak tree. He lifted her onto the back platform, and she clapped her hands for attention.

"Gentlemen," she shouted. "It's time to take a break. The day is dry and your throats must be filled with dust. Come, drink. We have lemonade and Cokes."

The field hands looked up and smiled. They always did when they saw Miss Sarah. Quickly, they put down their tools and walked towards her, led by a large black man of about sixty. His hair was white and his brown eyes sparkled with affection when he saw Miss Sarah.

"You shouldn't do this, Miss Sarah," old Jeremiah told her.

"And why not, may I ask?"

"No one else in the family ever done it."

"Perhaps that's reason enough, Jeremiah. Besides, I enjoy it."

"You have nothin' to make up for, Miss Sarah. The others, it's on their souls. They were—"

"Jeremiah," she cut him off. "It's not nice to speak ill of the dead. I'm sure they're paying a

16

heavy price for their sins." She handed him a cold Dixie cup. "Here, I know how much you like my homemade lemonade."

The old man took the glass gratefully, smiled, and moved on. Next came a young black man. This was his first season at Cherron.

"I hope you enjoy working here." Miss Sarah smiled at him as she handed him a bottle of Coke.

"I think I'll like it a lot," he said, and grinned.

"I'm very glad to hear that," she said. "Will we be seeing you at the Cherron party tomorrow?"

"Yes, ma'am," he assured her, eagerly.

The young man, whose name was Clifford Williams, joined old Jeremiah in the shade of the oak tree.

"She's nice," he said, sitting beside the old man.

"Yes, sir, boy. You're lucky you're working at Cherron now, with Miss Sarah. You wouldn't've liked it here before. Why this ball she gives every year for us workers—you never saw nothin' like that from the rest of the Bankrofts."

They sat in the shade and watched as Miss Sarah and Martin drove off in the pickup.

"Weren't the rest of the Bankrofts good people?"

"They were terrible, terrible people," Jeremiah said solemnly. "This whole idea of a party for the field hands was all hers."

"How'd Miss Sarah ever turn out like she did?"

"Miss Sarah's somethin' special, she surely is."

"She sure is special to look at," the young man grinned. "One good-looking woman. I wouldn't mind putting my shoes under her bed."

Anger rose in the old man's face and he grabbed

17

the younger man by the front of his shirt, so that their eyes met. Clifford was astonished at the fury in Jeremiah's kindly face.

"As long as you're here, boy," he yelled, "I don't want to hear that kind of talk from you. Ever. She is Miss Sarah to you. You got that?"

Williams was stunned by the strength in the old man.

"You hear that, boy? You never think those thoughts about her!"

"I'm sorry, Jeremiah, really I am. I didn't mean no disrespect."

The old man released his grip, but not before pushing Williams backwards against the tree.

"You just remember that if you want to get along here, boy."

They were passing back up the dusty road lined with cattails and clumps of blue irises, when Sarah noticed a small gray squirrel limping in the path of the truck. She insisted that Martin pull over to the side of the road and, as he did, the dogs began to bark loudly. "Hush up," she warned them as she stepped out and walked towards the tiny animal.

"Be careful, Sarah," Martin called out. "They can be vicious. He's hurt and scared; he could bite." But he knew from experience that his warning was of little use.

"Nonsense," she called back. Slowly she approached the wounded creature, speaking softly.

"It's all right, little fellow. I'll help you. We'll fix your leg."

"Sarah!" he called, but once he saw the glitter in

her eyes he knew she was beyond paying attention to him.

"Come on, come to Sarah," she said, putting out her hand.

The squirrel sat there watching her with beady eyes. After a moment's indecision, it hobbled towards her.

"That's right," she smiled. "You know Sarah would never hurt you, don't you?"

She picked up the squirrel and cradled it in her arms, careful not to injure its leg any further.

"Martin," she said, "I think you'd better get us to Uncle Luke's."

Martin did as he was told, watching Sarah and her newest friend from the corner of his eyes. The little gray squirrel lay in her arms as if he had known her all his life. It was amazing how animals took to his cousin right off. Perhaps they knew they were safe, cradled there in loving arms. That special gift with animals was only one of the many things that made him love her.

The town of Arcadia had not changed much since they were children. There was Main Street, flanked on either side by old buildings one or two stories high; and at the center of town there was a traffic circle where Main Street intersected with Route 39, a Florida state highway; and in the center of the circle was a monument and fountain dedicated to those soldiers of Arcadia who had fought for the Confederacy.

Martin and Sarah stopped in front of a yellow painted two-story building. The brass shingle outside read Luke Bankroft, M.D. Sarah went inside alone while Martin sat in the truck. She was relieved to find the waiting room empty. Her uncle's patients would not be pleased to know that Dr. Bankroft treated animals as well as people.

Luke Bankroft was a short, stout man with a warm, friendly smile and cheerful blue eyes. Unlike the rest of the Bankrofts, he had never been interested in tobacco or money. He had devoted his life to healing the sick. His office was modestly furnished in worn, dark wood. He worked behind a large desk, and shelves and drawers lined most of the walls. The drawers were labeled in Latin. There was a cracked red-leather sofa against one wall and two worn red-leather chairs faced the desk.

"Sarah," he sighed and shook his head when he saw the squirrel. "What have you got now?"

"He's hurt his leg, Uncle Luke. Will you fix it?"

"Child, have you any idea how many animals I've doctored for you?" But he noticed the look of concern on her face and relented. "Don't worry."

"Can you fix his leg?"

The doctor shook his head in amusement. "My patients would never understand this, but put him on the table."

Sarah kissed her uncle's cheek and followed him into the examination room. She placed the tiny patient on the table, but when the doctor reached out to examine him, the squirrel lashed out at him.

"Now you listen here," she said, eyes shining. "You let Uncle Luke help you."

This time, when Luke touched the squirrel, it

was docile and cooperative.

Luke Bankroft was quiet as he examined the tiny leg, and when he was through he turned to Sarah.

"It's a simple sprain, he'll be all right," he assured her as he tied a bandage around the tiny leg. "He'll be fine. Just keep him quiet if you can. In a few days he'll be climbing trees again."

Sarah picked up her new pet and thanked her uncle.

"It's what I do best," he shrugged. "Now what about you? Do you mind if I inquire as to your health?"

"Uncle Luke, I'm fine. I'm always fine."

The old man smiled and put his arm affectionately around Sarah's shoulder.

"I just worry that you work too hard. Running that big place all by yourself."

"Martin helps me."

"Martin does what you tell him to."

Sarah decided to change the subject. "You are coming to dinner tomorrow, aren't you, Uncle Luke?"

"I am if Mrs. Graves' baby doesn't decide to come into this vale of tears earlier than expected."

"Good, then we'll be expecting you," she said, planting a kiss on his ruddy cheek.

As Sarah stepped out of her uncle's office, still holding the wounded squirrel in her arms, she almost walked into two middle-aged women seated in the waiting room.

"What on earth have you got there?" Regina Quillam inquired. She was a tall, stout woman of about fifty with blue rinsed hair that matched her tight blue silk dress.

"It's a squirrel; he's sprained his leg."

From Sarah's manner, even a casual observer would have been able to tell that there was no love lost between Miss Sarah and Regina Quillam. Still, the older woman refused to be insulted.

"My goodness. Why must you pick up those things?" she said haughtily. "They're so dirty. I wouldn't touch it."

"He needs help, Mrs. Quillam. It's no trouble to me."

"The trouble with you is your heart. It's too big, child."

And the trouble with you is that your heart's too small, she thought, but didn't say, as she walked out to where Martin was waiting. All she wanted to do was to get her new little friend home.

Devon was sound asleep in his room. It seemed to Jessica Morrow that all her son did was sleep, and, when he was awake, he stared off into space. He seemed to lack any interest in life.

Not that she was much better, she realized. Keeping house for her niece wasn't very demanding, but it seemed to take all her energy. There was a girl from the village who came in every morning to do the cleaning, and Sarah would certainly let her have more help if she asked, but she didn't. She had very little interest in life at all anymore.

Maybe it was wrong of her to blame Sarah. After all, there were all those people who loved the girl, and God knows she'd suffered a lot in her young life. First the taunts of a family that wouldn't accept her, then the deaths of those closest to her. But she had suffered, as well as Sarah. Life was empty without Robert and somehow she was sure that Sarah was responsible for his death. But every time she tried to work it out in her head, she started to get these headaches. She couldn't concentrate.

She was sure that Sarah and Martin were up to something in the basement. She could hear them down there at night when they thought she was asleep. But Sarah had warned her to stay away.

Still, Sarah was in town now and she and Devon were alone in the house. It was now or never.

Slowly, she opened the cellar door beneath the great staircase. She descended the stone steps to the basement, feeling the cool air of the cellar all around her. It was quiet and still. She put her hand on the door to the basement room. It was locked.

"Aunt Jessica, what are you doing?"

It was Sarah. Jessica hadn't heard her come in the door, and now she was beside her on the steps.

"I—I was just looking for a mop," she said weakly.

"Since when do we keep mops in the basement?"

"I—I'm sorry. I—" Her voice trailed off.

"You know my rules. No one goes into the basement. You do remember that, Aunt Jessica, don't you?"

The strange tone in her niece's voice made Jessica Morrow tremble. Her eyes were fixed on the stone steps.

"Yes, I know. I'm very sorry. It won't happen again." She knew her apologies were feeble and she scurried up the stairs and off towards the kitchen before Sarah could say anything more.

Sarah was annoyed. She had warned her aunt many times not to go into the basement. She tried the door and was relieved to find that it was still locked. She turned and went to find Martin.

He was in the stable. The dogs watched him curiously as he prepared a small box for the invalid squirrel. She shook her head with displeasure as she placed the wounded animal in its new box.

"Aunt Jessica knows the rules, Martin," she said. "Perhaps it will take more to make her adhere to them." She seemed to be giving the matter more thought. "Yes, she must be taught a lesson. She must be."

Martin Bankroft nodded in silent agreement.

* * *

The Bankroft children and their friends were playing happily on the front lawn of Cherron. All were at play but one. Fat, homely little Sarah in her gingham dress watched her brothers and sister playing with a Frisbee. She was standing under a hickory tree and the ice cream cone she was eating was small comfort as she watched the others laughing and running. She made one more attempt to enter the game.

"Can I play too?" she asked shyly.

The others stopped their playing and stared at her as if she had suddenly lost all her senses.

"No," said her big brother Michael. He was thirteen and already strikingly handsome.

"Why not?" she asked, taking another lick of the cone.

"Because!"

"Because why?"

"Because you're fat and you're ugly," he said, giggling. The others followed suit.

"Ugly, ugly," they taunted.

Sarah's mouth trembled and tears filled her eyes. It was true she was not as pretty as the other little girls, especially her sister Monica. All the other Bankrofts were good looking. They did not have braces on their teeth. Their hair was perfect, and their features were nicely formed. Their limbs were strong and shapely; no gangling arms and legs there.

She watched her brothers, Michael, Everett, and David. All were tall and handsome. And her sister Monica, everyone said she was going to be a beauty.

She went back under the hickory tree and sobbed quietly to herself. She stared at the Frisbee in the air. Monica threw it to David. It would be nice if it hit that mean Michael in the head instead, she thought.

And it did.

Stunned, Michael rubbed his head. Now it was the other children's turn to laugh at him. Sarah, sitting under the tree a few yards away, did not join in the laughter. She was too puzzled by what had just happened.

She tried it again.

When David tossed the Frisbee to Everett, she thought about how funny it would be if it hit Monica right in the seat of her pants.

And it did.

The children all seemed to think it was hilarious that their Frisbee had taken on a life of its own. Sarah didn't attempt to join their game again.

Somehow, she was certain, she had made the Frisbee do what she wanted it to do.

* * *

All the bedrooms were on the second floor of Cherron. Martha Conroy Bankroft, still in her short white tennis dress, lined up her brood in the hall upstairs for inspection. They were having company for dinner and she wanted her children to do her proud. It wasn't every day that her husband's sister Jessica visited, and she wanted to show the children off. Except for Sarah. She was afraid there wasn't much to show off there.

She looked down at her now. The little girl still had ice cream all over her face. In contrast, Monica had already washed and put on her best green organdy party dress. The boys were in white summer suits, their hair slicked down, their shoes shined.

"Sarah," her mother said gently. "Wouldn't you like to play in your room tonight? I don't think you'd enjoy meeting your Aunt Jessica."

"Everyone else will be meeting her, won't they?"

"Yes, well, your brothers and sister might find her interesting."

"And I wouldn't?"

"No, I don't believe so! Go to your room now, dear."

"But I want to hear the stories about Europe," she cried. "Can't I come down later and see her?"

"No!"

"They don't want you to embarrass them. Don't you know that, stupid?" Michael hissed as she passed him in the hall.

"That's not true," she protested.

"Of course it's true, dummy."

She couldn't think of anything to say to him, so she stuck out her tongue.

Dejected, she went down the hall to her room. It was small and had simple white painted furniture. The walls had been covered with a tiny violet-patterned wallpaper and there were framed pictures of flowers on the wall.

She stood before the full-length mirror and stared at herself. What was wrong with her? She was overweight and wore thick braces on her teeth. Yes, she was not as pretty as all the other Bankrofts. But why did they feel the need to say things just to hurt her feelings? The words hurt so.

She stared at herself for a long time, trying to see the imperfections that made them hate her so, that made them exclude her from their games, their parties, their lives.

After a while she heard noises downstairs. Her aunt Jessica must have arrived. She waited in her room for her mother to call her to meet the guests, but the call never came.

Finally she combed her hair, placed a ribbon in

it, put on her prettiest dress, the yellow one, and ventured downstairs.

They were all there in the living room. Her parents were seated on one sofa and on the opposite sofa were her aunt Jessica and Jessica's husband, Robert. She was a tall, stately woman in a bright-red dress. She had high cheekbones, and her thick black hair was drawn back into a dramatic chignon. Her husband was equally handsome. The small boy who sat at her feet who seemed to be about four years old had to be her son Devon.

Monica, who was almost eleven, and Everett and David, who were twelve and ten, were all dressed up and sitting on the floor with Michael. All were staring in awe at their glamorous new relatives. This was the first time they had met Jessica and her family, who had been living in Europe for many years.

"There we were, standing inside of the Parthenon—" Jessica was saying, but she stopped short when she saw Sarah standing in the doorway.

"And who is this?" she asked in a rich, dramatic voice.

"Oh, Jessica, this is our youngest daughter, Sarah." Why did her father sound so apologetic?

"Come here, child," Jessica gestured with her hand. She had long red-painted nails and she wore gold bracelets on each wrist.

"How do you do, Aunt Jessica. It's a pleasure to meet you." Sarah curtsied as she had been taught, but the woman just laughed.

"My God!" she exclaimed, peering at Sarah as if she were a specimen under a microscope. "Are you

28

sure she's yours? Are you certain she's a Bankroft?"

Sarah was stunned.

"Yes, I'm a Bankroft," she said feebly.

"Well—it's just that—well, your sister is so pretty and you're, well, you are rather homely, aren't you?"

Sarah looked around for assistance, but none was forthcoming. She turned and ran from the room in tears, pausing only long enough to hear the hateful woman's last comment.

"She's rather unattractive, isn't she?"

"Ugly," Michael assisted, and they all joined in the laughing.

They had no right to taunt her, she told herself. Someday they would pay. She would punish them all for their cruelty—someday.

*   *   *

At least once a week Miss Sarah insisted that Uncle Luke, Aunt Jessica, Devon and Martin all sit down to dinner together at Cherron. There were so few Bankrofts left now, she would say, it was important that they stick together.

Dinner was served in the silk-walled formal dining room of the great house. They were seated at a long mahogany table and, as usual, there was a large centerpiece of magnificent roses from Miss Sarah's garden. Candles burned in the two heavy silver candelabra. Sarah sat at the foot of the table. She insisted that Dr. Luke, being the oldest male

Bankroft, sit at the head. His sister Jessica was at his right and Martin was at his left. Devon sat between Sarah and Jessica.

As usual, the old doctor and Sarah did most of the talking during dinner.

"How's my small patient getting on?" Uncle Luke asked as he spooned up the strawberries and cream that Jessica had prepared for dessert.

"He's doing quite well," Sarah assured him. "He has his own box in the barn. But I suppose in a few days he'll leave me. They always leave."

"Sarah, try not to think too much about your losses. Death is a part of life that no one can escape. Not even we Bankrofts."

"I know," she said wistfully. "It's all so sad, though. So many gone."

"You still have so much to look forward to," he insisted. "You're young, you're the mistress of a tobacco empire, you're beautiful, and you've got lots of suitors. Tell me, young lady, when do you intend to marry one of them? You can't put them off indefinitely, you know."

Martin began to dig into his dessert with unusual vigor as the old doctor spoke.

"I think I'll enjoy myself a bit longer, Uncle Luke. Besides, not many men would want their wives running a tobacco plantation. And how am I to know if they're merely marrying me for my money?"

"Child, it's not your money any self-respecting young man will see when he looks at you."

"Uncle Luke, I thank you for the compliment. I suppose someday I'll fall in love; although once

30

burned, twice shy, I guess."

Jessica and Devon stood up together and began to clear away the dishes.

"Sarah, my darling, you must forget that incident. Roy McEndrew was an immature oaf. I'm sure he never meant to hurt you."

"But as it turned out, he did just that, Uncle Luke."

"In that situation you acted more mature than he. Besides, he's suffered a great deal since then." The old doctor shook his head. "God help his poor wife."

"Yes, horrible," Martin agreed, exchanging a brief glance with Miss Sarah.

"All that is past, best forgotten," Sarah said quietly. "Believe me, they have enough pain in their lives. As for myself, the entire thing is in the past. I hold no ill will towards them."

"That's very generous of you, Sarah."

She smiled, but her smile faded as her aunt came back with a tray of coffee and three cups. She was still upset about finding Jessica at the basement door. She glared at the woman. Jessica's hand started to shake so that she nearly dropped the coffee on the rug. Sarah continued to concentrate her attention on her as she placed the tray on the table, then turned and left the room.

Sarah took the silver pot and began to pour the coffee. Martin watched her. They had been so close for so long that he was sensitive to her every mood. Only he seemed to notice the strange way her eyes were shining now.

Then they heard the scream.

"Ahhhh. Dear God, help me." The agonized cry came from the kitchen.

Luke Bankroft rushed through the kitchen doors, closely followed by Sarah, Martin, and Devon. They found Jessica in the kitchen on her knees, doubled up with pain, her hands clamped over her eyes.

"Jessica, what's wrong?" the doctor demanded.

She tried to look up at him, but she couldn't take her hands from her eyes. All she could do was moan with pain.

"Where? Where does it hurt, Jessica?"

"My eyes, my eyes are on fire. I can't see. Oh God, they're burning up."

"Martin, call an ambulance," he barked.

Sarah prepared a cold compress and held it on her aunt's eyes until the ambulance came. When it arrived fifteen minutes later, Luke Bankroft accompanied his sister to Arcadia General Hospital.

"What do you think is wrong with her?" Devon Morrow asked mechanically as the three of them stood in the doorway and watched the ambulance make its way down the drive.

"I have no idea," Sarah assured him. "But I'm certain Uncle Luke will discover what it is. Perhaps she's been using her eyes a bit too much. Maybe she needs glasses."

"Why don't you lock up now, Devon?" Martin suggested.

"Yes, Cousin Martin."

"Then you can go to bed," Sarah added.

"Thank you, Cousin Sarah."

After the boy had left, Martin looked at Sarah.

"I remember him as such a fresh little kid," he said.

She laughed. "He has mellowed, hasn't he."

Now that they were alone, she stepped behind him and began to massage his back, enjoying the feeling of his strong muscles under her small white hands.

"What's wrong, Martin?" she asked. "Did all that talk about my marrying upset you?"

"Yes," he said gravely. "If you were to marry, things would change between us."

She placed her head against his back, hugging his shoulders. "Don't you know you'll always be here at Cherron with me? Nothing will ever change that." She playfully stroked his dark hair. "Come now. I think it's time for us to visit the basement and then go to bed."

She followed him down the stone steps to the dimly lit basement. From her pocket she took a large iron key which she used to open the heavy wooden door. It made a hollow sound as it clicked in the lock, then the door opened. As they entered, Martin lit the sconces on the wall, bathing the room in a warm yellow light.

The basement room was as sumptuously furnished as any of the rooms upstairs. Only the stone walls gave evidence that a visitor was not in one of Cherron's finest parlors. There was an old-fashioned settee covered in dark pink velvet, and above it hung an oil portrait of Sebastian Bankroft. There were several Chippendale occasional chairs, as well as a long mahogany dining table set for dinner. There were other paintings of Bankroft ancestors on the other walls. Two of the loveliest were a pair representing Sarah's mother and father, David and Martha Bankroft. The side tables were decorated with china and with crystal bowls filled with Cherron roses of every color.

Sarah walked quickly through the room to a darkened doorway beyond. She paused there, then turned to her cousin.

"Martin," she said softly. "Where did you put their food?"

Chapter Two

Luke Bankroft was at his desk facing the young Northerner who had come to talk to him about his book. He was a good-looking young man, this Jonathan Evans. He seemed to be about thirty, with a slim but athletic-looking build. His dark brown hair was thick and his eyes were sea-green. He had a strong but gentle face with a small cleft in his chin. He claimed to be writing a history of the great families of Florida, and naturally he wanted to include the Bankrofts.

Luke tried to concentrate on what the young man was saying, but his mind kept wandering back to Jessica Morrow's sudden illness. It was the damndest thing. There she was, perfectly fine one minute and then suddenly stricken with those terrible pains in her eyes. He'd seen her himself, writhing there in agony on the kitchen floor. But by the time they got to Arcadia General the pains were gone. It had been a week now and they hadn't come back. Poor Jessica still seemed shaken up, though. Almost as though she was afraid to go home.

"You seem tired, sir," the young man was saying. "I could come back later."

"No, it's all right, Mr. Evans. I just have a case that's puzzling me. As a matter of fact the woman in question is my sister. She lives at Cherron. She's a widow and keeps house for Miss Sarah."

"I hope it's nothing serious."

"No, thank you, she's fine now. I'll be driving her home today. Now, you were saying that you want to write about the personal lives of the Bankrofts down through the years?"

"Yes. The personal side is very important," he said eagerly. "I want to know what sort of people they were—their temperaments, marriages, children, their business adventures, their entire lives. Since the Bankrofts are the oldest and most important family in Florida, I decided to speak to you. And, of course, to obtain your permission to write the story."

"For that, young man, you'll need to speak to my niece, Miss Sarah. She's the owner of Cherron now."

"Your niece runs the tobacco business?"

"Every part of it," he said proudly. "From the first planting to the auctions. And she still has time to be the best little gardener in Arcadia County. These roses are all from her garden." He gestured towards a large china bowl filled with bright red roses.

"They're lovely," Jonathan Evans agreed. He was eager to meet the girl who could grow tobacco and roses with equal skill.

"There is only one thing I must warn you about." Luke Bankroft paused as though he was preparing to talk about something painful to him. "We've had a great deal of tragedy in our family," he said sadly. "I wouldn't mind speaking to Miss Sarah for you, but I don't want any part of this story writing to upset her."

"I would be grateful if you would speak to your niece on my behalf, Dr. Bankroft, and I can assure you I will try not to upset her."

"Very well then, I'll talk to her this afternoon and, if she agrees, I'll set up an appointment for you."

They shook hands and, after the young gentleman left, Luke mused that he might be just the thing for Sarah. A handsome young writer might be just the man to get her mind off the past.

Later that afternoon Luke Bankroft helped his sister up the marble steps of the verandah. Jessica still seemed weak and nervous, and he noticed that her hand trembled when they saw Sarah standing in the doorway of Cherron.

"Aunt Jessica," she said brightly. "How do you feel?"

"I feel much better, thank you, Sarah," she murmured, but her voice was still timid.

"I'm so glad. Perhaps you would care to rest in your room for a few days." She turned to Martin. "Help Jessica upstairs. I'll have Devon bring up some tea."

That was Sarah all over—taking over, seeing that her sick aunt got right to bed, and fixing her tea. At least she would be in good hands here. Luke felt better already.

Sarah noticed the look of concern in her uncle's face.

"Did you find anything?" she asked.

"No, and frankly I don't understand it." He shook his head. "There was absolutely nothing physically wrong with her eyes. The tests were all negative. Yet they gave her such agonizing pain."

"How strange," she said casually. Then she turned to young Devon. "Oh, Devon, please prepare some tea for your mother and bring it up to her room."

"How is she, Miss Sarah?" There was no emotion in his voice.

"She's doing much better," Sarah assured him.

The boy seemed satisfied and asked no further questions. He turned automatically and went into the kitchen.

"I'm very glad she's well now," Sarah said.

"Don't hesitate to call me immediately if this should happen again."

"Who else would I call?" she laughed.

"Oh, I almost forgot!" Luke paused in the doorway. "A young man came to see me today. His name is Jonathan Evans. He says he's a writer from New York and he's writing a book on the old families of Florida. He wants to write about the Bankrofts. I told him I'd ask for your permission."

"A book! Really? That sounds fascinating."

"Then you'll speak to him? Now you don't have to, Sarah," he cautioned. "I mean, if it will distress you in the least to talk about the family."

She smiled sadly. "You were the one who told me that death is a part of this world, Uncle Luke. And since it's an unalterable fact, I must accept it. I don't like it, but there is nothing I can't cope with. I will speak to this Mr. Evans. Why don't you bring him around tonight?"

"Very well, Miss Sarah. I'll bring him by at eight; that is, if you can bear to have me twice in one day."

She laughed at her uncle. "Uncle Luke, you're welcome in this house any time you care to grace it."

She kissed her uncle goodbye and watched him start up his Buick. So a writer was going to visit Cherron. He wanted to tell the story of the Bankrofts. It certainly sounded most interesting.

She realized she had almost forgotten about Aunt Jessica until she saw Devon with the tray for tea.

"Oh, Devon, I'll take that," she said, lifting the silver tray from his hands. "I want to take a look at Aunt Jessica anyway."

She found her aunt propped up against some ruffled pillows. She lay under the blue goose-down comforter on her four-poster bed. Her eyes were closed as though she had dozed off.

"Here we are, some nice tea," she announced.

Her aunt looked at her with both surprise and fear as Sarah placed the tray on the table beside the bed and sat down on the edge of the bed.

"Do your eyes feel better now, Aunt Jessica?" she asked with concern.

"Yes, thank you, Sarah." The woman's words were restrained.

"I wonder why Uncle Luke couldn't find anything wrong with them?" She sounded puzzled. "Perhaps you saw something you shouldn't have."

The two women stared at each other as if they shared a secret. Finally Sarah broke the silence.

"You rest now," she said as she rose to leave. "But remember the rules, Aunt Jessica. No one goes near the basement."

She smiled pleasantly and left her aunt to her tea.

The McEndrew tobacco plantation bordered Cherron but it was smaller and less prosperous. Roy McEndrew told himself that it was just a matter of luck—the sun hitting right, the leaves ripening in the right order—but the truth was, he didn't care. He didn't care about much of anything these days.

He looked across the supper table at his wife, Kathy. When he'd married her six years ago she'd been the prettiest little girl he'd ever seen in his life. A real beauty, a Georgia peach that he picked and brought back to Arcadia to show all the locals what he could come up with when he tried. He wasn't going to get stuck with a dog like Sarah Bankroft no matter how his parents tried to force a marriage.

Maybe he had behaved like a heel, never telling

the girl he had no intentions of going through with a wedding. He waited until the last possible minute, then, that night at the Christmas party at Cherron, he'd laid it on her. He had married Kathy and that was that.

Kathy had been a bright-eyed, happy kind of girl, full of life and joy. It wasn't so much that she had changed physically, although she had. Her hair was shapeless, her skin was pallid, and she seemed to spend her whole life in that ragged chenille bathrobe. No, what really got to him was the fact that she behaved as though their baby was normal.

Every night, when he came in from the fields, she insisted on telling him about the baby's progress—how he was learning to talk, they would soon be taking him into town to show him around. Soon the kid would be learning the business from his dad, she'd say.

Couldn't she see that the kid would never be more than a pitiful, drooling, misshapen monster?

They'd been to doctors, but nothing could be done. And worse, there seemed to be no reason why it should have happened. They were both young and healthy. It had been a normal pregnancy, right up until the labor pains came that afternoon.

They'd been on a picnic up on Benson's Cliff with Miss Sarah who had behaved like a real good sport in spite of being practically jilted. And then suddenly Kathy started to feel the pains. They rushed her to the hospital and she delivered this monstrous child.

The doctors couldn't explain why the thing didn't just die. That was usually the case when such a thing happened. The baby would live a few weeks, or months, and then pass on. But this child wouldn't. The monster lived, and he and Kathy had become its prisoners.

Lately he found himself thinking about what life would have been like if he had married Miss Sarah, and joined the two plantations the way his parents had hoped they would. It was funny. She'd grown into a beautiful young woman. He'd see her in Arcadia or riding about Cherron and he would ache to touch her.

Sometimes this desire was the only thing that kept him from killing himself.

Jonathan Evans had already driven around the plantation and he had seen the great house from a distance. Still, when he entered it with Luke Bankroft, he was surprised by its beauty and grandeur, and he was even more surprised by the beauty and charm of its young mistress.

"Is something wrong, Mr. Evans?" she asked with concern after they were introduced.

"No, not at all," he assured her. "It's just that I wasn't expecting anyone like you to be running an empire like this. You are a remarkably beautiful woman."

"Thank you," she said, blushing slightly as she led them into the living room. There was a fire burning in the white marble fireplace. She indicated that the doctor and Jonathan should sit on the striped satin sofa that faced the fire. Sarah took one of the chintz armchairs and Martin sat in the other.

"My uncle tells me that you want to write a book about the Bankrofts," she said.

"Yes, the book will be about several old Florida families. I'm especially interested in the Bankrofts because your family has had so many tragedies."

"Mr. Evans—" Luke interjected.

"Please, call me Jonathan," he said. His eyes never left Miss Sarah's.

"Jonathan," she began. "We've had a number of misfortunes in our family, as has any family, I'm sure. Do you really think your readers will care to know about them?"

"Unfortunately, Miss Bankroft, they will derive a good deal of enjoyment from them."

"I see," she said sadly. "Yes, it is unfortunate that people seem to enjoy such things."

"I don't mean to exploit your family's misfortunes, Miss Bankroft. On the contrary, if there's anything you'd rather not discuss, I'll respect your feelings. You'll have the final approval on anything I write."

"I'm sure you'll respect my feelings Mr.—Jonathan." She seemed to be thinking for a moment. "I see no reason why you can't write about us. I think it might be quite exciting. A written history of the Bankrofts. It's never been done before. What do you think, Martin?"

Martin Bankroft had been sitting silently while Sarah talked to the visitor. He didn't like the look of the man and he didn't like the way Sarah agreed so quickly to let the man write about the

43

Bankrofts. He didn't think it was a good idea to start raking up the past. What was done was done. And he didn't like the way the man looked at Sarah; no, he didn't like that at all.

"Is your family with you, Mr. Evans?" Martin asked the visitor.

"My family? Oh, you mean a wife. I'm not married." He smiled at Sarah when he said this, and she blushed.

"Where would you like to begin, Jonathan?"

"How about at the beginning?"

"Martin is an expert on our family history," she said graciously. "I'll let him start."

"The story of the Bankrofts is tied to the history of tobacco in America," Martin began solemnly. "We got tobacco from the Indians. The explorers brought it back from the New World for its medicinal value. It was cultivated in Bavaria, Russia and China long before it was cultivated commercially at Jamestown in 1612. But for some reason it grows best in the western hemisphere, and that's where production has flourished."

"Actually, there are very good reasons why it thrived here," Uncle Luke interrupted. "The soil here was naturally rich. In addition, there were so many rivers and waterways in Virginia, where tobacco was first planted on a large-scale, that every planter could easily transport his crop.

"Slave gangs became the main source of labor, in that area, and because the slaves were unskilled and considered unteachable, the owners confined them to work on one crop. They brought those ideas down here to Florida with them."

"Wouldn't planting one crop like that wear out the soil?" Jonathan asked.

"Land was so cheap they didn't worry about that," Sarah told him.

Martin picked up his story again. "The tobacco trade was so profitable in Virginia that in 1621 the British Crown restricted tobacco cultivation in order to encourage food crops. By that time tobacco had become acceptable as legal tender."

"Many public officials and clergymen were paid in tobacco," Uncle Luke added.

"Imagine being able to grow your own money," Sarah laughed.

Martin glared at her. He could tell that his cousin was flirting with the visitor and he did not like it one bit.

"Sebastian Bankroft's father had a tobacco farm in the Connecticut Valley, the birthplace of the cigar-making industry in the United States. Mothers, fathers, and children would all sit by the fireside rolling the local leaf, which they would trade with the village merchants for store goods. The cigars they rolled were then packed several thousand to the barrel and shipped to seaport towns where they sold well."

"Meanwhile, all this time," Uncle Luke added, "Florida was still a Spanish colony, closed to Americans. Then in 1790 it was opened to general immigration. Hundreds of land-hungry farmers moved in, including Sebastian Bankroft. He started with a few acres and built up to the thousand we have intact today.

"By 1821 Florida was dominated by Americans

and it joined the United States. But by that time most of the South was growing cotton, which was even more profitable than tobacco."

"Especially for export," Sarah added.

"By 1850 Sebastian and his son were doing so well that they built this house, which he called Cherron," Luke said. "He named it for Charon, the boat man who ferried dead souls to the afterlife." Luke grinned. "He was a better farmer than a speller, but the name stuck."

"Did he make the cigars?" Jonathan asked Martin.

"Only for a short time. He was quite a promoter and rolled them in three sizes, what they called short sixes, long nines, and supers. But by 1860 he was out of that business and the real cigar making was going on in New Orleans. The Bankrofts have concentrated on producint the best leaf.

"Since 1900 Florida has become one of the fastest-growing states and it is now one of the ten most populated. But until the first world war, the Connecticut Valley, the Miami Ohio Valley, and Lancaster County in Pennsylvania were still the major producers of cigar wrapper tobacco. It's only since the end of that war that Gadsden County has become so important."

"And where does Cherron stand today?" Jonathan asked with interest.

"My niece here is sitting on a very desirable piece of real estate," Luke Bankroft answered. "The developers would love to get their hands on these thousand acres."

"But they never will," Sarah said firmly. "Not while I'm alive."

"Cherron has survived civil war, depressions, diseases and hurricanes. The Bankrofts have managed to hold on to Cherron, increasing their holdings until Miss Sarah's time," Martin said, staring directly at Jonathan as he spoke. "And they will hold on to it for another hundred years."

Jonathan sensed that he was being issued a warning.

"My father inherited Cherron from his father, and passed it down to my brothers in turn; but they all died young, and so it came to me," Sarah explained.

"And it took us a while to convince her to take over," Luke Bankroft added.

"You didn't want it?" Jonathan asked in amazement. He couldn't conceive of anyone rejecting a multi-million-dollar estate.

"Not at all," she assured him. "I already had what I needed. The people here love me. I had my family and my roses. I didn't need anything else. Material things don't interest me."

"I had to do a lot of fast talking," Luke said. "I told her how cruel her family had been to the people who worked for them."

"Uncle Luke!" she protested.

"Now, honey, it's the truth. He'll find out sooner or later." He turned back to Jonathan. "Why, when her daddy owned Cherron he'd work those poor devils sixteen hours a day, no concern for their health. We had some heavy arguments over that, I can tell you."

"We finally convinced Miss Sarah that she could help those people if she took over," Martin added, smiling proudly at his cousin. "And as it turned out, we were right."

The session lasted into the early morning, until the grandfather clock in the hallway chimed one o'clock, and Uncle Luke suggested that it was late and perhaps they could continue the genealogy in the morning.

"Yes, you're quite right," Jonathan agreed. "I'm sorry for keeping you so long, Miss Bankroft, but it's all fascinating to me."

"Please call me Miss Sarah; everybody does. I promise you first thing in the morning Martin and I will start looking in the attic. I'm sure there will be lots of information you can use."

"I appreciate this, Miss Sarah, and I'll be back in the morning to start work."

"By the way, where are you staying while you're here?"

"The Arcadia Inn in town."

"Nonsense," she said. "You must move in here. We've plenty of room."

He was tempted to refuse simply because he wanted to keep his objectivity, but when he saw the angry look in Martin Bankroft's face he decided to stay. Maybe the guy was just being overly protective, but something about Martin just rubbed him the wrong way.

Besides, this mansion was a lot more inviting than the gaudy hotel, and Miss Sarah was a lot more attractive than the weathered hostess in the hotel dining room.

"If you insist, Miss Sarah," he said. "I'll pack my things and bring them over in the morning."

"Good, then it's settled."

Sarah walked Jonathan and her uncle to the door and when she returned she found Martin sitting silently, staring at the remains of the fire.

"Now I suppose you think I'm rushing into something, don't you?" she said.

"Sarah," Martin said deliberately. "Are you sure you want him staying here?"

"What could possibly happen? I have you and Devon to protect me."

"Do you really think it's wise having him live here?"

"It's a bothersome drive from town to Cherron," she said, shrugging. "He'd have to make it every day. Why shouldn't he stay here?"

"You know why. He might learn too much."

Sarah smiled at her cousin as if she found his fears foolish. "Do you really believe that he would publish anything I didn't want him to? You of all people?"

"No, I suppose not."

"Why, Martin, I do believe you're jealous." She leaned over and kissed him. Dear, gentle Martin. Protecting her always.

*   *   *

"But I want to go, Father," Sarah pleaded. She was thirteen years old and she wanted to dress up and go to parties like her brothers and sister.

"You stay home with us," her father said.

"No one would invite you to a party," Monica teased. "You're not welcome anywhere." Monica was wearing a lavender silk party dress with lots of tucks and ruffles, and her long black hair was tied back in a big lavender bow. As always, she looked beautiful. And why not? She was one of the beautiful Bankrofts.

"Besides," her sister added, preening herself in front of the hall mirror like a little peacock. "No boy would want to dance with you; not if he were in his right mind."

"That's not fair," Martin yelled. He had heard everything. "Sarah's nice. Anyone would want to dance with her."

"Martin, I believe you're losing your mind," Monica jeered.

"She's nice, I tell you," he insisted. "And she's pretty, too."

"Martin! Have you been in the sun too long?" Monica laughed. "She's as fat as a whale and as ugly as sin."

"No, she's not," he shouted. "No, she's not."

"Stop it," her father commanded. "Enough from all of you. Monica, get in the car if you want to go to the party." He turned to Sarah and Martin "And you behave yourselves."

"I have to go to the party, too," Martin told her. "My father is making me."

Still, he tried to comfort the tearful girl. "Don't be sad, Sarah." He plunged his hand into his pocket and brought out three marbles. "Here, would you like these?"

She stared at them, a tear falling down her chubby cheek.

"Take them; they're blue, like your eyes."

She took the marbles timidly. They were pretty, all three a dark cobalt blue. She wiped the stinging tears from her eyes.

Martin put his arms around his little cousin lovingly. At least he cared about her; at least he loved her.

Later, after the children had left for the party, Sarah lay on the bed in her room. She was angry: angry at her brothers and sister for teasing her, angry at her parents for letting them. She hated them all and she hated all the people who wanted her to be a typical Bankroft. Only Martin was kind to her. She stared at the blue marbles he had given her.

They moved.

It was just like that day with the Frisbee, she thought. She had noticed it before. Sometimes if she stared at something, especially if she was angry, it moved. Today she was very angry and she thought again about all the reasons and why.

They moved again, lifting slightly into the air.

She'd done it.

Then they fell back down again, and rolled off the bed and onto the floor.

It was very strange, and she wondered what it meant.

* * *

"Have you fed our pets?" she asked Martin as he entered her bedroom.

It was a large room; blue-and-gold-striped paper covered its walls. There was something old-fashioned yet timeless about it. The white lace curtains hung from the French windows which led out to a balcony that overlooked the lawn of Cherron. Roses climbed over the balcony.

Sarah was seated at a dressing table made of dark wood. The legs of the table were covered with a frilly pink skirt. She was brushing her long blonde hair in front of the mirror while she talked to Martin. He was standing behind her, his hands on her soft white shoulders as he looked at her face in the mirror. Their faces were framed as in a portrait—his rugged and sad, hers soft and warm. They looked like the perfect picture of two lovers.

"I don't think he should be here," Martin said angrily as he grabbed her around the waist and pulled her towards him.

"Martin, you mustn't be jealous. He'll finish his story and leave." She smiled. "Besides, it'll be nice to have someone to talk to."

"You talk to me."

"I mean someone new, someone with different ideas."

"I have ideas," he said, as he held her tightly against him.

"Why," she giggled. "I do believe Mr. Evans has got you all excited. We'd best do something about that."

She began to kiss him on the mouth, but Martin was still distracted.

"Suppose he finds out about us?"

"Now don't worry; he's not going to find anything we don't want him to find, I'll make sure of that."

Before he drove out to Cherron in the morning, Jonathan had decided to speak to some of the people in town about the Bankrofts. His first stop was the National Bank of Arcadia, where he struck up a conversation with the president, a jovial young man named Bill Collins.

"Miss Sarah?" he said when Jonathan mentioned the name. "Does she know you're asking questions about her family?"

"Yes, Mr. Collins," he assured him. "I have her full cooperation."

Collins eyed the writer with suspicion; partly because he did not trust writers, partly because he did not trust Northerners, but mostly because he didn't trust handsome young men who showed an interest in Sarah Bankroft. Even though she had been leading him and some others a merry chase these last few years, he still hoped that she would come to her senses and do him the honor of accepting his oft-repeated proposal. Still, Miss Sarah had given the fellow permission to ask questions, so he'd better answer them. No sense in getting her riled up.

"The Bankrofts," he sighed. "They thought they were God's gift to the human race. Folks around here didn't much care for them. They felt themselves above us; they were snobs, you know. All but Miss Sarah, that is. Nicest kid you'd ever want to know. Funny thing is, they didn't have any use for her either."

"Why was that?" Jonathan found this surprising.

"As a child Miss Sarah wasn't—how should I put this?" He seemed to be struggling with the words. "She wasn't as attractive as they were. I've never seen so many kids with such perfect features. You kind of expect children to have pimples and cowlicks and such. Not the Bankrofts. Miss Sarah was the only one who wasn't perfect."

"And because of that they were cold to her?" Jonathan was still having trouble matching the beautiful blonde woman who was the mistress of Cherron with the chubby, unattractive little girl that Bill Collins described.

"They used to tease her all the time. Her cousin Martin was about the only one who was decent," he went on. "Poor little thing used to come here to town and spend practically the entire day talking to people; she was so lonely. She used to play with the poor kids in the shacks behind Main Street."

"The family didn't mind her spending so much time with the people there?"

"Her parents weren't happy about it, but I suppose they were relieved when she wasn't around to embarrass them."

"Embarrass them?"

"They thought she wasn't as intelligent as they were. Dull witted, her cousins used to call her." He shook his head.

Jonathan thought about what Bill Collins was telling him. The picture of her he was painting in his mind had no relation to the Miss Sarah he had

54

just met.

"But she runs that entire tobacco plantation on her own!"

"Just goes to show you. The ugly duckling grew up to be quite a swan. And talk about kind! There's nothing she wouldn't do for you if she could. See that boy out there?"

He pointed to a young man working at one of the teller's cages.

"He wanted to get started in the bank, but he had to drop out of college because of his financial situation. She loaned him the money to finish school and then talked me into taking him on here."

"I can understand your fondness for her," Jonathan agreed.

"Everyone in Arcadia feels the same way," Collins assured him. "She's got old Jeremiah's son in medical school, and she's helped God knows how many others I don't know about. She's probably helped every person in this town at one time or another. You see that library?" He pointed at a large red brick building across the street. "She built it for us."

Jonathan was impressed with Collins' list of Miss Sarah's kindnesses and charities. He marveled at the fact that someone who had been abused in her childhood could have grown into such a generous and talented young woman. Miss Sarah, he suspected, was turning out to be the most interesting of all the Bankrofts.

As he was leaving the bank, he bumped into another of Miss Sarah's admirers, her uncle Luke.

"Jonathan," the stout old man greeted him warmly. "I thought you were moving out to Cherron today."

"I am," he assured him. "I just wanted to talk to some of the townspeople about their feelings toward the Bankrofts."

Luke Bankroft smiled. "I'd like to hear some of their comments."

"They weren't particularly fond of the family."

"Nor was I."

"Really?"

"Since you're poking into their story, Jonathan, you may as well know the truth about them. They were strange, to put it kindly."

So he was beginning to discover!

"They believed they were above everyone else. Because of that, they believed that they had to excel in everything—beauty, brains, business, everything. The women had to be beautiful, the men had to be handsome and brilliant."

"All but Miss Sarah," Jonathan added.

"Oh, you know about that already? Yes, all but Miss Sarah. She was always different, not like the rest of the Bankrofts. But that gave them no reason to hurt the girl so." The old man shook his head. Even now, in his old age, human cruelty still shocked him.

"What about Martin? Is he a typical Bankroft?"

"No, I don't think you could say that either. Now my sister, Miss Jessica. She used to behave like a real Bankroft woman. You should have seen her in her prime. She lives out at Cherron and you'll meet her soon enough. But she's suffered a lot in the last few years, and I'm afraid there's little of the old Bankroft spirit left in her."

No doubt about it, Jonathan realized; the Bankrofts were a strange and fascinating family.

After his interview with Bill Collins and Luke Bankroft, Jonathan decided to head out to Cherron. As he drove along Route 39 he was struck once again by the beauty of the north Florida countryside. The open fields where the tobacco seedlings had recently been planted were covered with white cheesecloth tents flapping in the gentle breezes. Wild blue irises and clumps of cattails lined the roadside, and in the piney forests he could spot luscious magnolias and showy bougain-villeas.

His mind was still on the Bankrofts as he drove. So much death in one family. It was unusual, strange, really. He would have to know more about them. How had they all died? He hoped it would not upset Miss Sarah to talk about them.

Considering the heartaches her family had given her, it was a wonder she was not resentful. It could have had a profound negative effect upon her; but, in spite of it all, she seemed like a well-adjusted young woman. The fact that her family had deprived her of their love with outrageous demands for perfection did not seem to have turned her against them. He felt a sudden surge of anger towards people who had long since gone.

He could almost picture the girl in front of him as he drove. Lovely, delicate Miss Sarah. He saw those big blue eyes. Yes, there was definitely something magnetic about those eyes. Haunting, trusting and deep. He liked them. They had held him, caressed him. But then, he found he liked everything about Miss Sarah.

Miss Sarah insisted that she and Martin give Jonathan a horseback tour of Cherron. As they saddled up the horses—Miss Sarah on her pinto, Isis, and Jonathan and Martin on the Morgans, Jason and Medea—Martin spoke to Sarah.

"You're going to have to do something about your little squirrel friend, Sarah," he said. "He's driving the dogs crazy."

"He'll be gone soon," she assured him.

"Are you settled in the house?" Martin inquired politely enough, but Jonathan detected an underlying distaste in his voice. Nevertheless, he assured the cousin that he had settled in quite comfortably.

He asked Sarah about her aunt and cousin.

"They're family," she explained. "And since Aunt Jessica has no skills to support herself and Devon is too young to make a living, I could do no less than let them live here."

Once again he was struck by how much family loyalty meant to her. Here she had taken in her widowed aunt and given her and her son a home.

"I hope it doesn't bother you that I've been asking in town about your family?"

"Not at all," she said. "A writer must gather his material. I understand."

She showed him the beds where the tiny tobacco seeds were first placed, and the fields where they had recently been transplanted to be harvested in

July. The plants would grow six-feet tall, she explained. In a few weeks the workers would be "topping" them, that is, removing the top when the pink flowers begin to develop. That would increase the weight of the leaves and make them taste better.

She pointed out the large curing barns where the tobacco would be dried, and she showed him how they were then packed in large casks called hogsheads. Later in the summer she would take the hogsheads to the Live Oak auction, where Cherron tobacco was highly prized.

Jonathan was impressed with Miss Sarah's expertise and with the way she supervised every facet of the business; but most of all he was impressed with the way the men in the fields smiled and waved at Sarah as she walked by. The looks on their faces were sincere, and it was easy to see that they genuinely loved Miss Sarah.

The three of them had passed the tobacco fields now and were following the trail that led through the lush and unspoiled forest. There were cypress trees, thick groups of wilderness pine, dense thickets of cabbage palm, and abundant mangroves, red maples, tulip trees, and palmettos. Jonathan decided that this was the most beautiful forest he had ever seen.

Still, he was supposed to be working, and he continued his questions.

"I'd like to know more about the more recent Bankrofts, Miss Sarah," he said. "From your grandfather to the present."

"Grandfather Daniel was a perfectionist," she

said, picturing the stern old man who had made such an impression on her when she was a child. He was a tall, rail-thin man with a shock of white hair, and watery blue eyes. He had a brusque manner with those who did not meet his impeccable standards."

"Unfortunately, he believed that everyone in his family had to be perfect as well," Martin added bitterly. "A little impossible for mere human beings. I'm afraid it made life difficult for some of us."

"Nanna, our grandmother, was a small, sickly woman who took to her bed a good deal," Miss Sarah sighed. "She was always ill; at least that's the way I remember her. Her one great passion was books. She loved Charles Dickens."

Martin smiled as he recalled their gentle grandmother. "Sarah used to spend hours in Grandma's bedroom reading to her," he said. "She rarely left the house."

"She died when I was ten. Grandfather followed her soon after. His oldest son, Uncle Neil, inherited Cherron; but he died three months later. He'd never married."

"Which is not surprising," Martin added.

"Why?"

"Uncle Neil was not what you'd call a friendly man," Sarah explained.

"Uncle Neil was a miserable monster," Martin said.

"Martin, that's unkind."

"Maybe, but it's true." He looked at Jonathan. "He died while chasing one of the field hands. He was trying to beat him with a whip because the worker didn't have his horse ready for him on time. He tripped and fell, hit his head on a rock. Served him right, the bastard."

"Martin!"

The man's sad brown eyes were angry, and he seemed to grip the reins of his Morgan tighter than ever. He was still furious at the thought of it, years later.

"It did serve him right," he insisted. "He scared all of us when we were children. Him and his temper."

"Anyway," she said, smiling at Jonathan and obviously embarrassed by her cousin's outburst, "My daddy inherited Cherron from his brother. Aunt Jessica had married her dashing pilot by then and was living in Europe."

"That's the lady I met at the house?"

"Yes. You wouldn't believe it to look at her now, but she was quite a glamorous figure in her day." Sarah sighed. "A few years later, my parents lost their lives on the same day."

"After accidentally ingesting poison mushrooms?"

"You have been doing your homework, haven't you?" Sarah said, smiling. "Yes, that's true. My oldest brother, Michael, had died a year before or he would have inherited Cherron."

Jonathan sensed that these were events that still troubled Miss Sarah, and he avoided asking questions for a few minutes. They moved through the forest in silence. He noticed that not only was the forest rich in trees but there were many animals that seemed to be watching them as they passed through. He noticed a mother deer and a small baby deer, a raccoon, some woodchucks, and, of course, the birds. The forest was filled with songbirds.

"And you, Martin," he said at last. "You grew up at Cherron, too?"

"Yes," he said sullenly. "My father was the youngest brother, Jeffrey. He was an attorney and had an office in town, but I grew up here."

"And your mother?" Jonathan was sorry he asked when he saw the sadness come over Martin Bankroft's worn face.

"My mother stayed here as long as she could take being around the perfect Bankrofts," he said bitterly. "Finally she couldn't take any more. One day she left. We never heard from her again."

They had come to a bluff that looked out over still more forests. Below was a sheer drop of several hundred feet. Jonathan recognized the site from his research.

"I understand — that is," he hesitated to bring up another painful memory.

"Yes, Jonathan, this is where my brother Michael died," Sarah said quietly. She sighed. He had died so young, so brilliant and handsome. It was painful to recall.

"Michael wanted to be an ornithologist," she explained. "He would watch the birds from here with binoculars. I told mother he stood too close to the edge, but she would tell me that I should mind my own business, that Michael knew what he was doing. He was home from school on a two-week

62

recess. The morning of his second day home he came out here. He got too close to the edge of the cliff. I was there. I reached out to grab him, but he fell. They brought him up by mule the next afternoon."

"I'm terribly sorry to hear that," Jonathan murmured sympathetically.

"He was always a smart-ass bully anyway," Martin said.

"Martin! That's no way to speak about my brother!"

"He can't hear me," Martin said.

They rode back to the great house in silence. Jonathan was struck once again by how gentle and forgiving Miss Sarah was, but concerned about the bitterness in her cousin's voice.

*   *   *

It was early fall and there was a crispness in the air at Cherron. Fourteen-year-old Sarah Bankroft sat perched on a large rock on Benson's Cliff, swinging her chubby legs. Her adolescent face was marred by pimples, and her frizzy hair was blowing uncontrollably in the cold wind. Her brother Michael stood at the edge of the cliff, his binoculars glued to his eyes. He claimed to love birds, but his killing and stuffing them were not her idea of showing love for them. She thought it was barbaric.

"How are they getting on?" she asked.

"The eggs should hatch soon," he answered, not taking his glasses from his eyes.

"Aren't you standing too close, Michael?"

"No, I'm not standing too close," he said impatiently. "I wish I could catch her."

"Catch who?"

"The mother bird. She'd make a great addition to my collection."

This idea upset Sarah. "You shouldn't kill them," she insisted. "They're only beautiful when they're alive."

Michael Bankroft just sneered at his little sister. "What on earth do you know about beauty?"

"I know what's beautiful," she insisted.

"You? Now what would ugliness know about beauty?"

"You shouldn't say those things, Michael." She was angry and on the verge of tears. "You're my brother. You should be nice to me."

"I wish you weren't my sister. Don't you know you're an embarrassment. I'm ashamed to be seen with you. We all are." He turned away from her with disgust.

The chubby little girl just stared at the back of her brother's head. She was angry and hurt, and all her rage showed in her tearful blue eyes. Her pupils grew quite large, and the whites of her eyes began to shine as though a light had been turned on behind them. She sat as still as a statue, boring imaginary holes in the back of her brother's head.

Michael shivered and took several steps forward. Now he was just inches from the edge of the cliff.

"Don't say things like that, Michael. I warn you." Again her head lowered and she concentrated upon him. He took another step forward.

"You must never say things like that to me again."

Her brother just laughed, and the sound of his laughter echoed through the mountains, bounding off the moss-covered rocks.

It came so quickly. His foot slipped. Sarah reached forward and grabbed at his shirt, but it was too late. He looked back in horror as he went over the edge, but all he saw was Sarah, his little sister. She was smiling and her eyes were glittering strangely. It was the last thing he saw as he plunged several hundred feet down to his death.

* * *

Darkness had engulfed the great house, and most of its occupants were asleep. Miss Sarah descended the stone steps to the basement and crossed the floor to the large wooden door. Quietly, she reached for the big iron key and opened the door. It squeaked. She made a mental note to tell Martin to oil the hinges.

She walked in and lit each candle in the great crystal chandelier hanging from the ceiling, emitting a sigh of pleasure as her eyes swept around the room.

"A young man has come to Cherron," she said aloud. "A handsome young writer. He wants to tell the story of our family in a book. Isn't that nice of him? He likes me; I can tell he does. He finds me quite beautiful. How ironic that they all find me beautiful now."

She stepped around the table slowly.

"Should I tell him? Should I tell the true story of

the Bankrofts? No, I think not. It is too soon."

She glided around the room, still chattering.

"He wouldn't understand. That understanding takes time, doesn't it? Yes, you know that well."

Still there was no answer.

She looked back at the dining table. She ran her finger over a Limoges dish. It was dusty.

"Dust!" she shouted. "We can't have that. I'll tell Martin to wash the dishes. Everything must be perfect for you." She paused. "The party is tomorrow night. I know how much the men enjoy their yearly party at Cherron. They'll all be here with their bawdy talk and their hands stained with Cherron soil. They'll dance in the ballroom. They'll eat and drink and enjoy themselves. They'll make love on the lawn and laugh until all hours. How you would have frowned upon that. Having those common people in this house of perfection." Her tone was sarcastic.

"Well, I care about them," she said bitterly. "I love them."

As she backed out of the room she continued her one-way conversation.

"You'll see them tomorrow night. You'll hear them. You'll feel their presence and know that they are enjoying Cherron and that there is nothing you can do about it."

She began to laugh as she turned out the light, plunging the room back into total darkness.

Jonathan had decided to have a look at the area surrounding Cherron on his own, but he had promised he would return in time for the festivities

66

that evening. He was looking forward to the ball and to dancing with Miss Sarah.

The day was warm, but a vagrant breeze seemed to follow him as he walked through the woods at the edge of the lawn. This section had been left almost completely wild since, Miss Sarah had informed him, the swamp made it impossible to grow tobacco or anything else worthwhile.

He soon forgot her warning not to venture too far into the swamp, although he knew it was a dangerous place for a novice. The quicksand could swallow a man without leaving a trace and the alligators were supposed to be fierce. He had even heard rumors of panthers occasionally appearing in the darkness.

Nevertheless, he made his way undaunted through the swamp, watching the sunlight flicker through the tall cypress trees, their branches festooned with Spanish moss. The ground was damp and spongy, and the air was fetid.

He strolled for several hours while the foliage around him grew more dense. He had stopped to rest near some dark, mud-covered, fallen trees and to get his bearings when he heard it. A splash.

He whirled around and saw nothing. Then he realized with horror that what he had mistaken for a tree trunk was actually a large, old alligator. It was at least seven feet long and had a massive body that must have been two-feet wide at the back.

He stood paralyzed, praying that the old alligator would not notice him. It seemed hours until the huge creature was totally submerged beneath the muddy swamp water, leaving him free to continue.

Then he heard another sound, a hoarse, raspy sound.

He stood still, staring at the dense trees, realizing for the first time that the entire forest was alive with activity. The ground beneath him was filled with insects and lizards. There was an incessant din composed of the sounds of birds and frogs and the constant hissing of the steaming swamp mud.

Had he imagined the sound? No, the voice spoke again, sounding hoarse and gravelly.

"Stay away from her."

He turned but saw no one. Now he realized how far into the swamp he had come. His hands were clammy, and an odd coldness had entered the marrow of his bones. He was lost, and suddenly he wondered if he could find his way out again. What was this voice that spoke to him?

"Who's there?" he called to his invisible companion. "Who are you? What do you want?"

"Stay away from that place," the disembodied voice rasped at him again.

His head swung around quickly, and he caught a glimpse of something darting among the cypress trees.

"Hey, wait. Who are you?" he shouted as he pushed aside the jasmine vines and the Spanish moss and tried to follow. But the figure had disappeared. His heart was pounding as he stood there for a moment, puzzled. Then the voice came again, this time from behind him.

"That's the devil's home."

Jonathan turned to see a shriveled old man

crouching by a large tree. His arms were wrapped tightly around the trunk as if it were the only thing supporting him. His spindly legs shook badly. His wrinkled face was distorted with pain and red with oozing boils. Above his bulbous nose his bloodshot eyes were set deep in shadowed sockets. His filthy clothes were like rags, disintegrating on his body.

In spite of his wretched appearance, he spoke like an educated man.

"What are you talking about, old man?" Jonathan asked, taking a tentative step towards him.

"No," the old man shrieked, clutching the tree trunk tighter than ever.

"All right, calm down," he said patiently. "I won't come near you. Just tell me what you mean. What's the devil's home?"

The old man nodded his head in the direction of Cherron.

"That place—that place—it's evil!"

"You mean Cherron?" Jonathan asked, incredulous. It served him right for paying attention to the old fool. "It's a beautiful place," he said. "I'm staying there."

"I know, I know. Stay away if you know what's good for you. Stay away. Evil. Evil."

The wretched old man stood up to leave, leaning heavily on a thick tree branch that he used as a walking cane. Jonathan knew he could never follow him deeper into the swamp. He simply did not know his way.

"Please wait," he implored. "Why do you think Cherron is evil?"

"Because she's there," he whispered, his eyes shining madly.

"She? You mean Miss Sarah?"

Mention of the girl's name brought panic to the man's bloodshot eyes. He began to groan and to punch the air with his fists.

"Calm down. It's all right," Jonathan assured him.

"It is not all right," he insisted. "Nothing's all right. Not while—not while—she's alive."

"Now just a minute—"

"You'll see. You'll find out," the filthy old man warned him. "But it'll be too late for you. Too late, you hear." His red-rimmed eyes began to weep.

"Who are you?" Jonathan asked.

The aging hermit seemed to struggle to remember his very name. He hit himself on the head with the palm of his hand.

"Gibbons, Jason. That's me. I—I run the bank. The bank in town. Yes, that's who I am—I was, until that evil child. . . ."

Suddenly a glassy look came into his crazed red eyes. He seemed to be talking into space.

"What are you doing here?" he shouted to the air. "You go home now, girl. You go home now. What do you want here? What are you doing?"

The filthy old man looked terrified, and he jumped back as Jonathan watched in wonder. He seemed to be talking to someone who wasn't there.

"Don't look at me like that," he insisted. "What are you doing? Ohh, ahh." The anguish in his scream startled Jonathan. The old man seemed to be in genuine pain.

"What's the matter, Mr. Gibbons? What's wrong? Who are you talking to?"

The sound of Jonathan's voice seemed to reach the old man. He turned and faced him, but he still seemed dazed.

"I don't remember," he muttered. "She was there and I was here. I warn you, mister, stay away from her. It'll be too late. Ask Adela, she can tell you." He stopped suddenly, as if he realized he had already said too much. He turned away and ran off through the swamp, alternately howling and laughing. He moved swiftly, familiar with the swamp, and quickly disappeared into the mist and the moss.

Jonathan was confused and frightened by this encounter. The old man was definitely mad, though; of that he had no doubt.

He scanned the swamp. The trees seemed larger than before, towering over him. The foliage seemed even more dense than when he had entered. Which direction was he supposed to take? Suddenly he felt like a trapped animal. The enormous trees seemed to block his way deliberately.

He ran in one direction but saw nothing familiar to him. He started off in another, and still found nothing he recognized. He must jog his memory or he would be here forever.

Fear gripped him and he felt it rise from the pit of his stomach. Beads of sweat broke out on his forehead. He took out a handkerchief and wiped his face.

He could hear animal sounds off in the distance.

They seemed to be laughing at him, taunting him, daring him to find his way to safety. The sneering little creatures bared their teeth at him. And then there was that distorted wind whistling a jumbled melody through the trees. It seemed to say "We've got you now. You'll never get out. You'll never get out. You belong to us now."

He heard the swamp mud bubbling and saw steam rise from it in little puffs. There was more of that hideous laughing. Or was it merely a chipmunk? The thorns grabbed at his legs, holding and biting, ripping the material of his pants.

There was a malignancy about this place. It had a fetid, ominous atmosphere. He felt he had to get out soon or die. His head swirled; the trees went around and around; his eyes blurred. He felt surrounded and lost.

Suddenly he noticed a clump of blue irises. Hadn't he seen them before? Yes, he remembered. He had seen them on his way into the swamp. There it was, beyond; he could make out the great house, obscured by the overhanging Spanish moss.

With relief, he saw his way out.

Cherron was already ablaze with lights and alive with good spirits when Jonathan arrived. He hurried upstairs to change for the party. Great garlands of roses festooned the huge mahogany staircase and everywhere he saw and heard the sights and sounds of the Cherron ball.

There was a small orchestra playing in the ballroom, and the room and the patio beyond were crowded with dancers. The Cherron workers had brought their wives and sweethearts to the gala. He waved to Dr. Luke, who was dancing with his sister, Mrs. Morrow. He saw several young and pretty women flirting with Martin Bankroft, but the man seemed oblivious to their charms. It was strange, he realized, that Martin stayed on at Cherron. He had never married, yet he certainly seemed attractive to women.

Probably the only person who had not joined in the festivities was Devon Morrow, whom he found seated on the marble steps of the verandah, staring off into space, as usual. Now Jonathan realized what was so odd about the boy. He never blinked.

He did not have time to dwell on the strangeness of the boy, though. He still had not found Miss Sarah, and he was searching eagerly for her among the crowd.

He spotted her in the middle of the ballroom. She looked lovelier than ever in a long silk gown of a blue that matched her eyes. Her blonde hair was pinned up loosely, and several stray curls fell down her neck. She was wearing a necklace of heirloom pearls and she was dancing with Bill Collins. She was laughing at something he was saying and she seemed to be having a wonderful time.

Jonathan felt a sudden pang of jealousy. Really, he assured himself, that was ridiculous. He hardly knew the girl. He had no right to be possessive about her so soon.

Still, when she saw him over Bill Collins' shoulder, she did wink and, encouraged, he sailed across the dance floor, bumping into several couples on the way.

"May I cut in?" he asked politely. Although Bill Collins was obviously not pleased to give Miss Sarah up, he yielded for the sake of politeness.

"Are you having a good time, Jonathan?" she asked, as they moved across the dance floor.

"Yes, and I'm not the only one. All of your guests seem to be enjoying themselves."

"I hope so. I want to share the joy of Cherron with everyone who works for me."

The band paused, and he suggested that they stop at the barbecue that had been set up on the rear lawn, beyond the patio. Long pits had been dug and filled with pine chips and hickory wood that blazed now with a fragrant fire. In them were roasting dozens of whole chickens and several whole pigs. Jeremiah was tending the pit, and he smiled when he saw Miss Sarah and Jonathan.

On a long table nearby were great bowls of greens, buttermilk biscuits, cornbread, okra, fresh fruit, and Key Lime pie. The food was disappearing fast.

Jonathan and Sarah made their way along the table and, when they had filled their plates, they sat on a wrought iron bench under a nearby magnolia tree.

He wondered if he should mention the strange man he had encountered in the swamp. She seemed to be having such a wonderful time and she had worked so hard on the party that he did not want to dampen her mood. Still, if the man was spreading this kind of vicious gossip, she should know it.

"Jason Gibbons!" she said when he told her

about his adventure. "You actually spoke to him?"

"Yes. I saw him in the swamp."

"You shouldn't have ventured so far in there, Jonathan," she warned him. "People have disappeared in there."

He was touched by her concern about his safety, and he decided not to tell her the part about being lost in the swamp. She'd only worry.

"I hadn't intended to go so far," he explained. "My mind wasn't on my progress."

"So he thinks I'm the devil?" Sarah seemed amused at the thought.

"He seems to be afraid of you."

"I have no idea why. The last time I saw him I was just a child."

"Does it bother you?"

"Why should it? No one listens to him. He's just a crazy old man. A sad, crazy old man."

"I guess you're right." He spooned up the last of the Key Lime pie. Inside, the band had resumed and they could hear the music pouring out the opened French doors.

"He seemed to think he was still in charge of the bank," he added. "He mentioned a name, too. A woman called Adela. Does that mean anything to you?"

"Adela? Oh, that old witch," she said and smiled. "I'm afraid you're going to meet all our local eccentrics. She used to live in the swamp too, but I haven't seen her around in some time."

He looked at her tenderly. He felt that he must protect this delicate girl from the ravings of a sick old man. Surely this was not a devil, but rather an angel.

* * *

The other children gathered in a tight little group and spoke in secret whispers to each other while twelve-year-old Sarah stood alone, watching, wanting so badly to be a part of them. Occasionally one of them would turn to look at her and giggle.

"You want to play a game with us?" her brother Everett finally asked.

It was a miracle. They were allowing her to play with them. They recognized her existence. The chubby little girl's dull eyes brightened.

"Sure I do."

"O.K. We'll play hide-and-seek," Everett took her by the hand and stood her facing the hickory tree. "Now you count to one hundred and we'll hide. Then you have to find us. Keep your eyes closed tight now. O.K.?"

"O.K." Her heartbeat quickened as she placed her chubby hands over her eyes and counted out loud. As she did so she heard the other children chuckling and mumbling, then there was only silence. When she reached one hundred she turned around and began to look for the other children.

They were nowhere to be seen.

She looked all over the grounds of Cherron, skipping lightly through the woods, peering behind the rocks, and coming finally to the edge of the swamp. She saw no one. She called out their names.

"Everett!"

No answer.

"Michael!"

No answer.

"Monica!"

No answer.

Now she realized that they had played another joke on her. They had run away leaving her to stand there alone, hurt and humiliated. Why? Why did they do these things?

"Run out on ya, did they?"

She turned around to see a short, hunchbacked old woman standing in front of her, her hands on her hips. Her stiff black hair was greasy, sticking out from both sides of her head. Her eyes were mere slits set deep in her withered face. She wore a rusty old black dress that hung like a sack on her scrawny body. Her hands were gnarled and her long nails were dirty. A scruffy gray cat stood next to her, staring at Sarah with the same kind of slitty eyes its mistress had.

Sarah stared back curiously at this strange figure. She wasn't sure whether to laugh or run.

"Them kids are always doin' that to you, ain't they, girl?"

Sarah still didn't answer.

"You scared of me, girl?"

"No."

The old woman started to laugh, but it came out as a dry cackle, a shrill broken cry like nothing that Sarah had ever heard before. Sarah began to regret that she had ventured so near the swamp.

"Most folks are afraid of me," the old crone assured her. "Surely they are."

"I'm not afraid of you," Sarah said firmly.

"What's your name?"

"Adela, and my cat here's named Elvira."

"Mine's Sarah."

"I know, girl. I know all about you."

"How can you?" Sarah was surprised. "I've never seen you before."

"I watch. I'm watchin' all the time. I seen what they do to you. They hurt you, don't they?"

"Sometimes." She still wasn't sure she liked the idea of any witnesses to her humiliations.

"All the time!" The old woman started to cackle again. "They're always pullin' that crap on you. I watch. I see."

"Where do you live?" Sarah asked.

The hag seemed to enjoy the girl's openness.

"In there," she said, pointing to the interior of the swamp.

"Nobody can live in there," Sarah said.

"I do. You want to see my house?"

"You have a house in there?" Sarah was amazed that anyone could be living in the swamp, much less in a house there.

"I surely do, child. You come with Adela now. Adela will show you things you never dreamed of." The old woman turned around and, without hesitation, Sarah followed her into the swamp.

"You really ain't scared of me, are you girl?" the old woman asked her when they had gone a few yards.

"No. I'm just glad to have someone to talk to." Adela liked her, she could tell. Finally she had a real friend. She was sure that Adela would never make fun of her or play cruel tricks.

"Oh, Adela will talk to you all right," the old woman assured her, as if reading her mind. "She'll be your friend." The old hag threw her head back and laughed.

Sarah had been warned never to go into the swamp, but her new friend seemed unafraid. She showed the little girl how to walk gingerly on the wet, spongy ground and how to avoid being sucked into the bubbling mud holes.

It was becoming difficult to see through the undergrowth. The tall grass and the Spanish moss that overhung the tree branches seemed to shut out most of the sunlight. Although it could be only two o'clock in the afternoon, it already seemed like midnight inside Adela's swamp.

Once Sarah put her foot on what she thought was an old tree trunk, and suddenly it moved. She screamed, but Adela just laughed.

"If you're goin' to come into the swamp, you best learn to recognize an alligator before you step on it," she cackled.

The heavy scent of the trees and wild flowers mingled with the rotten smell of the swamp mud. The chattering of the songbirds, white egrets, and mockingbirds was deafening. The atmosphere was heady.

Sarah noticed a small raccoon at the foot of a cypress tree. The little animal stared at her through its masked eyes, but when she bent down and called to it, the creature refused to move.

"Make it come to you," Adela told her.

"Make it? How can I make it?"

"Use your mind. You can make it do anything

you like, if you know how."

The old woman bent down and tightened her grip on Sarah's tender shoulders.

"Now concentrate," she ordered. "Think very hard. Look at it. With your mind, tell it to come to you."

Sarah still did not understand what the old crone was talking about, but she did as she was told. She fixed her eyes on the little raccoon and thought very hard.

"That's it," Adela encouraged her. "Don't take your eyes from it. Make it come. That's it. That's good."

Suddenly the little raccoon came forward hesitantly and sat down right at Sarah's feet. She reached out and picked it up, but it wriggled, trying to free itself from her arms.

"Keep concentrating," Adela ordered. "Make him sit quiet."

Sarah forced herself to concentrate, and, in a moment, it had ceased its protests and lay still and content in her arms.

She still wasn't sure what had just happened. But she remembered her strange experiences with the Frisbee and the marbles. Maybe she hadn't been imagining them after all.

"You can make anything happen if you want," Adela assured her. "If you truly want."

They moved on deeper into the swamp and Sarah began to worry. Suppose she was somehow separated from the old woman? She would never find her way out. She would die a horrible death. Maybe she would starve. Or perhaps she would be sucked up by one of the mudholes or attacked by the alligators. She clutched Adela's hand.

At last they came upon a small clearing of solid earth in the middle of a marsh. On it stood a ramshackle wood shed with a flat tar paper roof. It looked ready to collapse. Around it, in what could be described as a yard, were tin cans, cups, wood, old inner tubes, cardboard cartons, newspapers, string, and all sorts of odd junk. In the center of the yard was a small campfire, and over it hung a large iron pot.

"You hungry, girl?" Adela asked her.

She nodded. She was always hungry. She watched as the woman stirred some foul-smelling stew that had been simmering in the pot. She dished out the mess onto three dirty tin plates for themselves and Elvira. Adela and Sarah sat on the ground and Elvira curled up by her mistress.

"Do you live here?" Sarah asked, trying to hide her disgust as some of Adela's stew dribbled down the old woman's chin and onto her stained dress.

"Different from your house, ain't it, girl?" The old woman laughed again.

"What's your last name?" She still couldn't understand where the woman had come from.

"Ain't got one," she snapped.

"Why do you live here?"

" 'Cause it's my home. Besides, ain't too many people would want me around them. I ain't their sort," she sniffed. "I'm an outcast, like you."

"How'd you know that raccoon would come to me?"

"I seen you around. I knew you could do it," she

81

said casually. "You can make people do what you want 'um to do, too. I want 'um to leave me in peace and they do."

"I want them to like me."

Adela studied the girl. "Would you like to get even with them kids for what they do to you?"

"I can't."

"Sure you can, if you want to. But you gotta want it bad, real bad, in your guts. I can help. I can teach you how."

"You mean like a game?"

The old woman smiled at the little girl.

"Yes child," she agreed. "Like a game. But you gotta try very hard. You have to practice all the time. If you do, they'll never hurt you again. Would you like that?"

Sarah thought about this. She didn't know what sort of game would stop people from hurting her, but it would be nice. She wrinkled her brow and squinted her eyes. Perhaps it was worth a try.

"They really shouldn't do those things to me," she said. "It's not right. O.K. I'll play the game. What are the rules?"

"The first rule is that you listen to me," Adela snapped. "The rest of them, they don't even know what's inside their own heads. The power's just sittin' there, and they don't even use it."

"Why not?"

" 'Cause they don't know it's there," the old crone laughed. "They only got book learnin'. They go no further. They stop at what them books teach them. If they could reach deeper into themselves, past that first bit of book learnin', they'd know the power that was a waitin' for 'um."

"Do you know how to use it, Adela?"

"A part of it."

"You mean there's power behind a door that no one knows about?"

"Somethin' like that. If you can unlock that door you can reach into your own mind. Then you can reach into the heads of other people. Make 'um do anything you like."

"How?" she said, still skeptical.

"Just like you did with that raccoon. I'll teach you. We can start right now, if you want." She rose and led Sarah into the shack.

It was dark inside, and the candle Adela lit didn't give much light. The house held a musty, putrid smell that turned Sarah's stomach. There was only one small room and it had a dirt floor, part of which was covered with a filthy, threadbare rug. There was a dusty couch, a battered chest of drawers with its third drawer missing, and some old pictures of movie stars and fashionable women stuck on the wall with nails.

As Adela led Sarah to the couch, the girl felt a cold chill creep into her.

"Now you lay quiet," she warned. "Close your eyes. Relax, I ain't gonna hurt you. I'm just trying to help you." Sarah lay back, relaxed her shoulders, and closed her eyes. "Good, that's the way."

Adela blew out the candle and placed pieces of old cardboard over the windows to block any light. She sat on a chair beside the couch and began to massage the girl's forehead gently.

"All right, now," she said. "I want you to concentrate." She spoke in a hushed voice. "You're walking down a corridor. It's the corridor of your own mind. Can you see it?"

"I — I don't know."

"Think," Adela said softly, still massaging the girl's forehead. "Use your mind's eye. Can you see it now?"

"Yes, I think so. Yes, yes I can," she exclaimed. "It's gray."

"Fine. Now keep on walking. Deeper, farther into yourself. You'll touch places you never dreamed existed."

Sarah was frightened of this journey into the unknown and Adela seemed to sense this.

"Don't be scared," she said gently. "This is your own mind; it can't hurt you. Keep walking."

The musty, fetid odor of the cabin overpowered her senses, invading her very core. She felt sick, nauseous.

"I'm dizzy, Adela."

"You're doing fine. Keep going; don't stop now. Keep walking."

"I'm dizzy I tell you. I don't feel well. I'm going to be sick. Let me up, please, Adela. I'm scared."

"No need to be, child. Just lie still."

Sarah relaxed again.

"You're walking down that corridor, that long gray corridor."

"I'm not walking anymore, Adela. I'm floating."

"Good! Deeper, go deeper, girl."

There was a long silence, then Sarah spoke up again.

"I can't go any further."

"Why not?"

"I can't. There's something there. Something that won't let me pass. It's blocking my way."

"That's it, child," the old woman said eagerly. "You've come to it, to your door, your locked door. Now think, think hard. Remember the pain people give you every day—the hurts, the insults, the humiliation. I know you got it in you to break through. You got reason to."

Sarah thought about how they tormented her. She remembered their cruelty, remembered how they had humiliated her by hiding from her today and leaving her there on the lawn, counting, thinking she was finally part of their game. Her anger began to rise and she began to pant. Her chest heaved faster and faster as she thought about how mean people had been to her.

"It's there girl, just beyond," Adela said, egging her on further into her own being.

The old woman leaned close to the girl's face, gently touching her cheek, talking into her ear.

"It's right there behind that door, girl. The power to stop them. To stop their words and actions. You must go through it."

Sarah began to squirm, her arms flying into the air savagely. Adela fought to hold her still, but her entire body jerked in violent spasms.

"Nooooo. Ahhhhh, noooooo." She screamed, arching her body convulsively, wrenching, kicking. "Nooooo. Noooo. I can't. No, I can't go in there."

"You can, child. You must, or they'll hurt you for the rest of your life. You'll have nothin' but pain to look forward to. Imagine that pain for the rest of your life. But the power's there to stop them. When you break through, you'll know. You'll have the power. Fight. Go through. Fight. You have the will, I know. I saw it in you."

"Nooo, ahhhh, God, no." Sarah's screams could be heard far into the swamp, but there was no one to help her. She was alone, within herself. She was in a far place where no one had ever ventured before. Adela fought to hold her as she thrashed about in pain on the couch.

"Now!" she ordered. "Now, child, break through. Open that door to your mind. Do it!"

Sarah's whole body vibrated. Spasms shot through her like electric shocks. She kicked and screamed. Her small, pale body was drenched in sweat.

"Ohhh, God, God," she cried. "No, no, no." Her breathing was labored and she was gasping like a drowning woman. "It's pushing me, Adela. The wind, it's pushing me away. Hold me back."

Suddenly she gave a shrill cry from deep within her body and then she relaxed completely. Her breathing returned to normal and her face broke into a satisfied smile.

"I can see it now. The door is open."

"You're through now, girl," Adela sighed, and released Sarah's arms from her strong grasp. "You can rest now."

"Is it over?" she asked weakly.

"No, child. For you it's just beginning."

Adela rose and lit the candle again, as Sarah pushed herself up to a sitting position. The room was now illuminated by an odd glow. Funny that she hadn't noticed it before. Perhaps it had not been there when she first entered the shack. Or perhaps she was now seeing things in a different way.

"What do I do now?"

"You use that power. You practice. Draw the energy you found from your mind. Use your eyes to place it wherever you want to go."

"I don't understand."

"I know you don't. Not yet, anyway. It ain't been long since I found it myself. You keep coming back here and Adela will teach you all she knows about it."

She opened a cabinet and brought out a dusty bottle. She poured a small glass for Sarah and one for herself.

"Dandelion wine," she explained. "This calls for a celebration."

Sarah sipped the sweet drink.

"Can we test it? Can we play the game?"

"Sure, if you want to. We can start with somethin' small. See that spoon on the table? Make it come to you."

Sarah stared at the spoon, her eyes transfixed. She reached into the depths of her mind and commanded the spoon to move. From around her darkened pupils came a glow, a flowing light which came to rest on the object. Nothing happened.

"Harder child, harder," Adela coached.

The spoon began to move across the wooden table. Slowly, then faster, it moved across the room and landed at Sarah's feet.

"Good!" Adela said, satisfied. "That's a beginning. How far you go will depend on you. You must practice."

Sarah was astonished at what she had just done, but the old woman seemed to take it for granted. She picked up the spoon and fondled it.

"But how can this help me with people?"

"Don't you see? You can channel that energy, that force. You focus it on people. Reach into their minds with your own."

She was beginning to understand. Her new power would protect her. It would be her defense. She could control the others with it.

The girl smiled at her mentor.

"It'll take time and hard work, child. I know. You come back tomorrow. We'll try it again."

"Are you a witch, Adela?"

"Lordy, no. I'm like one of them scientists. I just discovered somethin' new."

Sarah was still not convinced, but she let it go. If Adela was a witch she certainly did not want to anger her.

Adela guided her back to the edge of the swamp, and, as she crossed the lawn back to the great house, she considered her new power. The idea of controlling people's very thoughts frightened her, but it fascinated her as well. She would try. She would practice. After all, she had moved an inanimate object. Surely that was something no one else could do.

In the months that followed she visited Adela almost every day. She learned the dangers and the beauty of the swamp. Her brothers and sister and their friends hardly noticed she was gone.

There was no one she could confide in except Martin, and he was away at school. But when he returned she would tell him about her adventure. Meanwhile, she guarded her secret carefully, wondering when she would be ready to use it on people.

Her time finally came.

It was Saturday and her brother David was going into town. Father was going to drive him. There was a horror double-feature at the Arcadia Theatre, *Island of Terror* and *Valley of Mystery*.

David had, as usual, refused to let her join him. Perhaps this might be the time to play the game.

"David, can I come with you today?"

"I told you, no."

"Why?"

"Because you're a nuisance."

"Please let me come," she pleaded. "I won't say a word. You won't even know I'm there."

"I won't know because you won't be."

Yes, she realized. It was surely time. After all, what did she have to lose?

She watched as David walked to the big Chrysler Imperial. Her father had started the motor. She focused on David's forehead, concentrating harder. It took a few minutes, but finally she was through. She had managed to reach into his very private thoughts. Yes, she could see something. Dark, negative thoughts about her. She could read them like words on a page. She tried to transfer her own thoughts into her brother's mind.

"You want to take me with you. You want me to

come more than anything."

Her eyes flickered and glowed as she watched him, seated in the front seat next to their father. She saw him shake himself, as if trying to rid himself of a pesky fly. She did not halt the flow of energy. She was determined to make it work. Adela had told her she could.

"You want me to come. I must come with you or you will feel great sadness."

The Imperial began to move down the paved circular drive, but suddenly it came to a sharp halt. Sarah watched as David opened the door and called out to her.

"Hey, you want to come along?"

Sarah said nothing.

"Come on, Sarah. I want you to come with me. Please come."

She felt a great wave of satisfaction.

Dan Bankroft stared at his son, but no one was more amazed by what had just happened than David Bankroft himself. He had no idea what had gotten into him, but suddenly he wanted his fat, ugly little sister to come to the movies with him. It was very important, and he knew that he would never be able to enjoy the movie without her.

But Sarah knew why he felt that way, and she couldn't wait to tell her new friend what had happened.

Adela was delighted with her little friend's success. The girl giggled when she related how David had pleaded with her to come along.

"That's fine for a beginning," the old woman cackled. "But you've got to try something harder next time."

The chance came a few days later, while she was playing with some of the children in town. They were throwing their ball against the brick wall of the National Bank of Arcadia when Mr. Gibbons came running out. His face was red with anger. He was always furious with the children.

"You kids go play someplace else," he roared. "You're annoying me with your racket. Now go home, all of you. Get out of here."

The children had scattered and Sarah was standing there alone. He looked down at her with distaste.

"And you, Sarah. You should be ashamed. Playing with that trash. Go on, get home."

She stared at him.

"Didn't I tell you something?" he said. He didn't like the way the girl was looking at him. In fact, he didn't like looking back at her. She was a very unattractive little girl. She reminded him of a monkey.

"It's after three o'clock, Mr. Gibbons," she said. "The bank's closed. We're not bothering anyone."

"Cheeky, aren't you?" he said nastily. "You know, you look like a monkey? Now go home."

Yes, she realized. The greater test was at hand. She followed him back into the bank. It was deserted now, and still, and quiet. She followed him on tiptoe down the hallway and into his large office. She watched as he took his place behind the elaborate mahogany desk.

Sarah took a deep breath and looked right into

91

the banker's mind. She summoned the force from within her. She saw the banker squirming, becoming restless in his chair. She was reaching him through space and time.

He looked up and saw the girl standing in the doorway.

"What are you doing in here, girl? Get out of here before I call your daddy. Come on, you're not supposed to be in here."

Sarah was undaunted. She reached far into the recesses of his mind. The thin sliver of light from her eyes was aimed at the banker's head.

Gibbons noticed that the girl was staring at him strangely and he saw the odd, inhuman glow that seemed to come from the whites of her eyes. He began to feel a stabbing pain in the back of his brain. He tried to turn away from that awful light, but he was powerless. The girl's eyes had locked with his own.

"What is that? What are you doing?" he cried. "Stop that. Stop that, I said."

But his voice was weakening.

The child controlled him now and he knew it.

"Whatever you're doing, stop it. I'm sorry. I didn't mean to hurt you."

"So I look like a monkey, do I?" The little girl smiled and her eyes glittered brighter than ever.

The banker began to jump up and down, scratching his side for imaginary fleas, just like a monkey she had seen in a zoo. She was making him do it, she controlled him now. She could do anything she wanted to do with him.

"Stop it," he pleaded. "Have mercy. Please, I

beg you." His skin had begun to explode in oozing boils, and each one felt like a searing flame that had been pushed under his skin.

His pleas were wasted on her, and finally he seemed to realize it. He raced past Sarah and out into the late afternoon sun. Screaming and crying, he ran down the street, deep in madness.

* * *

From his front porch Roy McEndrew could hear the noises of Miss Sarah's party for the Cherron workers. It seemed to get bigger and louder every year, or maybe he was just getting old.

He could see the Japanese lanterns that had been strung through the magnolia trees around the lawn and the tennis court and he could hear the music of the orchestra drifting through the night. He could hear the laughter and the sounds of happiness.

Inside, he could hear Kathy talking to the thing. He couldn't even pretend to think of it as his son anymore. It was just a thing to him, a horrible monster, the quintessence of misery.

His last moment of happiness, he realized, had been that picnic at Benson's Cliff with Miss Sarah and Kathy, just before Kathy went into labor. He remembered how happy the three of them had been, awaiting the birth of a child conceived in love.

Lately, though, when he tried to remember every moment of that afternoon, he found that he had blank spots. When he struggled to fill them in

93

he got blinding headaches. It was as if a red hot poker was searing his mind. He couldn't think or recall anything then.

He wondered sometimes what he had ever done to deserve this monster child—what he and Kathy had done. Who could have wished this thing on anyone?

He looked again across the lawn at the party at Cherron, trying to delay the inevitable moment when he would have to join his sad little family.

Regina Quillam was watching the party at Cherron, from her car, which she had parked alongside Route 39, not far from the gates to the plantation. It was still a free country; and even if Miss Sarah didn't think she was good enough to be received at Cherron, she could certainly take a look at the festivities.

Not that she could ever understand why that girl insisted on entertaining field hands in the big house. If poor Martha Bankroft could see what her daughter was up to, she'd be turning in her grave. In fact, the whole family graveyard must be filled tonight with spirits troubled at the idea of that ugly little child turning belle dame on them all, and throwing all standards to the winds.

She rolled down her car window so that she could hear the music. It must be quite an orchestra, from the sound of it. And she could make out the barbecue from the light of the lanterns that had been strewn across the lawn. Yes, Miss Sarah had gone all out.

Now the truth was that she didn't begrudge the poor girl any happiness in this world. Lord knows she'd suffered enough when she was a child, even Regina would have to admit that. And if the girl wanted to abandon any sense of family pride and tradition and throw Cherron open to the entire world, she wouldn't say a word. She would however, continue to be excluded from the festivities. Even though she had been a great and good friend of the entire Bankroft family, and especially of the child's dearly departed parents, she could accept that the child was just never going to invite her to Cherron, not even for a glass of lemonade.

No, what really got her goat was those roses.

She'd spent her life growing roses; breeding, pruning, cultivating her roses until she was the acknowledged rose queen of the southeastern states. That is, until Miss Sarah had taken a fancy to building a rose garden.

She could not understand what that girl was doing, but those roses just seemed to be the biggest, brightest flowers she'd ever seen. They seemed to take all the prizes at the Gadsden County Rose Fair and it was driving Regina crazy.

And the worst thing was that every time she saw that girl all she could think about was the roses. And the girl seemed to sense it. If she didn't know better, she'd think the girl was reading her mind.

At three in the morning the last of the guests had thanked Miss Sarah and departed. Jonathan watched her as she bid them a gracious goodbye from the white marble steps of the verandah. He thought she was the loveliest thing he had ever seen.

"Well," she sighed, closing the big mahogany and stained glass door. "I'm glad that's over with for another year."

"I admire you for doing it," he said. All night people had been telling him how no other Bankroft would have thrown a party like this for mere employees.

"It's such a beautiful night," he said. "Would you like to take a walk?"

They walked in the rose garden, their way lit by the moonlight. He took her small white hand.

"I love Cherron best when it's like this," she said softly. "Quiet and serene."

He touched her face gently, his hand lingering on her neck. She smiled at him and, encouraged, he drew her close to him and kissed her, pressing against her full, sensuous mouth. He suddenly wanted to possess her, engulf her with his love.

"Sarah," he whispered urgently. "I'm falling in love with you."

To his surprise, she pulled away.

"Please, Jonathan, don't say that."

"But it's true," he insisted. "I know I haven't known you very long, but believe me, it's true."

"Be careful, Jonathan," she warned him. "The Bankrofts are a tragic family. I wouldn't want to see you hurt."

"All right," he said, trying hard to understand. "Let's go back."

From an upstairs balcony, Martin Bankroft watched as his cousin and the stranger walked slowly back to the house. He had seen Jonathan kiss Sarah and he had seen her let him. The look on his face was pained and slowly a tear began to run down his cheek. For the first time, he feared that someone else could shut him out of Sarah's world.

Chapter Three

It was morning and Jonathan found Miss Sarah tending her rose garden. She wore a faded blue denim skirt and a madras shirt, and her blonde hair was braided and covered by a red bandana. Even in these clothes she looked elegant to him.

"Good morning," she said as she looked up at him, shading her eyes from the sun.

"Sarah, about last night." He was a little ashamed of himself.

"Please, it's forgotten."

He knelt beside her and watched as she weeded vigorously. "This is quite a garden," he remarked sincerely. "What kind of fertilizer do you use?"

"Bone meal," she said, smiling. "Martin helps me with it."

"You know, I get the feeling that Martin doesn't approve of me. I felt that he was giving me very hostile looks at breakfast this morning."

"He's just worried about me, Jonathan. He doesn't want me to be hurt again."

"I'd never hurt you, Sarah. You know that, don't you?"

"Actually, Jonathan, I know very little about you," she said as he helped her to her feet.

"My life's an open book. What would you like to know?"

"Whatever you'd care to tell?"

"Well, I was born in New York and went to school there. I come from a nice middle-class family. I have one brother, Ron, who lives in New York and runs a real estate agency. My parents are both living. I went to City College and became a freelance journalist. I've never been in love, at least not seriously, until now."

She stared at him as they stood there in the middle of the rose garden.

"And are you in love—now?"

"I think so."

"You haven't known me very long, Jonathan."

"How long does it take?"

"I don't mean to offend you, but I've only known you a few days."

"The message is slow down," he said.

"Yes."

She seemed to realize that he was hurt and she softened. "Where are you rushing to? We've known each other less than a week. You can't expect people to fall in love overnight, Jonathan. Besides, you have to work on that book of yours."

"Perhaps you're right. But I won't stop trying."

"I don't want you to," she laughed. "How is your

book coming?"

"Slowly, but now I don't mind."

"I have to drive into Arcadia for supplies. Care to come along?"

"Your wish is my command."

Later, after they had loaded Jonathan's car with groceries and supplies, he suggested that they stop for lunch at the Palmetto Leaf Café. He didn't want to go back to Cherron just yet. He was becoming uncomfortable with the disapproving presence of Martin Bankroft and the ghostly looks of Mrs. Morrow and her strange son.

The woman seemed to avoid him, running out of the room when he entered, pretending not to see him when he waved to her from the lawn. Martin seemed to resent his presence completely, as though he was jealous of his friendship with Sarah. In fact, the only one who seemed happy to have him there was Miss Sarah.

He smiled at her now as they sat in a booth at the Palmetto Leaf Café. She had changed into a black and white checkered wrap dress and her hair was pulled back in a pony tail she had tied with a black ribbon.

The restaurant was a typical small-town coffee shop with a fountain and candy counter in the front and booths in the back. It was two o'clock. The lunch hour crush was over, and they seemed to have the restaurant to themselves. He ordered a hamburger for himself and a chicken salad plate for Miss Sarah. He also ordered two ice teas.

Suddenly he noticed a stout, fussily dressed

woman approaching them like a battleship on the high seas. She was about fifty, and her blue flowered dress did not flatter her square shape. She was wearing a white straw hat and white gloves.

"Sarah!" she called out.

He could tell by the way that Sarah winced that she didn't like the woman, but if Regina Quillam noticed it she certainly didn't show it. She was too busy looking him over, trying to figure out who he was. Reluctantly, Sarah introduced him.

"Mr. Evans is writing a book about the Bankrofts," she said proudly.

"Such a tragic family," Mrs. Quillam clucked as she put her gloved hand to Sarah's face, a gesture that made Sarah cringe. "This poor child has had such a bad time of it. I've known her since she was a baby. Tell me, Mr. Evans, were you at the party last night?"

"Yes, ma'am, but I don't remember meeting you."

She laughed. "You didn't. I'm not privileged to be invited to Cherron. Why, I haven't been invited to Cherron in years."

"The party was just for the men who work for me," Miss Sarah said with irritation.

"I understand that," the woman said. "But I do wish that you would invite me up sometimes. After all, I used to be such a great friend of your mother's."

Jonathan noticed that Sarah was glaring at the woman, who rattled on, unconcerned.

"And besides, dear, I'd like to get a look at that rose garden," Regina Quillam was saying. "I just promised myself that you're not going to beat me again at this year's rose show."

Regina had every intention of standing there until kingdom come if necessary, until that stuck-up little girl invited her to sit down. Unfortunately, she started to feel a slight itch. She scratched her neck vigorously, and then she noticed the girl staring at her. Embarrassed, she tried to ignore the itch, but it wouldn't go away. She felt as if a small, hungry fly had bitten her on her neck and then again, under her arm. She scratched harder and then, to her great embarrassment, she realized that she was scratching herself all over as though she had become a rest home for fleas.

"Well, my goodness, you'll have to excuse me," she managed to say as she made a quick exit, scratching hard.

Sarah glared at her until she was out the door and then she turned back to Jonathan who had almost finished his hamburger.

"She seems like a pleasant lady," he remarked.

"Pleasant like a cobra," she said and her bitterness surprised him. "She's no more concerned about me than she is about a mockingbird. She's just jealous and angry because she isn't invited to Cherron. She reminds me of my parents."

"How so?"

"Always looking down on people. She considers herself the most socially prominent person in town. The fact that I throw a party for the men who work in my fields make her just furious. She can't understand why those dirty people, as she calls them, can visit Cherron and she can't."

He realized that this was the first time that he had ever heard Sarah speak badly about her family, but he could understand. She had obviously had enough of her parents' friends when they were alive. If Regina Quillam was a social climber, she was not going to climb on Sarah's back.

"It makes her mad, too," Sarah added, "that my roses are the best at the rose fair every year. When I was a little girl, she was always the prize winner, but now everyone knows that mine are the best."

"You handled her very well," he assured her.

"Yes, didn't I?" Sarah stared at the door again as she sipped her ice tea.

Jason Gibbons was wandering through the swamp. He knew it like it was the back of his hand. It had been his home for more than ten years. Once, a long time ago, he had lived in a great white house not far from town. And he had walked to town every morning in his fine pinstriped suit and everyone along Main Street would nod to him. They respected him, or feared him at least. He held many of their lives in his hands. He did when he was the president of the bank, at least. But that was a long time ago.

Now his mind was as tangled and confused as the swamp itself. He saw and heard things, but they made no sense to him. Once he had found a scrap of tin foil and he had managed to discern his reflection in it. His heart had almost burst at the sight of his face, distorted by oozing boils, the nose red and mottled. He hardly recognized himself.

Somehow, he knew that Bankroft girl was to

blame. She was there when he got his first spell, standing there, staring at him with her funny eyes. But no one believed him when he told them that. They all dismissed him as a crazy old man.

He had seen her coming to visit Adela in the swamp and he had heard them muttering over Adela's campfire. He had watched as they had played with the swamp creatures, making them leap and fly and do anything they wanted them to do. He knew the two of them had some kind of power, but he could not figure out what it was. He could not concentrate, and, when he tried, he would get his spells. Then the whole forest would come alive and it would seem as though all the creatures in it were rushing at him. He'd start to feel that searing pain again, as though his face were afire. It was more than he could bear.

There was something else. Sometimes, late at night, he would wander close to Cherron. He had seen that Bankroft girl and her surly cousin doing things in the graveyard. They were up to something, he knew it.

But the pains started to come again, and Jason Gibbons started to weep.

Sarah had set up an office of sorts for Jonathan in the library of the great house. He worked at the long table. From there he could look out the French window at the green lawn and the rose garden. A honeysuckle vine grew right outside the window and scented the air as he worked.

"How are you doing?" she asked, peeking in. The two Labradors were at her feet. They walked over to Jonathan eagerly, and he petted them vigorously on their heads.

"I can't get over how friendly your dogs are," he remarked.

"Oh, they're well trained."

"Did you ever hunt with them?"

She looked at him with irritation. "My brothers believed in hunting, but Martin and I don't. I've managed to get all that out of them. Now they're — friends.

"You know, Sarah, there's something else I've wanted to ask you."

"Yes?"

"This morning, when I was rummaging through some of these Bankroft papers, I found a letter from your brother Everett. I didn't realize that he owned Cherron at one time."

"Well, he did."

"I'm just surprised that no one mentioned it." He noticed that her face had gone pale. "Sarah, is something wrong?"

She smiled sadly and shook her head.

"If you must know, when I became mistress of Cherron I forbade anyone in the family to speak of Everett. He tried to destroy Cherron. Can you imagine?"

"Is this one of the things you don't care to talk about?"

She sat in the chair next to him and put her elbows on the table, holding her chin in her hands.

"Jonathan," she said. "It's true my family wasn't kind to me, but no matter how cruel they were I always knew one thing: no matter what happened,

Cherron would always belong to us: it belonged to the family; it would go on forever."

She paused and gazed out at the rose garden. Jonathan hesitated to say anything because he realized that this was a painful subject.

"After my parents died, Everett dropped his bombshell. He intended to sell Cherron. To sell everything right out from under us, to the first buyer who met his price."

"What happened? Obviously he didn't sell it. You're still here."

"It was on the market for over a year, but Cherron costs a lot of money. The land and the tobacco business were estimated to be worth forty million dollars."

Jonathan whistled.

"No one could afford to buy it. I guess we all hoped that no one ever would. Meanwhile, Everett neglected the business. He was much better at spending money than at making it."

A bumble bee had landed on the honeysuckle vine, and she stared at it as it extracted the pollen. Then it flew away and she returned to her story.

"Then one day Everett called us all together right here in the library and told us he had a buyer. Some rich Texas oil man. That started the battling between David and Everett all over again. Sometimes at night I still dream about their quarrels, I can still hear them arguing."

"It must have been terrible." Jonathan nodded sympathetically. Sarah had her hands on the table now and he took one and held it as she continued.

"Several weeks before the deal was to be closed,

Everett went riding near the swamp. His horse must have spooked, because he reared up. Everett was thrown to the ground. Before he had a chance to get back up, an alligator slithered out from the swamp and began to tear him apart."

"Oh, my God!"

"It was horrible. When we realized that he was missing we went looking for him. We found him, or what was left of him."

Jonathan's heart ached at the story of the girl's misfortunes.

"I'm sorry, truly sorry, Sarah, that I brought all this up."

"There was no way you could have known," she assured him. "We were all hurt deeply by Everett's actions. My brother David never spoke about him after that. He took over the business and it remained where it belonged, in Bankroft hands."

"What would you have done if Everett had succeeded?"

"I honestly have no idea. But I'm glad I didn't have to make that decision." She smiled for the first time since entering the library. "Come on, now, you'd better get back to your book. I'll leave you to work."

With a sad little smile, she left the room, followed by her dogs.

* * *

A family meeting had been called and so they had all gathered in the library: Uncle Jeffrey, Martin, Aunt Jessica, Robert, Devon, Everett, and

107

David. Sarah and Monica were still dressed in black. Their parents had been dead only a few days.

"Who the hell do you think you are?" David screamed when Everett made his announcement. "This is our home. How dare you sell it?"

"Cherron belongs to me now," he said quietly. "I can do anything I please with it."

"What about the rest of us?" David insisted. "What part of the money do we get when you sell Cherron?"

"You didn't hear me clearly. All of you," Everett yelled. "Cherron belongs to me. All of it. Why should I share the money with you or anyone else."

Sarah felt sick to her stomach. Her own brother was going to sell the family home. Where would she live? Where would any of them go? She looked around the room at the others.

Her uncle Jeffrey was furious and Martin's face was red with anger. Aunt Jessica seemed on the verge of tears and her husband, Robert, put his arm around her to comfort her. Sarah tried to do the same thing for Monica, who was sobbing quietly, but she pulled away.

"You miserable son of a bitch," David shouted. "We're going to be left out in the cold."

"Father made no provision for anyone else in his will," Everett said coldly.

"Of course not. He expected you to do your duty and keep Cherron going."

"I'll do with it as I damn please. I don't want to discuss it anymore and certainly not with you."

Suddenly David leaped on Everett, knocking him

108

to the floor. "I'll kill you, you bastard," he shouted.

Aunt Jessica screamed and Monica became hysterical. Only Sarah remained calm, watching as the two young men struggled on the floor, until Uncle Jeffrey and Uncle Robert managed to pull them apart.

"Act like Bankrofts, for God's sake," Martin shouted. "Have a little dignity. I'm shocked at you, Everett. What will happen to the rest of us if you sell?"

"Frankly, cousin, I don't much care," Everett said, wiping the blood from his face with a handkerchief. "The house, the land, and the business are all for sale. The rest of you can fend for yourselves. I don't give a damn what happens to you."

"If I had any guts," David roared as Everett left the room, "I'd kill you myself."

Everett turned and smiled. It was a cruel and evil smile. "But you don't David, and you know it."

Sarah had remained quietly in the background during the whole awful scene. She knew her intervention would do no good. The smell of greed filled every corner of the room.

She followed Everett to the stable where he brought out his Morgan, a big beautiful horse he called Ranger.

"Everett, can I ride with you?" she said.

He smiled. "You won't get me to change my mind about selling Cherron."

"No, I just want to talk to you," she assured him.

She saddled up Isis, her pinto, and together they rode towards the swamp. It was evening, but the full moon lit the lawn with an eerie glow.

"Well, little sister," he said. "It won't be long before you're out of a home."

She had always believed that Michael was the cruelest member of her family, but this was too much even from him.

"You're not really going to sell, are you Everett?"

"Of course."

"Everett," she cried. "How can you be so brutal? For two hundred years Cherron has never been owned by anyone but Bankrofts. Why would you sell it to strangers?"

"For money, my dear sister," he laughed. "A great deal of money."

"But you can make lots of money running the business."

"That's work," he said, sneering. "Besides, I have no interest in the business. Tobacco should be smoked. I leave the growing of it to someone else."

"You shouldn't sell it, Everett. It's wrong of you."

"Don't dare tell me what's right or wrong."

"No, I suppose you're like all the rest. No one can tell you anything."

She stared at her tall, handsome brother atop the magnificent horse.

Suddenly the horse bucked and Everett fell to the ground. He stood up, a little shaken, and began to brush himself off. Then he reached for his whip.

"Goddamned horse. I'll teach him to throw me,"

he muttered as he raised the whip.

Sarah stared off into the swamp. If Everett had been watching her instead of his horse he would have seen the odd glow in the whites of her eyes, the strange fixed expression on her face, the look of concentration. He might have seen the huge alligator before it was too late, before he felt it grip his leg.

He looked at it in horror, vainly trying to use his horsewhip, but its thick, leather-like hide was impervious. It refused to release his leg. Instead, it sank its sharp white teeth deeper into his flesh, ripping it away from the bone. Sarah watched as her brother fell to the ground. He had lost his whip now in the soft mud and he was fighting the alligator with his bare hands.

"Help me, Sarah," he screamed. "Please, for God's sake, help me."

Sarah didn't move. She sat atop the pinto, quietly watching as the huge alligator tore at Everett's arms. Soon his limbs were strewn across the muddy, bloody grass and his white shirt was soaked red with blood. She watched as his guts spilled out onto the grass, but by this time, mercifully, Everett had lapsed into unconsciousness.

At last the alligator, gorged, looked up at Sarah as if awaiting a nod of dismissal. The glow still shone in her eyes. He turned and slithered back into the swamp.

She turned away and rode slowly back to the stable. It was apparent that Everett would not be selling Cherron after all.

Chapter Four

Sarah Bankroft was walking on the rear lawn of Cherron. It was a warm, cloudless morning and occasionally she would stare up at the blue sky. For a moment she watched as the birds sailed carelessly, playfully through the sky. She wished she could sail with them on silver wings.

"Sarah!" a voice hissed at her.

She turned, and her smile of contentment became a look of horror.

When she had been in love with Roy McEndrew he was a strong, strapping man with a broad grin, a shock of blond hair and shining blue eyes. Now he stood before her, a tired, decaying old man. His clothes were baggy and they hung loosely from his scrawny body. He was practically skin and bones. His face was haggard; puffy bags lay under his eyes, and his cheeks were hollow.

"Sarah!" He put his hand on her arm, but she

shrank from his touch. "How are you?"

"I'm well, thank you, Roy. What brings you to Cherron?" She felt that, under the circumstances, she must be hospitable.

"I wanted to see you, Sarah," he said. "Maybe we could have dinner some night?"

The longing look in his eyes made her uncomfortable. After all, Roy had a wife and a son.

"That would be nice, Roy," she lied. "Bring Kathy around some evening."

"You know that's not what I mean," he said and grimaced. "Besides, Kathy never goes anywhere now."

She sympathized with his situation, but, after all, he was the one who married Kathy. Didn't he remember that it was for better or worse? He wanted to marry her because she was beautiful and Sarah was not. Maybe his taste had changed in the years since.

"I need you, Sarah," he whispered.

"I'm afraid it's no concern of mine what you need. You have a wife. I suggest you go home to her."

"I can't," he cried. "It's like walking into hell every time I open the door."

"I can't help that, Roy. You made your choice."

"Sarah, have pity on me. She sits there in that dark room: all the curtains are drawn; all the lights are out. She just sits in that rocking chair. Sometimes her mind wanders. Sometimes she even seems to think he's normal. It's like living in hell. It's awful."

"I'm sorry for you." She wanted to get away

113

from him, but he grabbed her arm and pinned her against the tree.

"What do you think you're doing?" she demanded.

"Sarah, I need you. Please don't turn me away."

"Roy, let me go." She struggled, but even in his present condition she was no match for him.

"Remember how it was before I left."

He seemed to have deluded himself into believing that there had been a real romantic attachment between them, instead of an engagement arranged by their parents.

"I remember, Roy. I remember everything quite clearly. That's the trouble. I especially remember the time you came back only to tell me that you were married and expecting a child."

"Forgive me for that, Sarah. I was arrogant and stupid. It was pride, that's all."

She stared at him. Did he really believe that was all? She could remember how he had flaunted his beautiful bride all over Arcadia. She recalled his smug smile as he showed the whole town what kind of bride he could get if he chose. Well, it hadn't turned out happily ever after, the way he'd expected. And now he was crawling to her, asking for love?

"You disgust me, Roy. You're a cruel, self-centered man and you always will be. You chose your lovely bride; now you can live with her and with your son. Let's not forget your son."

"Please, Sarah, I need you," he said urgently.

"Sarah! Are you all right?"

It was Jonathan's voice. She heaved a sigh of

relief as poor Roy loosened his grip, then she ran towards the reporter.

"What's going on here?" he said, glaring at Roy.

"It's all right, Jonathan," she assured him. "This is Roy McEndrew; he's an old family friend."

Jonathan found it a little hard to believe that this scrofulous wreck of a man could have been a friend of the discriminating Bankrofts, but he let it go.

"I'd best be going now," Roy said, embarrassed by his own behavior.

"Yes, I think that would be a good idea," Sarah agreed.

He turned away, a lonely, sad figure as he walked down the drive.

"What was that all about?" Jonathan said when the man was out of hearing distance. "Is he really a friend of yours?"

"Not exactly. I was engaged to him once."

He looked at her in shock. "Engaged? To that old man?"

"He's not that old; he's the same age as Martin, about thirty."

"Gee, he must have had a tough life."

"I guess he has. He seems to have very little reason to live anymore."

"What happened to him?" Jonathan was curious about how a healthy young man good enough to snare Miss Sarah could have deteriorated so rapidly.

She sighed, as if recalling the painful details of Roy McEndrew's sad little life.

"His son was born hideously deformed. A

biological freak of nature Uncle Luke called it. The doctors tried to talk Roy and his wife into institutionalizing it, but they decided to keep it instead. Guilt, I guess. Now they're locked up with him twenty-four hours a day. Kathy, his wife, just sits in that dark room with the boy, talking to something that can't understand her."

* * *

It was Christmas Eve at Cherron, and it was a special night. Not only was her brother David now head of the family, but Sarah expected that Roy would make his announcement tonight at the big party David was giving. After all, they had been engaged for several years. To think that she, the ugly daughter, would be getting handsome Roy McEndrew!

So what if David insisted it was only because the families wanted to combine their interests. She knew that Roy loved her. And so what if Martin said that Roy wasn't good enough for her, that he didn't trust him. She knew different. Why, he was tall and handsome and wise and funny. Even Monica was jealous.

She dressed with special care that night in a long white strapless formal gown with a huge red sash at the waist. She put her blond hair up and stuck a piece of holly in it. It was too bad that Mother and Father and Michael couldn't see her now. She was a beautiful young woman now. How surprised they'd be.

The great staircase of Cherron was festooned

with boughs of holly. As she descended the staircase on Martin's arm she could hear the voices of
the party guests in the ballroom. They were
laughing and the orchestra was playing. She knew
this would be a Christmas party that she would
always remember.

She walked into the ballroom and saw Roy,
standing head and shoulders above the crowd. He
was even more handsome than she remembered.
She smiled at him and he smiled back.

She started to make her way across the room
towards him. Then she saw the pretty, dark-haired
woman beside him.

"Sarah, I'd like you to meet someone. This is
Katherine, my wife."

The smile froze on her face, and suddenly the
music and the laughter of the party seemed very
far away.

"I—I'm pleased to meet you." The words caught
in her throat.

"Roy's told me a few things about you," the girl
said.

She was petite and delicate, with short black
curly hair and dark brown eyes. She was wearing a
loose-fitting red dress.

"Shall we dance, Mrs. McEndrew?" Martin said
politely, steering the new bride away and leaving
Sarah to confront Roy.

"I don't understand," she said, leaning towards
him so that the others could not hear. "We were
engaged."

"Sarah, that wouldn't have worked out between
us," he said blithely. "Although I must admit,

117

you've changed in the year I've been away. You've become a beautiful young woman."

It was small comfort. To think that she had really believed he loved her, and all the time he had been courting someone else.

"I had to marry her," he assured her. "Kathy's in a family way."

She couldn't believe it. All the time he had been courting her he had been making love to someone else. He had betrayed her. Didn't he realize that anyone who betrayed her paid a price? Obviously he did not. But someday, she vowed silently to herself, he would.

No one but Martin seemed to notice that anything was wrong that night. Certainly Kathy and Roy did not. Sarah carried on like the perfect Southern belle: charming the guests, flirting with the men—all of whom were impressed with how beautiful she had become in the last year. The chubby little girl with pimples and braces and stringy hair had become a blond, sensuous young woman. None of them seemed to notice that she had also become a monster.

In the weeks that followed, Sarah graciously invited the newlyweds to join the Bankrofts at Cherron. They were surprised at her generosity. Kathy confided in Sarah. She told her all the details about her meeting Roy, their courtship, and the coming baby, Sarah seemed to eat it all up.

All the time she was planning her revenge.

She insisted on helping Kathy decorate the baby's room. They chose a wallpaper with little ducks on it and a precious little mobile of brightly colored balls that would hang over the baby's crib. Sarah suggested a picture window to brighten the room.

Kathy was due to give birth in mid-June. They were all enjoying a Memorial Day picnic together near Benson's Cliff when it happened. Kathy didn't seem to notice how Sarah concentrated her gaze on Kathy's stomach. She had been doing this for weeks, but no one had noticed.

"I think Grayson is a beautiful name," she rattled on. "Don't you think so, Sarah? It can be for either a boy or a girl. Grayson McEndrew has a ring to it. Don't you think so?"

"It sounds lovely," Sarah assured her.

"Sarah," the girl said. "I'm so glad that you're my friend. When Roy told me that he was almost engaged to you I just didn't know how you would take our getting married and all."

"Nonsense," Sarah assured her. "The engagement was arranged by our families when we were very young. That kind of thing never works out."

"I must admit, though, that you're not exactly the way Roy described you. He told me you were—plain. But you're not really; you're very pretty."

"Thank you."

"Oh, Lord," she patted her bulging stomach. "Three more weeks. I think I'll go crazy. We can't wait for the baby to come."

"Perhaps you won't have to," Sarah mumbled.

"What?"

"Nothing, just thinking out loud."

Sarah was thinking that perhaps she could do something about the long wait. All during the picnic she continued to watch Kathy McEndrew as she busied herself at the picnic table. Sarah concentrated all her attention on Kathy's unborn child.

"I think we'd best pack up now," Roy told his wife, giving her an affectionate kiss on the neck.

"Yes, I think you're right. I've had enough fresh air for one day." Kathy began to clean off the table, stopping several times to sit down and catch her breath. She seemed quite tired.

Sarah just stared, thinking about the scene with Roy McEndrews at the Cherron Christmas party, thinking about the way Roy had led her to believe that he loved her. Slowly the anger in her rose up and her eyes began to shine. Beams of clear, brilliant white light seemed to pour from her eyes.

"Ohh, oh, my God, Roy," Kathy cried out in pain.

"Honey, what's wrong? Is it time?" Roy asked, as he leaped to his feet.

"Oh, my God. It hurts. It hurts so bad." She bent over in agony. "Something's wrong. Roy, something is terribly wrong. It doesn't feel like the doctor told me it would."

"All right, Kathy, stay calm. We'll get you to the hospital. Can you walk?"

She tried to stand up straight, but could only moan in pain.

"No, no I can't."

"All right, hold on." He picked his wife up with great effort and carried her to the car.

Sarah drove them to the hospital while Roy sat

in the back seat with Kathy, timing her contractions. When they arrived he ran into the hospital and, in a moment, two orderlies came rushing out and carried Kathy McEndrew into the delivery room. Roy followed close behind.

After parking the car, Sarah sat in the empty waiting room and idly glanced at the magazines. After about a half hour she wandered down the hall to the coffee machine. She was sipping her coffee when she heard the screams, horrible, frightening screams.

They took Sarah completely by surprise. She turned towards the opened door in time to see Roy McEndrew running down the hospital corridor still in his delivery-room garb. His mask was off his face and he was sobbing.

Sarah sipped her coffee thoughtfully. She could still hear screams coming from the delivery room; they were a woman's screams. She strolled down toward the room. In the excitement the door had been left ajar and she peeked inside.

Kathy was sitting up and she looked exhausted from her ordeal. She was holding her new baby in her arms, a smug grin on her face. But the tiny creature in her arms was a monster with a huge, misshapen head and a pitifully malformed body. It would never be normal. It writhed uncontrollably in its mother's arms.

The doctors were speaking in hushed voices in a corner of the room when suddenly the air was torn again by Kathy's ear-shattering scream.

"No, no get it away from me," she screamed,

holding the baby out to the nurse. "Please, take it away. Take it away. It didn't come from me; it didn't; it couldn't."

Sarah saw the entire scene, then turned and went back to the waiting room where she finished her coffee undisturbed. A few minutes later, her uncle Luke came in. All the color had drained from his face and he looked as if he might be sick.

"Uncle Luke! My God, what's happening?"

"I—I don't believe what I just saw," the old doctor shook his head. "In all my years as a doctor I have never seen anything like it."

"What is it, Uncle Luke? What happened? Is the baby all right?"

"The baby," his eyes widened. "My Lord, the baby."

"Is it dead?"

"It might be better off dead; death would be merciful."

"Is it that bad, Uncle Luke?"

"It's deformed, horribly deformed."

"How sad."

Little Grayson McEndrew was kept in a room separate from the other newborns, so as to avoid frightening anyone unnecessarily.

Sarah was allowed to visit Kathy only once during her hospital stay. The girl was in deep shock, the doctors told Sarah. Perhaps a visit from a friend would help.

As she entered the room she saw Kathy on the bed. She lay very still, staring up at the ceiling. She hadn't uttered a word since that scene in the delivery room.

"Kathy?" Sarah said. "Kathy, how are you?"

The girl turned her face to the wall.

"You must pull yourself out of this. It's not good for you or Roy or the baby."

Kathy was silent.

"You know, you're a mother now and your son needs you. It's a shame, but as it turns out he needs you more than other babies need their mothers. You brought that child into this world; you and Roy did. You are responsible for him."

Sarah sat down on the hospital bed. Kathy turned to stare at her with unblinking eyes.

* * *

"I tried to visit them once, after Kathy came home," Sarah told Jonathan. "Roy thought it might do Kathy some good."

"Did it help?"

"No, I'm afraid it was useless. Poor Kathy just sits in the darkened house year after year in an old housecoat," she sighed. "When she saw me she just became hysterical."

"How awful for you, when you were trying to help," Jonathan said loyally.

"She just sat in that nursery, crooning to the baby. It made some kind of unintelligible sounds as if someone were speaking with a mouthful of cotton. I also heard a thumping, as if it were beating its head against the crib. That was the last time I saw them, until today."

They stood there, looking out over the green

lawn of Cherron, and each thinking about the sudden, unexpected tragedies in life. Finally, Jonathan broke the silence.

"It's so beautiful here, Sarah," he said. "Florida's going to spoil me. I don't want to go back to New York."

"Then don't," she said, smiling.

"I have to."

"Why?"

"It's nature's law. It's called survival."

"You're a free-lance journalist, Jonathan," she said. "You can work anywhere."

"That's true, but most of the excitement is in New York."

"We have excitement here, too," she protested. "Florida is filled with things to write about. After all, you're not writing about the old families of New York, are you?"

"Are you trying to tempt me to stay, woman?" Jonathan smiled. "It is a temptation, I have to admit. The weather, the Florida scenery, and you."

"In that order?"

Jonathan laughed. "No, not in that order."

Sarah seemed so relaxed that he decided to bring up something that had been bothering him for several days.

"Sarah, Bill Collins gave me the idea that you were—ah—that is—" He was supposed to be a writer, and here he was, at a loss for words.

"Engaged?" she said, smiling.

"Yes."

"Jonathan, a Southern girl likes to have a lot of beaux."

"So there's on one special?" He sounded relieved.

"No, not now."

Encouraged, he took Sarah's hand and led her back in the house.

Chapter Five

Jessica Morrow didn't blame her son. Devon was only fifteen and he hardly remembered the way things used to be. He spent most of his time now staring into space. It wasn't normal for a young boy to just stare that way, as if all the life had gone out of him.

"Come on, Devon," she coaxed him. "Eat something; otherwise you'll get sick."

They were sitting at the white kitchen table. There was a small bowl of Miss Sarah's roses in the center of the table. Jessica had made chicken okra gumbo just the way Devon used to like it when he was a little boy. But he was no more interested in that than in anything else.

Sometimes she still tried to convince herself that she was lucky. Where else could they go? Robert had left her no money and Devon was too young to work. As for herself, all she had ever learned was how to enjoy life, to travel, to run a great house. So here she was, running Cherron for her niece. No, she was lucky that Miss Sarah let them stay. But Devon didn't understand that.

"I want to leave," he said plaintively. "Why can't we leave this place?"

"You know why as well as I do," Jessica told him, glancing at the kitchen door.

"She's upstairs; she can't hear us."

"She doesn't need ears to hear us; she can read our thoughts."

"She can't keep us here. She shouldn't be allowed to keep us here. Can't we go?"

"You know better than to ask that. We can never leave here. She would always find us," Jessica said nervously as she spooned the chicken okra gumbo into two bowls. "Now stop talking about it. You know how dangerous it is to talk about leaving."

Devon poked at the soup listlessly.

"We're prisoners, no more than slaves," he insisted.

"That's the way she wants it and she always gets her way."

"We'll be here always, until the day we die." He paused. A thought seemed to occur to him, and for just a minute he brightened. "Or until the day she dies."

"Devon!" Jessica said sharply. "Please don't say things like that. Don't even think them."

"Yes, Devon, don't even think them."

The mother and son looked up to see Sarah Bankroft standing in the doorway to the kitchen.

"As your mother says," she went on, "that can be very dangerous."

"He didn't mean anything by that," Jessica said quickly. "We're grateful that you've given us a home. We're really very grateful."

"Are you?" Sarah stared at Devon. "You know, Devon, talk like that can be very hazardous to your health. We wouldn't want anything to happen to you now, would we?"

The boy said nothing.

"Would we, Devon?" she insisted.

"He didn't mean anything, I swear he didn't," Jessica pleaded.

"Let Devon answer for himself," she said sharply.

"No, Cousin Sarah, I wouldn't want anything to happen to me."

"Good." Sarah's eyes were glowing with a surge of light, an odd stream of that intense light that seemed to pour out of the whites of her eyes. She stared at her young cousin.

"And you'll never think about leaving here again, will you?"

"No, Cousin Sarah."

She looked at Jessica. "And you?"

"No, Sarah, never again."

"Good. Now I have to go. We mustn't forget our obligations to our relatives, must we?"

"No," the mother and son spoke in unison.

"Dinner will be at eight, I assume?"

"Yes, of course," Jessica told her.

Cameron Sanitorium was a large brick building

set on several acres of rolling hillside not far from Arcadia. It was hidden from idle curiosity-seekers by the tall live oaks that surrounded it. Not that too many strangers would want to visit a home for the mentally ill unless they had business there. Miss Sarah had business there.

She was greeted at the door by Dr. Seamus Cameron himself. He was a portly middle-aged man who favored casual golf clothes like the bright blue pants and shirt he was wearing today. He felt it put the patients at their ease.

He and Miss Sarah were old friends. She had been coming here for years now. He certainly admired the girl's loyalty. She never missed a visit, and she always brought a bouquet of roses from her garden.

"Has there been any improvement, Dr. Cameron?" she asked him as they walked down the corridor. She asked the same question every month and the answer was always the same.

"I'm sorry to report, no. She still remains in the room with very little light and allows only certain of our people to administer to her."

"I'm very disappointed to hear that," Sarah sighed. "Do you think there will ever be a time when she'll be able to lead a normal life?"

The doctor shook his head sadly. "In her present state of mind, I think that's highly unlikely."

"I'll never be able to accept that my beautiful sister is gone, doctor. Yet it seems so futile."

Nothing is ever futile where there is life," he assured her.

"May I see her now?"

"Yes, of course."

The room was dark and quiet and it reminded Sarah of the McEndrew house. Her eyes took a while to adjust to the dim light. She seated herself in a leather chair and looked at her sister. As always, she began the conversation.

"Well, how are you today?"

The ghostly figure sat huddled in the far corner of the room, as far away as she could get from her sister and from even the slight sliver of light that came through the crack in the curtains.

"Are you feeling better?"

The shadowy figure twisted uncomfortably.

"Answer me."

The figure muttered something unintelligible.

"You can do better than that, Monica. Are you feeling better?"

"Yes." The voice was distorted, speaking with difficulty.

"Dr. Cameron says otherwise. He says you still refuse to socialize with the other patients. You should, you know. Get out of the room; take a walk with the orderly; go to the game room. Do something, anything."

"Nooooo," the figure moaned, and huddled closer to the wall. The voice sounded as if it were being forced through clenched teeth.

"Come now, Monica. It's been three years since the accident. There's nothing to keep you in this room. You should get out and see people."

"Noooo." The ghostly figure rose from the chair and started to pace the room like a caged animal.

"You must get over this attitude, Monica. It's

time you saw people again. Remember how you used to love being with people. And the boys! The house was always filled with your admirers."

The pacing animal shook her head pitifully, but Sarah continued.

"So many boys came to Cherron to see you. You used to go to so many parties. You must remember them, the parties I was never invited to. All the girls with their pretty party dresses and the boys, so handsome."

Sarah watched the figure before her.

"What if I were to tell you that I wouldn't pay for your care here anymore? What if I think it's time you came home?"

The ghostly figure shook her head violently and moaned. "Nooooo."

"Why not? The doctors can do no more for you here than we could. This place has become nothing more than a baby sitter, and a rather expensive baby sitter at that. Perhaps if you came back to Cherron and saw some of your old friends—"

"Noooo."

"Don't you think they'd be glad to see you?"

"Dead," the figure murmured. "They think I'm dead."

"Yes, I know. But we could explain to them that it was your idea to tell everyone you were killed in the accident. I'm sure they'd all be quite happy to discover you're not dead at all."

As she talked Sarah moved briskly about the room, emptying a large vase of withered flowers, stepping into the small lavatory to fill the vase with fresh water, and filling it with the fresh bouquet she had brought from Cherron.

"I hope you like the roses from my garden," Sarah said, setting the vase on the bedside table.

"Yes, they're lovely."

"You know, if you came home you could enjoy walking in my rose garden."

"No. I can't go back there."

"I don't see why not. You won't go through anything I didn't go through when I was a child. You get used to people staring and laughing at you."

"No, please."

"It's costing me a good deal of money to keep you hidden away here, Monica," Sarah said firmly. "And the doctors can't do anything about the way you look. We could give you the same care at home and it would cost a lot less."

"If I have to go back I'll kill myself." The girl struggled to get the words out, but there was no doubt that she meant them. "I can't let people see me this way."

"Yes," Sarah sighed. "You always did take great store in the way you looked. You never let me forget that I was the ugly one. How things have changed!"

She moved to the window and began to pull at the curtains.

"Lord, you need some light in here."

"NO! No light." The girl's hand sprang out to stop Sarah from opening the curtain.

"Nonsense, I can't see a thing. I don't want to talk to a shadow." She opened the shutters a crack and a beam of sunlight flowed into the room. She could see the girl more clearly now.

She was a young woman, a little older than Sarah. Her hands flew to her face as soon as the sunlight touched it.

"Stop that. I know what you look like. You don't have to hide from me."

She sat down on the bed.

"We missed you at the party, Monica. You really should have come. I remember how much you used to love to dance at our parties. And Bill Collins was there. You remember Bill, don't you? He's begging me to marry him. But I don't know, I have so many admirers, I think I'll play the field a little longer."

There was no mirror in the room, so Sarah took out her compact and began to fuss with her make-up.

"How the tables have turned. I used to watch you brushing your silky black hair and I was so envious of you. That lovely face. It used to drive men crazy." She laughed. "I suppose if they saw it today it still would."

Suddenly Sarah flung the shutters open all the way and the room was flooded with sunlight.

"Noooo," the woman wailed. "Please shut them." She tried to cover her face with her hands, and when that failed she pulled a blanket over her head. Sarah tugged at the blanket and pulled it off.

"Stop this nonsense," she said, grabbing her sister and taking her face in her hands.

"My, that glass certainly did a job on you, didn't it?"

It was difficult to tell that this had ever been a human face, much less the face of a beautiful young girl. Thick red scar tissue distorted it. There was a gaping hole where a beautiful, shining blue eye had once been. There was an indistinguishable nose and the lips were gone completely, making it difficult for the girl to speak at all.

Ironically, her body was still a young woman's body. She still had a sensational figure with graceful legs and hands that had been untouched by the accident. She still had a glorious mane of thick, black hair, listless now from lack of care. Only the face was that of a monster.

It was a face that would have repulsed anyone, but not Sarah. She took delight in it. Her eyes glowed at the very sight of it.

"That glass came at me as if it had eyes, Sarah," the girl said bitterly. She had finally summoned the strength to speak.

"It was as if it was deliberately cutting my face," the girl insisted.

"What's that?" Sarah cooed. "You have to speak more clearly. I have trouble understanding you."

"Why did that car go out of control so suddenly? David couldn't move the steering wheel. I've been sitting here trying to put it together for years."

Sarah's eyes glowed, and a beam of white light seemed to shoot from the whites of her eyes as she listened to her sister struggle to assemble the bits and pieces in her mind.

"I vaguely remember David fighting for control of the car, Sarah. But when I try to remember the rest I get these awful burning pains in my head. It feels as if red hot nails were being driven into my brain. But I think you did something. You did, didn't you?"

"Calm down, you're upsetting yourself."

"Oh, my God," the scarred girl began to scream. "What did you do to me?"

"Please, Monica. If you don't calm down I'll have to call the orderly. He'll have to restrain you. You don't like the straitjacket. Remember how it felt when we brought you here?"

The girl forced herself to calm down. "I'll behave, Sarah. Really I will. Please don't call the orderly."

"I won't," Sarah said. "Besides, it's almost time for me to leave." She rose to go, then she remembered something.

"Oh, I almost forgot. Another young man has come to Cherron, a writer. He's going to tell all about the Bankrofts, how beautiful they all were. Would you like me to send him to you?"

"No, Sarah, please don't," the girl begged.

"I understand. I'll see you next month, dear. I'm sure you will understand if I don't kiss you good-bye."

"I understand."

"Goodbye, dear sister."

"Goodbye, Sarah."

Jonathan was working in the library, but he was finding it hard to concentrate. Sarah had gone out on some mysterious errand and he could see Martin working outside in the rose garden.

The more he learned about Sarah Bankroft, the

more convinced he was that he was in love with her. He had tried several times to tell her so, but she brushed him off. Yet she cared about him, he was convinced of that.

Why did she choose to spend her life here in this small town, devoting her time to running a business and supporting her dreary relatives? Maybe her early tragedies, her miserable childhood, and the tragic deaths of so many of her family had traumatized her. That was it, he told himself. Poor Sarah wanted to cling to the family she had left.

He also found himself thinking about the old derelict he had met in the swamp. Even though Sarah denied knowing much about him, she seemed upset when he mentioned his name. And the old man seemed obsessed with Sarah. He seemed to hate her. Yes, there was certainly a lot going on here.

Sarah and Martin quietly descended the stone staircase to the basement. They locked the door behind them. With Jonathan in the house they had to be especially careful.

"I saw Monica today, Martin," Sarah said as she placed fresh roses at the center of the dining table.

"How is she?"

"The same. My mother used to say that when she walked into the room she brought the spring flowers with her. Now it's more like dead twigs. Oh, that face!"

She could still picture the way her sister looked, the distorted, twisted flesh that looked like a hideous red mask, that one pitiful eye staring out at her.

"I don't care. I'm glad she's paying for what she did to you," Martin said.

"Thank you, Martin, I know that you have always loved me."

"Did you tell her about Jonathan Evans?"

"Of course. I always share good news with her."

"I'll bet that made her angry."

"She cried."

"Good."

"Martin, you haven't said much lately. Is something wrong?" There was concern in her voice.

"You know what's wrong," he said, turning to her with an anguished look. "You're falling in love with that writer, aren't you?"

"Oh, Martin, if you're going to get all riled up just because a gentleman pays attention to me—"

"This is different," he insisted. "And you know it. I can tell you feel something for him that you never felt for any of the others."

She knew he was right. Yesterday, when Jonathan asked her to come to New York with him, she had wanted to say yes with all her heart. For the first in many years she cared about someone besides Martin, and he could tell.

"Don't worry, Martin," she tried to reassure him. "I'd never leave you."

He came towards her, and kissed her gently on the lips.

"I hate it when I have to share you with someone else, Sarah," he whispered. "When is he going to leave?"

"When his book is finished, and that should be soon." She smiled at the thought of all those strangers finally reading about how cruel the Bankroft family had been.

"Can I come to you tonight?"

"Yes, but try to be quiet. We don't want Jonathan writing about us."

"No," Martin agreed. "Remember what happened when David and my father found out?"

"Yes, but I took care of them, didn't I?"

"Yes, Sarah, you did."

Jonathan was waiting for them at the top of the staircase.

"What's so interesting down there?" he asked. Then, when he saw the startled look on Sarah's face, he added hastily "I didn't mean to frighten you."

"I thought you were working in the library," she answered coolly.

"I took a break to speak to you."

She turned to Martin. "I think that's all for tonight." It was a dismissal, and he understood. Reluctantly he took his leave of them both.

"So, what's down there?" Jonathan asked again.

Sarah shrugged. "Some Bankroft heirlooms and my family's personal effects. That's all."

"Do you think it's healthy, Sarah, to spend so much time with those things?"

"They're part of my life, Jonathan."

Jonathan decided to drop the subject. He hadn't searched her out to argue, but rather to apologize.

"Sarah, this afternoon I wasn't the most

understanding guy in the world. I know this is your home and you don't want to leave it."

"I'm glad you finally see that," she said, her voice softening.

"I just don't want you to be angry with me anymore."

"I'm not."

He kissed her and she responded in spite of herself.

"Can I see you tonight?" he whispered.

"No, Jonathan, not tonight."

Sarah was sitting by the open French windows, gazing at the moon, when the soft knock came at her door. Martin entered.

"You'd better lock the door," she warned him.

He did so, then walked quickly towards her, taking her in his arms and kissing her eagerly, passionately, pressing her body to his.

"Oh, God, Sarah, it seems like so long since we've been together. He's interfering in our lives. you know that, don't you?"

"I thought this night was supposed to be ours, Martin."

"Yes," he relented. "Just you and me tonight, like it used to be." He kissed her eyes and picked her up and carried her to the bed.

"You don't love him, do you Sarah?"

"I don't want to talk about him, not now."

The night belonged to them and no one could interfere.

Chapter Six

Jonathan had finished typing his notes, but he was restless and unable to sleep. He decided a snack might help and he walked quietly downstairs to the kitchen. To his delight he found Jessica Morrow at the table. The ghostly woman had been avoiding him, but finally they were alone together.

She rose to leave.

"Please don't go, Miss Jessica," he said. "Can't you sleep either?"

"No, Mr. Evans, I felt restless."

"So did I. Care to share a snack?"

"No, thank you."

Jonathan opened the refrigerator and stared at the contents as he talked to Jessica.

"We haven't been able to talk much."

"About what, Mr. Evans?"

"Please call me Jonathan," he said as he took out some milk and the makings for a roast beef sandwich. "I'd like to talk about you. Dr. Luke tells me that you've traveled extensively."

"Yes," she said sadly. "I lived in Paris, Munich, Rome, many wonderful places. But that was a long time ago."

"Your husband was English?"

"Yes, I met him in London. Robert, my husband, and Devon and I came back here to live several years ago," she explained. "Sarah's brother Everett was running Cherron then, and when he died Robert stayed on to help out."

Jonathan had finished preparing his sandwich and he brought it to the table and sat down beside the woman.

"They didn't treat Miss Sarah very well when she was a child, did they?"

"No, I'm sorry to say they did not," she answered. "I'm afraid that I was as guilty as the others."

"She's been very kind to you, though, hasn't she?"

"That makes me feel even guiltier," she said cryptically. "My husband had invested in some rather disastrous business deals before he died. He left us very little."

"If it doesn't upset you, Miss Jessica, I'd like to know how Mr. Morrow died."

Jessica Morrow stared sadly into space as if trying to recall the painful moment. She signed and then began.

"Robert loved to fly and he had his own small single-engine plane," she said. "One afternoon he had taken off from the Arcadia airport and he was flying over Cherron, showing off for Devon, when his engine blew up." She winced with pain at the memory of it. "The plane went down in flames right out there on the lawn. Devon and Sarah and I saw the whole thing."

She flinched even now as she recalled the great burst of fire and then the crash on the lawn. She could still see her beloved Robert being dragged from the plane, a burning corpse. She could still hear his cries.

"I'm very sorry, Miss Jessica." Perhaps this tragedy explained the strangeness of the mother and son.

"Then Miss Sarah allowed us to stay on at Cherron," she concluded. "Now, if you don't mind, I'm feeling quite tired now; I think I'll go to bed."

"Good night and thank you, Miss Jessica."

Jonathan thought about what the woman had told him. She seemed friendly enough and calm on the surface, but there was an underlying distress. Something about the strange tone in her voice bothered him. She talked and acted as if she were walking on eggshells all the time.

There was something else disturbing him. Lately, he had an overwhelming desire to go back to the swamp. He wanted to see the old hermit again. The old man's words had upset him. The old man was insane, Jonathan knew that. Yet he couldn't forget him.

Tomorrow, he told himself, tomorrow he would find the man again.

The next morning, Jonathan decided to take a look at the Bankroft family graveyard behind the curing barns. The entire area was surrounded by an old iron fence, and as he pulled at the iron gate it made a horrible screeching sound. He shivered.

There must have been at least ninety gravestones, some dating from the end of the 18th century, but he had no trouble finding those of Miss Sarah's immediate family. She had already told him about the small mausoleum she had built for them and he spotted it immediately at the center of the plot.

It was a sad little building of solid granite. At its door was a statue of Charon, the ferryman, who would carry the dead souls of the Bankrofts into the next life.

At the door of the small crypt was a series of brass plaques, and beside each plaque was a niche in the wall. Each niche held a fresh bouquet of roses. Jonathan read the plaques with interest.

DANIEL SEBASTIAN BANKROFT
1927–1970

MARTHA CONROY BANKROFT
1929–1970

THEIR BELOVED CHILDREN

MICHAEL CONROY BANKROFT
1951–1970

EVERETT CONROY BANKROFT
1952–1971

DAVID ERVIN BANKROFT
1953–1977

MONICA VIOLET BANKROFT
1954–

SARAH LOUISE BANKROFT
1955–

Now that was odd. There was no date of death for Monica Bankroft. He was sure that Sarah had told him that all her brothers and her sister were dead. Even if she were not interred here, it seemed only logical to give the date of her death.

An odd feeling began to creep over him as he looked at the sad little plaques. They must have been a happy family once. Yet now they were all gone except for Sarah, the one they hated.

He stood there as if rooted to the ground. He felt that something or someone was trying to reach him. He was not alone. All he could think of was Sarah and the way she had spoken about her family, not when she was defending them, dismissing their cruelty to her. No, there was that one moment in the soda fountain, the day they met Regina Quillam.

She hated them all.

Now he thought he understood. Yes, she did hate them, and being the kind of person she was, she could not admit it. God knows she had every right to hate them. Her uncle Luke, Martin, and even Miss Jessica had all admitted that the family treated her badly.

That was why she was staying on at Cherron. That was why she spent so much time in that basement room that no one let him see. Jessica had hinted that it held old relics and heirlooms of the Bankroft family.

His heart almost broke at the idea of poor Sarah sitting alone among the last remnants of her family, torn between her love for them and her justifiable rage at the way they had treated her.

Now he realized what he had to do. He had to sit down with her and help her realize that she was entitled to hate them, that there was no need to feel ashamed.

And he would also like to ask her what happened to her sister Monica.

"You are a fool."

The voice startled him, and then he realized it had come from the old man in front of him, who was still clothed in disintegrating rags. The boils that covered his body seemed to have gotten worse. They looked like running sores. Jonathan thought he noticed lice crawling in the old man's hair. In the sunlight, Jason Gibbons cut an even more miserable figure than he had in the dark swamp.

"Why have you come back here?" the old man hissed. "You should have gone away when I told you to."

"I have to talk to you, Mr. Gibbons."

"No talk is going to help you, boy. Go away."

"Mr. Gibbons, please, I have to talk to you, " he insisted. "All I want to do is ask you what you meant about Miss Sarah. Why are you so afraid of her?"

Gibbons stared back at him with red-rimmed eyes.

"Why should I tell you?" he said, and a mad glimmer came into his eyes. "You won't believe me. You'll believe her. You must believe her. You'll have no choice."

"No choice? Why do you say that? I can make up my own mind."

"Lots of people thought they could. But then they're not in control of their minds any longer." The old man began to gesture with his hands. "She crawls into them, seeping into their very thoughts. They have no defense, none. They are helpless against her. They can't do anything, they can't fight; and when I tell them, they think I'm insane."

Jonathan had had enough of the old man's ravings and he wanted to get away, away from the filthy old man, away from the gloom of this sad little cemetery.

"Are you trying to tell me that Sarah Bankroft can control minds?"

He was angry with himself for even talking to this old man who was obviously deranged and had no idea what he was saying.

"You see, you see," the old man began to cry. "They didn't believe me either."

"Who are they?"

"Her family. That's why they're in that place."

"You mean the mausoleum?" Jonathan asked.

The old man began to laugh, slowly, at first, as if someone had just told him a funny story. Then his laugh grew wilder and louder until he seemed hysterical. He could not stop until Jonathan slapped him on the face, hard.

Sobered, he stared at Jonathan with his mad eyes. Jonathan still held him tightly by his bony arms.

"I saw them; at night it was," he said, lowering his voice so that it was almost a whisper. "Black as her heart, the night was. Doing the Devil's work. Them two, skulking out there, taking the very bodies from the ground."

"What are you talking about?"

"They're not in there. They don't rest; they can't; she won't let them."

"What are you saying?" Jonathan realized that he was a fool to try to make sense of anything this madman told him, yet he kept on prodding him.

"You'll see; you'll understand one day, but it'll be too late. She'll have you, too." The old man struggled to break away from Jonathan's grip, but Jonathan wasn't through with him.

"You're not running away this time, old man," he warned him. "I want you to tell me what that all means. Tell me, tell me."

"She put them in there, then she took them away."

"She put them in where?"

"Charon. The ferryman took them to the other side, but she brought them back," the old man insisted. "But you won't believe me; no one does. She'll have you too, like she has all the others. She'll control you. Adela knew, but she's gone. No one can stop that girl now."

He finally managed to break from Jonathan's

grasp and pull away. Jonathan watched as the old man ran back towards the swamp, leaving him more confused then ever.

Jonathan still didn't know what the old hermit meant. He only knew that his words had troubled him deeply.

He found Sarah working on the rose garden. The sun was shining on her blonde hair making it look as if it were made of spun gold. She smiled when she saw him.

"Where have you been?" she asked cheerfully.

"I went to the cemetery."

"What on earth for?"

"I wanted to get a feeling for the dead Bankrofts," he said half joking. "But now I've got a small mystery on my hands."

"What's that?" she asked, standing up.

He took her arm and led her to a marble bench beneath a nearby magnolia tree.

"I hope this doesn't bother you, Sarah," he said gently. "But I noticed there's no date of death on the mausoleum for your sister Monica. Isn't she interred with the others?"

Sarah seemed reluctant to answer him. She stared into space for a few minutes.

"Is it something you don't wish to discuss, Sarah? I've told you before that I won't write about anything that you don't want me to."

"Jonathan," she began sadly. "You've become more than a writer who wants to publish our history; you've become a friend."

"And more to you, I hope."

Sarah smiled.

"Jonathan, Monica is not buried there because she's not dead."

"What? But I thought you said—"

"This is the way she wants it."

"You mean she's still alive, but she wants people here to think she's dead?"

"Yes."

"But why? I don't understand."

"It happened three years ago," Sarah sighed. "David and Monica were driving into town. The car went out of control and smashed into a tree. David was killed instantly, but poor Monica survived.

"Then why on earth does she want people to believe she's dead?"

"Because of what the glass did to her. You see, Monica was once a beautiful woman. She was considered to be the most beautiful of the Bankrofts. The glass from the shattered windshield mutilated her so horribly that she is ashamed to have anyone see her. She prefers to be thought as dead."

"Where is she really?"

"In a sanitorium," Sarah said sadly. "She's been there ever since the doctors decided nothing more could be done. They simply can't repair the damage to her face. It's like some hideous mask of scar tissue, and it resists everything they've tried. Now she just sits there in her dark room. It's very sad."

"And you visit her?"

"Yes, every month." Sarah's eyes had flooded with tears so that they glittered in the sunlight.

"And that's where you were yesterday, wasn't it?"

"Yes," she sighed. "I've tried to talk her into coming home to Cherron. I thought seeing her home and friends would help her adjust to her affliction, but she refuses."

"It must cost a fortune to keep her there."

Sarah shrugged. "That doesn't matter. I'd prefer her to be here among the people who love her. Perhaps someday she'll come back to us."

Jonathan took her small white hand and held it. He could see how deeply her sister's tragedy had affected her.

"Sarah," he said gently. "Have you ever been to New York?"

"No."

"Would you like to go?"

"What for?"

"Because I want to marry you."

There was a trace of sadness in her blue eyes as she stared up at him. "We've been over that, Jonathan."

"I know you want me to take things more slowly, but what's wrong with our getting married and living in New York?"

"First of all, Cherron is my home. Who would run the tobacco business if I went away?"

"Martin."

"He doesn't want it. And what about Aunt Jessica and Devon? I have responsibilities."

Somehow Jonathan's reporter's instincts told him that those were not the reasons.

"Sarah, is there some other reason? There is, isn't there?"

"Like what?"

"Like you don't love me."

With all her heart she wanted to scream *No. No. I do love you, Jonathan Evans, more than I've loved any other man.* But for some reason—was it fear? or shyness? or just good sense?—the words would not come. Instead, she spoke sensibly.

"I've told you, it's too soon, Jonathan. I do care for you; maybe I love you, but I cannot leave my home."

"Can't or won't?"

"What's the difference?"

"The difference is that if you loved me you'd consider coming with me to New York."

"And if you loved me you wouldn't ask me to prove it by leaving my home. That's not love."

"I do love you."

"Then you can stay here at Cherron with me."

"Leave New York?"

She smiled and her voice took on a playful tone. "It's quite different now, isn't it? You see, it works both ways, and I'm afraid you can't have everything your own way."

Jonathan still was not satisfied.

"I feel you're hiding something, Sarah," he said. "There's something else, some other reason why you won't leave this place, isn't there?"

"I do not choose to leave. This is my home and I have every intention of enjoying it."

"Darling, I don't mean to fight with you."

"Then, please don't." She rose to go.

"Sarah—" he called her.

"I don't wish to discuss it."

"Sarah, please."

"I told you, the discussion is over. I'll hear no more about it." She walked briskly away, leaving poor Jonathan watching her sadly.

* * *

David found his sister in the stable, saddling up Isis for a ride. The two Labradors had followed him inside.

"I want to talk to you, Sarah."

She could tell he was angry.

"What's wrong?" She had never seen a look like that on him before.

"Come here." He pulled her by the arm to the back of the stable. The dogs began to bark loudly.

"Hush," Sarah commanded them, and the noise subsided. Then she turned to her brother.

"You're hurting me, David, What is it?"

"I saw you and Martin last night!"

Sarah caught her breath. She felt a sinking feeling in the pit of her stomach.

"I don't know what you're talking about," she told him brusquely.

"How could you? How could the two of you do such a thing?"

"What thing?"

"You're cousins, for God's sake. It's sick; it's depraved."

"And what right do any of you have to talk about depraved?" She was struggling to remain calm.

"Both of you must be sick!"

"Don't you dare say that," she screamed, showing emotion for the first time. "Martin is the only one of you who ever cared, ever loved me, ever showed me one single moment of kindness. The rest of you only laughed at me, insulted me. None of you ever cared, no one except Martin."

"That's no excuse for what the two of you did."

"How do you know we did anything?"

"I looked in your room; I saw. And I have every intention of doing something about it."

Suddenly she was really afraid. David was the head of the family now. He could do anything.

"Doing something, David? What are you going to do?"

"I've contacted a psychiatrist. He's coming here Friday to examine both of you. And I have no doubts that the two of you will be put away somewhere; A madhouse, I'm certain, where you'll never be able to touch each other ever again. Your conduct has been outrageous."

"Have you told this to Uncle Jeffrey?" If Martin's father knew, things would be even worse.

"Not yet. I thought I'd have the psychiatrist break it to him. I fully expect that the doctor will recommend that we commit the two of you."

So that was what her brother wanted for her. To lock her away in some cold, dank room where she would never be able to touch Martin again.

"Until Dr. Sheffield gets here, I want you two to behave yourselves," he warned, "or it will only go worse for you."

"Why are you doing this, David?"

"Why?" he shrieked. "For God's sake, what the

two of you did is unnatural."

"Reaching out for love is not unnatural. We love each other."

"I told you, I don't want to hear this filth. This situation will be taken care of immediately. Now I'm going to get Monica. We're going in to town. It'll all be settled in the next few weeks."

No, it must be settled now, Sarah realized. She could not bear the thought of life without Martin, his gentle touch, his understanding. If the rest of the Bankrofts had ever shown her the same kindness and affection that Martin had, he and she might never have fallen in love. But they had, and she would never allow David or any psychiatrist to come between them.

Still shaken by her encounter with David, Sarah went downstairs to the basement. She had to warn Martin: that was the most important thing.

As a child, in her loneliness, she had made a small playroom for herself and Martin had often joined her there. As the years passed, they had fixed it up together. It was their room, their private space. They spent so much time together here; maybe that was where David had seen them. When she was mistress of Cherron she would put a lock on their hideaway.

When she was mistress of Cherron!

Yes. She had never wanted it, never coveted it; but soon it would all be hers, very soon.

She found Martin waiting for her in the basement room. It had been simply furnished with cast-off furniture that David and Monica considered unsuitable for the upstairs rooms.

"Martin," she said. "David knows about us!"

His face went ashen. She could see that he felt the same way she did. He would do anything she suggested. Nothing must stand in the way of their happiness.

"The bastard!" he said angrily. "Did he tell my father?"

"Not yet, but he has a psychiatrist coming Friday."

"Friday, that's only three days away! What will we do?" Martin was not ashamed of what he and Sarah had done, but he was terrified of his father's wrath.

"Don't worry, Martin. I'll take care of it. All you have to do is take your father into town Friday. No matter what happens, get him out of the house!"

She left Martin and went back upstairs. The door to Monica's room was open, and she walked in timidly. Monica was seated at her vanity table, brushing her long black hair and practicing smiling in the mirror. When she saw Sarah she frowned.

"Oh, it's you. Well, stay; you can help me decide what to wear."

She had laid out several dresses on her bed. Sarah looked at them wistfully. Each one was prettier than the next.

"Why do you take so much time to dress, Monica?"

Monica sighed. It always depressed her that her sister showed so little of the Bankroft style.

"Sarah," she said, trying to be patient. "I can't

155

disappoint my admirers, can I? I have to look perfect."

"You always do," Sarah assured her. "This is a nice one. It matches your eyes."

She pointed at the powder-blue dress with the full, flouncy skirt.

"Please, Sarah, don't touch it. I don't want you to soil it."

"I'm not dirty."

Monica didn't seem to be listening. She began to rub some cream into her smooth skin.

"Isn't this new cream marvelous?" she chattered. "It makes my skin smoother than ever. Don't you think so?"

"Yes."

"Perhaps you should try some." She looked at her little sister. "No, come to think of it, nothing could help you."

David called up from the hall downstairs. He was waiting in the car for Monica, and if she didn't hurry they were going to be late.

"Tell him I'll be right down, will you?" she said. "Men will never understand that it takes time to be so beautiful."

"Is that all you care about, Monica? Being beautiful on the outside."

"Lord, you are a dull-witted thing aren't you?" she said, laughing. "Of course it's important. Men want to love a beautiful woman, not someone like you."

Although actually, Monica realized as she watched her sister in the mirror, Sarah did not look half-bad lately. This was probably due to the good example she herself set.

"I don't suppose it would do me any good to ask you if I could come too?" Sarah asked.

"No, it wouldn't. Haven't you gotten it through your head that we don't want you with us?"

"Yes, Monica. It's gotten through all too clearly."

Monica stood up to join David in the car. She shooed her sister out of the room.

"Now stop bothering me and leave my things alone. You know how I want everything to be perfect."

Sarah stood out on the lawn, watching David's big yellow Cadillac move slowly down the drive. In her mind she was there with them. She saw the steering wheel and she saw David's hands on it. She could see it so clearly, how easily he turned the wheel. She heard her sister telling David how Sarah had begged to come along with them. They were laughing.

She heard and saw and grew more angry. She thought about David's plans to separate her from Martin, and as she did her eyes began to shine. A powerful white light seemed to come from the whites of her eyes. She focused her mind on the steering wheel of David's Cadillac and in her thoughts, she turned it slightly.

Inside the car, David felt a slight resistance from the wheel. He tried to turn it the other way but it refused to follow. His foot moved to the gas pedal and pressed down. It was as though a huge weight was on top of his foot and he couldn't lift it off that pedal. He watched as the speedometer started to rise: sixty, seventy, eighty. He couldn't seem to control the car.

The speedometer now was at one hundred and he could hear Monica begging him to stop driving so fast. They were barreling down the great drive of Cherron, and he was weaving; but he couldn't stop the car. He tried to put his other foot on the brake but nothing happened. The brake was useless.

His arms were tense as he fought for control, but it was impossible. All he could hear was Monica screaming that they were going to die.

"David, stop the car, please," she begged.

"I can't. God, I can't," he cried. "It won't move; the wheel won't move."

The car was a yellow blur as it flew down the drive at one hundred and twenty miles an hour, faster and faster. They were heading for a huge live oak and there was nothing he could do about it.

Now she was inside the car with them. She could see their faces twisted with fright; she could hear their screams.

"God, no! God help us!"

"No one can help you," she told them.

They hit the tree and the huge car crumpled like a cheap tin can. David was killed immediately. His bloody body lay slumped over the steering wheel. But she was not finished. The glass from the windshield shattered and the shards went straight for Monica. Each piece had but one purpose, to cut Monica's face.

Monica could see them coming at her as if in slow motion, their jagged edges ripping away at her soft flesh. Sarah saw it all as if she were inside the car, although physically she was still standing on the verandah of Cherron with Uncle Jeffrey and Martin. When the car hit the tree, they rushed down the drive to the wreckage.

Jeffrey pried the front door open and blood spilled out on the ground. They pulled David from the car, but he was already dead. Then they heard low moans. It was Monica.

Together, Jeffrey and Martin managed to free the girl from the wreckage. She was still breathing, but her face was a bleeding lump of pulpy flesh. Glass was still embedded in her cheeks and it gleamed as the sun peaked through the clouds and bounced off each tiny piece. One large, jagged piece was sticking out where an eye had been.

Sarah had seen it all.

Monica was going into deep shock when the ambulance arrived to take her away. A white-faced Jeffrey Bankroft went with her to the hospital.

Martin's only thought was for Sarah.

"Did you do this?" he said gently.

"I told you not to worry," she smiled. "Nothing will happen to us. Just do as I tell you."

They stood there together, watching as the ambulance, with its human wreckage pulled away.

Chapter Seven

Before Jonathan Evans had arrived at Cherron, Sarah had encouraged many suitors. But in the weeks since the Cherron party she had not even seen Bill Collins. That was why she had invited him out to play tennis. There was safety in numbers. It would make Martin feel safer to know that Jonathan meant no more to her than any man and it would show the writer that he was not the only man in her life.

They were waiting for her on the court now: Jonathan, who would be her partner; a grinning Bill Collins, obviously delighted to be back at Cherron, and a somber Martin. The men were all in tennis whites and she was glad that she had decided to wear her new tennis dress. She waved at them as she approached.

"Am I late?" she asked.

"Oh, no," Bill assured her. "Jonathan and I are

just geting to know each other."

Jonathan grinned. In spite of himself he liked the burly young bank president. He seemed so normal, so easy to figure out, unlike the enigmatic Martin.

"Well, let's go then. Jonathan, you're my partner; Martin and Bill, you'll be opposite us."

At first Jonathan was concerned that they would be outweighed, a man and a girl against two men. But any doubts he had about Sarah's strengths as a player were dispelled as he watched her step back behind the baseline and prepare to serve. She tossed the ball into the air and swung at it effortlessly, sending it spinning into the opposite court. It formed a perfect arc as Bill Collins rushed up to the net and hit it, sending it back so quickly that Jonathan barely realized what was happening. He recovered and leaped into the air, returning the ball to Martin.

He was obviously in the big leagues now, he realized. It had been months since he had played and he could feel the rustiness in his legs and in his reflexes. He allowed a steady stream of service returns from Martin and Bill to float back across the net, practically handing the points to them. Sarah was too much of a lady to say anything, but he sensed that she was disappointed.

"Well now, city boy," Martin gloated. "I guess we country folks still do some things better, wouldn't you say?"

The sun burned hot on the clay court and the sweat poured from him. The teasing only strengthened Jonathan's resolve not to be beaten.

He had only himself to blame. He should have cut off their shots at the net, if not all of them, at least some. He had made up his mind he was not going to lose in front of Sarah.

Sarah watched him with interest as he moved closer to her side of the court. He was poaching and she knew it. She liked the idea that he was trying something so risky. It was true that you could tell a lot about a person by watching him on the court. Now, to her surprise, she realized that Jonathan Evans was a man who would take risks and who would push himself to the limits of endurance in order to do so.

If he moved across the court too soon, Bill would hit the ball behind him down the alley. If he moved too late, then he would miss the ball completely. He must wait for exactly the right moment.

She wondered if she should give him some help. She decided not to just yet. The ball came towards her and she laced a return at the feet of Bill Collins. He would have to hit the ball up in order to clear the net, and that would be a weak shot. He went for it, and Jonathan went for the poach, sending it back. Bill missed the shot.

Jonathan smiled at Sarah as if he realized that with that shot he had redeemed himself. At that moment he felt that they understood each other. They were both playing to win. And now, not only had he scored points but he had rattled Bill and Martin. Knowing that he liked to poach, they would wonder for the rest of the game whether he was going to do it again, or whether they should simply hit the ball down his alley. Thoughts like that could bother even experienced players and make them hit shots everywhere but in the court.

They continued to play for an hour, until Bill and Martin conceded the third set. Then Sarah insisted they come inside for lemonade. Martin declined, saying that he had to feed the dogs, but Bill and Jonathan eagerly followed her into the house.

It had been a good game and Jonathan was exhilarated from the workout. Only one thing bothered him. Occasionally, as he watched Sarah serve or gracefully reach for the ball, he got the strangest sensation. The ball seemed to linger in the air a little too long, as it if were being controlled by something other than gravity. But he dismissed the thought. He had simply had too much sun.

"You play quite a game for a city boy," Bill said as he took a frosted glass from the tray Sarah was holding and leaned back on the living room sofa.

"Thank you, you're good at the net yourself."

"I owe it all to Sarah, here. When I can tear her away from her business, and if Martin lets her play, she's a lot of fun."

Sarah smiled. "My family always told me I'd never learn, but I managed."

Jonathan decided that Bill Collins was not so bad. In fact, it was pleasant to talk to him here with Sarah probably because the glowering Martin was not around.

He had slowly come to realize what was disturbing him. It was the relationship between Sarah and her cousin. They not only spent a good deal of their time together, but even when they weren't with each other he sensed a strong psychological dependency on Sarah's part.

She had already told him that she was close to Martin because he had comforted her when her family mistreated her. But he had begun to believe that there was something more there, some unspoken secret that they shared.

Was he simply jealous of Martin's closeness with his cousin? Was this getting in the way of his seeing things clearly? He knew now that he was in love with Sarah Bankroft and he wanted desperately to be the one she confided in.

It was important for her to break away from Martin, not only for his own selfish reasons, but because she had to break away from her past. She was no longer the ugly, neglected little sister. She was a beautiful intelligent young woman. She had to free herself from her past and he, Jonathan Evans would help her.

He decided that the first step would be a talk with Martin; and as soon as Bill Collins left, he went to find him.

Martin was working in the stable. The dour, brooding fellow did not looked pleased to see him, but he had made up his mind that he was going to get Martin to talk to him this time.

"Cleaning the stable?"

"Yes," Martin said dryly. "That squirrel Miss Sarah rescued left quite a mess. He brought every stick in the yard in here."

"They like chewing on those things."

"I know." His voice was tight, as if he was struggling to be cordial.

"You don't like me very much, do you, Martin?"

The man seemed surprised by Jonathan's frankness.

"I never said that," he insisted.

"No, but I get that impression. You'd just as soon I wasn't here. Am I right?"

"You are." He decided to match the writer's honesty with some of his own.

"Would you mind telling me why?"

"Because I don't want to see Miss Sarah hurt again, that's why."

"Do you think I'd hurt her?"

"I don't know that for certain. I don't want to take any chances."

"That decision belongs to Miss Sarah."

Martin had finished with the sweeping and he was now brushing down his Morgan, Medea.

"Sarah is too trusting of people sometimes," he said gruffly. "She never believed Roy McEndrews would hurt her either, but he damn near destroyed her."

"I can assure you that I'm nothing like that poor soul," Jonathan said angrily. "I've already asked her to come to New York with me."

"Miss Sarah will never leave Cherron."

Jonathan worried that Martin might be right. He had already learned how much Cherron meant to her. It wasn't just her home; but she also genuinely cared about her workers. He knew that if he forced her to make a choice between Cherron and himself it would tear her apart.

If only Martin were less possessive and really

thought about what she was doing here, wasting her life, withering away.

"If you really care about Miss Sarah, Martin, why do you let her spend so much time in the basement?"

Martin's eyes grew large and he looked at Jonathan in amazement. The question had obviously unsettled him.

"What are you talking about?" he cried.

"You know what I'm talking about, Martin. I know you keep family heirlooms down there. I suppose Sarah goes down there and just sits and looks at them while the memories come flooding back. Do you think that's healthy? Do you imagine that it makes her happy?"

Martin seemed to have recovered his composure. He answered Jonathan calmly.

"What she does in the basement is her business."

"But it's not healthy. She should get rid of them."

"Why don't you tell her that?" Martin said and walked away quickly.

Sarah had suggested that she and Jonathan take another ride around Cherron. He saddled up Jason and she rode Isis. Midway across the lawn, Isis broke into a gallop. Jonathan watched with awe as Sarah rode effortlessly over the grounds, her long golden hair blowing freely in the wind.

"Wow," he said when he'd caught up with her. "You're too much for me. I'm just a poor city-kid, remember. Slow down."

"I'm sorry," she laughed. "I forgot not everyone

loves riding the way I do. I feel so free on a horse. When Isis is at full gallop we try to beat the wind."

"Ever win?"

"No," she laughed again. "But we've come close."

They were trotting now, together, and he could talk to her while still admiring the beauty of the scenery around them. In the distance he could see the white, cheesecloth-covered tobacco fields, and, more closely, the great lawn of Cherron with its abundance of flowering trees. And of course, Miss Sarah's rose garden, a brightly colored maze surrounded by a white picket fence.

"Tell me, Sarah, does your cousin have a girl friend?"

She smiled at the idea.

"No. He used to date, but I think he's afraid of getting mixed up with the wrong kind of woman. He saw the trouble Everett had with his wife, and I suppose he just doesn't want to get involved."

"I didn't know your brother had married."

She shrugged. "They were divorced after only a few months. Mother and Father didn't approve. They said she was after our money, and it was one of the few times they were right."

"What happened to her?"

"After Everett died she came back here to see if she could get any more money from us. I think she really believed she could get a piece of Cherron."

"Did your family have to settle with her?"

"Lord, no. Uncle Jeffrey threatened to put her in jail if she pressed her claim. It must have frightened her off. One night she just left the hotel in town without a word, and we never heard from her again." She turned to face him, her eyes glittering in the sun. "Come on, let's really let the horses out."

"You go ahead, Sarah. I'll catch up."

"Coward."

"Every inch of me."

He watched as Sarah and Isis took off at full gallop. The girl and the horse were perfectly matched; her blond hair and the horse's brown mane both floated in the wind. They stopped at the edge of the forest. As Jonathan trotted up to them he couldn't help glancing into the dense wood, hoping for a glimpse of the old hermit.

"Looking for something?" she asked him.

"Sarah, I have a confession to make. I went back to the swamp to see Jason Gibbons."

"Now why would you do something like that?"

"I don't really know myself. He spoke about that woman again, that Adela. Did you know her?"

"Yes, I did," she admitted. "I had spoken to her several times. She's just a harmless old woman who lives in a shack in the swamp."

"And the old man insists that you're in league with Satan," Jonathan added.

Sarah laughed. "I don't know why you bother yourself with him. You know he's not right in his head. No one here takes what he says seriously. I don't understand what fascinates you about him in the first place."

"I don't know myself," he said quietly.

Sarah pulled her horse up sharply.

"Do you really believe I've made some sort of

deal with the Devil?"

"You know I didn't mean it like that," he said apologetically. "Come on, I'll race you back to the house."

The winds howled that night sounding like souls in torment. Sarah placed her cape around her shoulders and descended the great staircase. Martin was waiting at the bottom of the stairs and, without a word, he followed her out the front door, across the green lawn, and into the swamp.

Sarah made her way deftly through the marshy land without fear or anxiety. She knew every inch of the swamp after her many visits over the years.

She did not like the way things were going. Most people simply ignored Jason Gibbons, but he had started Jonathan thinking and questioning. There was no telling what the old fool would say next.

She should never have let it go this far. Something would have to be done soon, before he caused any more trouble.

Through the darkness of the night they saw a clearing, and then a tiny light, a candle flame inside the tar-paper shack where Gibbons lived. Sarah stood before the shack, her eyes narrowing slightly, the wind tugging at her cape as a child tugs at its mother's sleeve. Martin stood a few feet behind her as she waited for Gibbons to come to her.

The old man was confused. It was a cold night and he had not intended to leave the shack; but suddenly he was walking through the door, carrying his candle. The biting cold made him shiver, but he could not turn back. He moved out into the clearing.

He could make out two figures, but he couldn't tell who they were; it was too dark. He brought the candle closer to see who had summoned him. It was her, the devil! Her face was distorted by the candlelight, and her eyes were shining like nothing on earth.

Horrified, he trembled and shrank backwards, falling to the muddy ground. The wind blew out his candle.

"Noo, noo," he moaned. "Go away, go away. Leave me in peace."

"Have you left me in peace?" she demanded.

"I've done nothing to you, nothing," he whined. He was rolling in the mud now like a pitiful animal. It was hard to believe that this man had once been the head of a bank, and one of the most powerful men in Arcadia.

"You've been talking to Jonathan Evans," she shouted at him. "You've been telling him things about me, things that are better left unsaid."

"Please, I won't talk to him again, Miss Sarah. I swear it."

"Must I prove my powers to you again?"

"No," he begged. "I know what you can do. I won't talk to him. I swear it. Just leave me alone."

Sarah raised her arm and pointed a finger at him. He slithered in the mud, trying to escape, but it was useless.

"You'll never speak to anyone again."

"Please, please, Pl—Agh." The old man grabbed his throat and tried to make an intelligent sound. "Agh, agh." He looked up to Sarah with such fear that his whole body trembled. He could not speak.

She stared down at him, her blue eyes glittering; and then an odd glow came into the whites of her eyes. They burned at him like two blinding stars. The muddy ground around him began to smoke and bubble and, as he twisted and turned, he sank deeper into it. He was desperately trying to force words from his throat. When none came he began to cry. He made a pitiful, whining sound as gradually he was engulfed by the soft mud.

Sarah watched until nothing was left but his head. His horrified face stared at her, still pleading for mercy. Jason Gibbons was a drowning man and he knew it. Finally, his eyes bulging, his face an awful shade of purple, he gasped and then died.

Sarah stared until the mud bubbled more furiously, pushing the lifeless body of the tormented old man up, up, out of the mud until it floated, face down on the surface of the swamp.

Later, she and Martin returned home with their bundle. Martin took her cape and hung it up. Then she reminded him about the pets.

"Did you feed them, darling?" she asked.

"Not yet."

"Good," she smiled. "Let's do it together."

* * *

What with the funeral and all, Friday came quickly. Sarah waited for the knock at the door all morning. Thank goodness Martin had managed to

171

get his father out of the house when it came.

"How do you do?" said the distinguished man. "I'm Dr. Calvin Sheffield. David Bankroft is expecting me."

If she ever bothered herself with trivial matters such as picturing what a psychiatrist looked like she could not have imagined anyone better. Calvin Sheffield was a large, self-assured man. Sarah sensed that he was a man who thought he had no problems. Well, he was wrong; he had a problem now.

"How do you do, Dr. Sheppard," she welcomed him graciously. "I'm Sarah Bankroft."

"Oh!" His tone told Sarah that he had heard her name before. He was obviously surprised that she was attractive. She wondered what David had told the doctor about Martin and herself.

She led the doctor into the living room. He sat on the red velvet sofa and she sat opposite him on a small chintz chair.

"I'm afraid I have some bad news for you, Doctor. My brother David was killed a few days ago in a car accident."

"I'm terribly sorry." He had an oily, ingratiating way of speaking that he supposed would make her trust him.

"Is there anything I can do for you?" she went on.

"Perhaps. If it is you I came to see, Miss Bankroft."

"Me? Why, I'm as fit as a fiddle," she laughed.

The doctor began to fill his pipe thoughtfully, as if measuring how much he should tell her. He was blissfully unaware that she already knew all about him.

"I'm not a medical doctor, Miss Bankroft. I'm a psychiatrist. It seems that your brother was concerned about you and your cousin. He called me several weeks ago and invited me here."

"I don't know of any problems."

"Under the circumstances, perhaps it would be better if I were to speak to the young man's father."

"Uncle Jeffrey is out at the moment. As a matter of fact, no one is in this house except us. I don't see the need to discuss it with anyone else."

"I would like to speak with him," Dr. Sheffield said firmly. "Do you know when he'll return?"

Sarah threw up her hands in a gesture of impatience.

"Doctor, I have tried to be patient. However, I'm not happy with the fact that my brother has been discussing my personal life with a stranger. Now, exactly what is this problem that I'm supposed to have?"

"I think I'd better discuss this with your uncle."

"Doctor, are you saying I have no right to know what this is about?"

"You're perfectly right, Miss Bankroft," he relented. "Your brother was upset by a particular incident he saw."

"What incident is that?"

"I think you know very well. Mr. Bankroft told me that he inadvertently discovered you were involved, sexually, with a close relative."

"And you've already made up your mind that

what my brother told you is the truth," she snapped. "Perhaps it's David who had a problem. Don't you think there might be something wrong with a man who spies on two lovers?"

"Then you admit that the problem exists?"

"There is no problem," she snapped. "Martin Bankroft and I have been lovers for years."

Calvin Sheffield had been trained not to show any emotion, not even surprise. However, he was certainly surprised that this beautiful young woman not only had a relationship with her cousin, but seemed positively proud of it. She seemed to be daring him to do something about it.

"Do you love your cousin?" he asked gently.

Sarah smiled and, for the first time, she seemed to relax.

"I love him more than anyone in this world. Now, can you say that's wrong?"

"Miss Bankroft, in our society incest is a sin and a crime . . . ."

"I'm not interested in society. Martin and I are hurting no one."

"You're hurting yourselves."

Sarah found it outrageous that this stranger thought he could come in here and tell her what was right and wrong. What did he know of her loneliness? In the vast wilderness of loneliness she had found a haven, a kind, gentle soul. Martin had comforted her, wiped away her tears, and given her strength to hold on. He, and he alone, had looked past her plain exterior and into the heart within.

"But you're blood relatives," the doctor was insisting. "From what you and your brother have told me I think you should go into therapy immediately. Both of you."

"Never!" she insisted. "Don't you understand that we're happy the way we are, that we love each other. Martin gives me more love every morning than anyone in my entire family ever gave me in my entire life."

Dr. Sheffield rose to go.

"Perhaps it would be better if I returned to my hotel and waited for your uncle there."

"Nothing I've said has made any difference to you, Doctor, has it?"

"No, I'm afraid not."

It was time and Sarah knew it. Her eyes began to shine with anger.

"Doctor," she said softly. "Are you familiar with psychokinesis?"

"Yes, it's supposedly the controlling of objects through intense concentration."

"Would you believe me if I told you I had telekenetic powers, and that you will never leave this house?"

The doctor moved towards the door. He had had enough of Miss Bankroft. "I would not; and if you're threatening me, it won't work."

"It's warm today, don't you agree, Doctor?" she said politely. "As a matter of fact, it's very hot."

The doctor took out his handkerchief and began to dab at his eyes.

"Yes, you're feeling it, aren't you? It's so hot, you'd like to come downstairs where it's so much cooler, wouldn't you?"

Dr. Sheffield found himself agreeing with the girl.

"Yes, I — I would like that."

"Good. Let me show you." She led him to the cellar door. "Right down here."

The doctor wiped his forehead and face and followed her down the stone steps obediently.

She unlocked the door and led the way into the basement room. The doctor followed her into a simple parlor.

"Do you like my little hideaway, Doctor?" she asked. "Someday I hope to have it fixed up like a little jewel-box with my family's heirlooms and paintings. But for now, this will have to do for Martin and me."

Dr. Sheffield stared at the young woman. She was quite mad, he decided, and the best thing to do was humor her.

"Yes," he agreed. "The room is quite lovely."

"Then you must see my friends in the other room." She indicated a doorway that led to a darkened room beyond.

"Your friends?" He had assumed they were in the house alone.

"Yes doctor." She was staring at him, her eyes glittering. "Of course you want to meet them."

He stood transfixed. He seemed to have no will of his own. "Yes," he admitted. "Where are these friends?"

"Right in there," she pointed at the doorway. "Go ahead."

He walked slowly through the door into the black velvet darkness. Then he could feel himself

176

falling. He moaned, and then he began to scream.

Outside the room, Sarah listened to the doctor's cries of pain and terror. A great feeling of pleasure filled her. She had saved herself and Martin with her power. Their friends would do the rest.

In a few minutes the cries faded. She waited a few minutes more before going inside. Dr. Calvin Sheffield had threatened the one happiness in her life, and she had destroyed him. Now she and Martin had nothing to fear from the Dr. Sheffields of this world.

Her thoughts about Dr. Sheffield were disturbed by a noise upstairs. She wasn't alone! She stood still, listening hard, but her heart was beating wildly.

"Sarah? Is that you?"

Thank God. She breathed a sigh of relief. It was Martin standing in the doorway.

"Sarah, are you all right? You look pale."

"Yes," she assured him. "I'm all right now."

"I left Dad in town. I thought you might need help."

"Now I do." She led him into the other room and pointed at what was left of Calvin Sheffield. Martin looked at the whitened bones of what had once been a man.

"Dr. Sheffield, I presume," he said.

"That's right. He's not our problem now."

"Well, his car is. It's parked outside."

Sarah was unconcerned. "You can drive it to the edge of the swamp. They'll think he lost his way in there."

She turned her attention back to the pool as

Martin stood watching her. She was already putting the bones of Dr. Sheffield into a large damask table cloth.

"What are you going to do with them, Sarah?"

"Bones make good fertilizer," she told him, carrying the makeshift sack up the stairs. Dr. Sheffield had turned out to be surprisingly light.

While Martin started up the doctor's car, Sarah laid the bones on the kitchen counter. She began to feed them to a large machine. It was not quite a blender, not quite a grinder. She remembered how her mother's cook, Clemmie, used to use it to grind flour and corn meal. No one had used it for years.

She watched in fascination as the hard, white calcified bones turned to coarse gray powder.

Yes, with this kind of bone meal she was going to have the finest rose garden in Gadsden County.

* * *

Jonathan was standing in front of the mausoleum, still running Jason Gibbons' words over in his head. The old man had insisted that he had seen two people skulking around in the dark taking bodies from the ground. What bodies?

He looked again at the names of the persons memorialized in the graveyard. It disturbed him to think that the magnificent Bankroft family had dwindled down to this handful of eccentrics cared for by one beautiful but lonely young woman. What had happened to them all? Somehow he felt the answer was here in the graveyard. Perhaps Jason Gibbons had seen it.

He could not seem to drag himself away. It was as if some unseen hand held him there in its grasp. Was someone trying to tell him something? Sometimes he almost believed that the spirits of the dead were reaching from their graves, touching him, he felt as though there was something they wanted him to understand. But what? What was it that these dead souls wanted him to know?

"What on earth are you doing here?"

The sound of Miss Sarah's voice startled him. He hadn't heard her come into the little graveyard, but here she was.

"Did you think I was one of my restless relatives?"

"To be honest, Sarah, yes."

"Don't worry, Jonathan. They're all quite dead."

He pointed at the roses that decorated the graves and the mausoleum. "The flowers are beautiful."

"Thank you. I tend them myself. I like to think that my loved ones will never be without fresh roses." She smiled at him and her blue eyes glittered in the sunlight.

"But you haven't answered my question, Jonathan. What are you doing standing alone in the middle of the cemetery?"

"I don't really know. I guess I was drawn here by the past."

He watched as she placed her flowers in the niches of the mausoleum.

"I just thought that crazy Jason Gibbons might have been bending your ear again with more stories," she said. "You take what he says so much to heart. He shouldn't tell such stories."

"I'm not taking him seriously anymore," Jonathan insisted. "It's all nonsense."

"I'm glad you finally see that." She smiled at him. "Come on, we'll walk together to the house."

She took his arm and they strolled through the magnolias and the jasmine vines. Encouraged by her outgoing mood he decided to ask her about the old woman, Adela.

"I've been asking in town about her and people tell me she was a witch."

"And you're going to believe that?" she laughed.

"Of course not, but I wanted to know what you thought."

Miss Sarah frowned. "She was a wild-eyed, dirty old woman. Everyone stayed away from her."

"Except you?"

"I was terribly lonely. A child needs someone to talk to."

"You had Martin."

"And when Martin was at school I had no one," she said sadly. "She was a fascinating creature to me. And to you too, I can see."

"I admit it. She lived alone in a swamp; people feared her," he acknowledged. "She's a curiosity and I'm a curious writer. I wonder whatever happened to her. Do you think she's still in the swamp?"

Sarah was becoming impatient with his persistence.

"I told you before, Johathan. I have no idea what happened to her and I care less."

He realized that he had better change the subject. He got back to the Bankroft family.

"Did Martin grow up at Cherron with you?"

"Yes. Grandfather didn't approve of Martin's mother. He insisted they live here so he could make sure that Martin was raised as a real Bankroft."

"Your grandfather sounds like a hard man."

"He was too strict, a perfectionist. I think he made my grandmother ill. She knew people could never live up to what he expected of them. She saw the pain that he caused, but she was powerless to do anything about it; so she just withered away and died."

* * *

Ten-year-old Sarah knocked gently on the bedroom door and a frail voice bid her enter. The large bedroom smelled of lavender. The heavy draperies shut out the afternoon sunlight and the room was dark.

"Nanna, I have the book."

The tiny woman lay in the center of the huge bed, propped up on two large feather pillows. Her white hair was swept up in an old-fashioned bun and she wore a pale blue silk bed-jacket that matched her faded blue eyes. She motioned weakly for the girl to come closer.

Sarah sat down on the bed next to her grandmother.

"Would you like me to finish the story now, Nanna?"

"Yes, dear," the old woman whispered.

Sarah opened the book to the the place where they had stopped after the last reading.

"Remember, Nanna, this is Oliver Twist," she said, wondering how many times she had read like this to her Nanna. She couldn't remember. It brought them both the only pleasure they had living in this large, lonely house.

"Oliver has just been sold from the orphanage because he dared to ask for food," she began, and then she seemed to realize what it was she had just said. "You know, Nanna, all Oliver is looking for is someone to love him."

The old woman understood. "The same as you, child," she whispered.

"What?"

"I heard the way the children were teasing you today. I heard it from my window."

"I'm used to it," she shrugged.

"You poor child. You've never been happy with them, have you? All you're looking for is a little love, just like Oliver."

She stroked her granddaughter's chubby face with her ancient, gnarled hand. "My poor baby, my heart aches for you."

Sarah embraced the hand lovingly.

"I have love, Nanna. You love me."

"Not for much longer," she said, closing her tired eyes but still clinging to Sarah's hand. "I'm old and tired. I can't fight them anymore. I never could, really. And when I go, you'll be all alone, won't you? And I'm afraid I must take the blame. I brought them into the world."

"Nanna, don't," she protested. "Save your strength."

"You're so young, Sarah. You've had no joy in

your life."

"Sure, I have. I like reading to you." She was terrified. If Nanna left she would have no one. "I won't let you die. I'll never let you go."

"We have no choice, child. I can't go on any longer; perhaps I don't want to. It'll be a blessing. I see what my family has become. No one can be perfect, no one, not even Grandfather. And you'll be alone. That's what hurts even more, child. I'll leave you to their mercy."

"Let me read to you, Nanna." Anything to get her mind off death and onto life.

"Read my favorite, read *A Christmas Carol.*"

Sarah hurriedly turned the pages of the book until she came to the story; then she began to read. She sat there most of the afternoon. Several times she heard her grandmother whisper her name as if in a dream.

"Sarah, I must leave you alone now. Call me by my favorite name. I want to hear it again before I go."

"Nanna, my Nanna." Tears streamed down the girl's chubby cheeks, as she watched the old woman close her eyes.

Sarah closed her book and bent over the old woman. She kissed her.

"Good night, Nanna."

The only spark of love in her world was gone.

* * *

Chapter Eight

Jonathan found Sarah in her small office. Although it was next to the library where he was working he had never been inside. This morning the door was open and he stood in the doorway watching her at her desk.

It was an efficient but still feminine room with blue, patterned wallpaper, a fireplace lined with blue-and-white Delft tile, and French doors that were opened to frame an exquisite view of Miss Sarah's rose garden. She was working at a large, white painted table piled high with papers. The only non-business item on the desk was a crystal vase filled with yellow roses.

He knocked gently on the door frame and she looked up and smiled.

"Welcome!" she said cheerfully. "Now you see what I do all day."

"I see, but I can hardly believe," he said. "What

in the world are those?" He pointed at the two painted wooden statues that stood at each end of her work table.

"Oh, these?" she laughed. "Don't tell me you don't recognize cigar-store Indians, Jonathan."

"Sure I do," he defended himself, suddenly realizing that one of the statues was definitely an American brave in all his multi-colored glory. Then he pointed at the other statue. "But that's no Indian."

"Don't you recognize Jenny Lind?" she said, laughing.

Of course. The Swedish nightingale, with her long blond hair and blue dress resembled an old ship's figurehead more than a cigar-store ornament.

"The cigar stores didn't just use Indians," she explained. "There were Scottish Highlanders, Turks, Blacks, and many contemporary celebrities, including Miss Jenny Lind."

"She's really quite beautiful," he said, coming closer to examine the carving work.

"The cigar-store owners considered them an important part of the business at one time," Sarah explained. "In fact, they usually put a lot more money into these statues than into the rest of the store. I keep them around because they are so well done, a real American folk art."

"I've always wondered what happened to them," Jonathan remarked.

"Oh, public tastes change, and by 1890 the big cities were getting so crowded that these became sidewalk obstructions. And by that time the industry had begun to concentrate on national advertising."

"The business has changed a lot over the years, hasn't it?"

"Yes, I'm afraid it has," Sarah sighed.

"And where does that leave you and Cherron?"

Suddenly she stiffened and her eyes became wary. "What do you mean?"

"Oh come on, Sarah," he chided. "The cigar-making business is a dying one. I see how many workers you have. I know what your commitments are. How long can you meet your payroll?"

"Cherron will go on as long as I have a breath in my body," she shouted. "And not one Cherron worker will ever lose his job if I can help it."

"Is that you or Martin talking?"

"What do you mean?"

"You know what I mean, Sarah. It's his way of keeping you to himself, his way of controlling you. As long as you're tied to Cherron, you're tied to him."

"Really, Jonathan, you don't know what you're saying."

"Oh, yes I do. Why does he stay here? Why doesn't he get married and leave?"

"I told you, Martin is happy here. He has everything he wants. Why should he leave? Did it ever occur to you that he doesn't want to get married? Some people don't you know."

"Does that apply to you, Sarah?" he said grimly.

"Here we go again," she said, throwing up her hands in a gesture of exasperation. "Please try to understand, Jonathan. Martin loves Cherron as

186

much as I do. Why, I think he'd kill for it."

"I'm sure he would," Jonathan said brusquely.

"You don't understand at all, do you, Jonathan?"

"I'm sorry," he said, turning to leave. "Consider the subject dropped."

"I see I now have a new rival," Bill Collins said sullenly. He had succeeded in getting Sarah out for a night of dining and dancing at the Crystal Room, the finest restaurant in Arcadia; but he could tell her thoughts were elsewhere.

"I don't know what you're talking about, Bill," Sarah insisted.

"Oh, yes you do." They were dancing to the sound of "The Way We Were," but he could tell that she was thinking about that Yankee writer. "It's all right, Sarah. I've made up my mind I'm just going to wait until you come to your senses and marry me."

She barely heard him. She was thinking about Jonathan again. His questions were beginning to disturb her. Why was he so insistent about Jason Gibbons, when everyone in town agreed that the old man was crazy? It made her uneasy to think that that awful old man had poisoned Jonathan's mind, making trouble for her with this crazy talk.

But there was something else, something more serious. She had often teased Martin about the possibility that she would marry. Uncle Luke was right: she had many suitors, and even Bill Collins, holding her now, was a prize catch. Any girl in Gadsden County would be thrilled to have him. And he was devoted to her.

He would make an excellent husband: handsome, wealthy in his own right, and in love with her. But he meant nothing to her. None of them did, except Martin. They had shared so much, loved each other so long, that it didn't seem possible that she could share her life with any other man. Yet, suddenly she had willfully encouraged Jonathan Evans. Even Bill realized it.

She had hurt Martin, willfully inviting the stranger into their little Eden. She knew it hurt Martin, and still she had done it, and still she encouraged Jonathan. The truth was that for the first time in her life she felt real passion for a man. She also felt fear because she realized that this feeling she had for Jonathan Evans was not something she could control. She shivered.

"Is something wrong, darling?" Bill asked with concern.

"No, no, but I'd like to sit a while, Bill, if you don't mind. I just had the strangest sensation."

"Perhaps someone walked on your grave," he said, trying to make a bad joke.

But to Sarah it was no joke.

That night a rejected but undiscouraged Bill Collins said good night to Sarah on the veranda of Cherron. She stood in the doorway and waved as he started up his Buick and then disappeared down the long, winding driveway. Then she hurried upstairs to her room.

Martin was waiting for her and he took her in his arms and kissed her as soon as she closed the door.

"I missed you," he whispered.

"And I missed you; every time we danced I thought of you," she lied. Most of the evening she had found herself thinking about Jonathan Evans.

"I want you, Sarah," he insisted. "I need you. Why are you tormenting me by flirting with this stranger? Don't you know it's killing me?"

As they stood together in the moonlight she looked into her cousin's sad, brown eyes. His jealousy was touching. Sometimes he could be a tower of strength, protecting her, fighting for her one minute, and totally vulnerable to her the next. She liked that. She wondered if Jonathan Evans was that way too.

"I go crazy when I think of you in his arms," Martin said.

"Please, Martin, don't think about it. Not when we're together."

There was a soft knock at the door and they looked at each other in amazement. Jessica and Devon would never dare disturb them here.

"Who is it?" Sarah called out, her heart beating wildly.

"It's Jonathan," he called through the thick oak door. "May I come in? I'd like to talk to you."

She saw the anger and disappointment on Martin's face. She placed her small hand over his mouth, fearful that he would blurt out something.

"Not tonight, Jonathan," she answered.

"Sarah, please," he pleaded. "I need you tonight."

"I'll speak to you in the morning. I'm very tired right now."

"Are you angry with me?"

"No. Please, Jonathan, go to bed. We'll talk in the morning."

Jonathan stood in the dark hallway. He couldn't bear that she was sending him away. "I need you. I want to touch you, Sarah, to hold you. . . ."

Sarah took her hand away from Martin. He was obviously too distraught to even speak. His face was flushed with anger, or perhaps it was pain. She was terrified that he would fall into an uncontrollable rage. If Jonathan continued to shout through that door he was going to destroy them all.

"Jonathan," she pleaded. "Stop this and go to bed."

There was silence, then the sound of reluctant footsteps echoing down the hall.

She removed her hand from Martin's mouth. "Don't let that upset you, darling," she said as he sat down on the bed.

"How many times have you been with him?" he asked, his face still dark with anger.

"None — yet."

"But you want him, don't you?"

"Really, Martin, you're the one who awakened the sexual desires in me when I was a girl and transformed me into a woman." She sat beside him and took his hand in hers.

"You were a woman before I ever touched you, Sarah," he said firmly. "He's been asking you to leave Cherron, hasn't he?"

"You know he has."

"Have you ever considered it?"

"Not even for a minute." She reached out and

touched his rough cheek.

"Are you sure you don't want to go with him?" he prodded.

"I've never been so sure of anything," she lied.

"He won't stay here at Cherron; you realize that don't you?"

"Yes." But she faced his departure with mounting dread.

"Will it hurt you when he leaves?"

She still couldn't bring herself to tell Martin the truth. Instead she lied again. "I don't know," she teased. "Are you afraid I'll go rushing off after him?"

"I don't want to lose what we have here."

"Martin, have I ever lied to you?"

"No."

"Well, I won't start now. I'll always remain here with you, no matter what happens with Jonathan."

"Do you promise?"

Really, his insistence on questioning her about Jonathan was becoming wearing. How could she tell him the absolute truth when she wasn't even sure of it herself? Still, her dearest wish was to spare him any pain.

She put her arm around his shoulder and leaned her head against him. "My word of honor."

"You won't use your powers on him to make him stay, will you?"

"No. I've never used them on you, have I?"

"You never had to, Sarah. I've always loved you. And I never wanted to be any place but here."

"And I've always loved you." She sighed. "Why is it we spend so much of our time when we're together talking about him?"

"We have to stop that, don't we?" He drew her down onto the bed with him. "Still best friends?"

"All that and more," she assured him as she responded to his embrace, reveling in his touch as he moved his mouth along her neck and gently began to open her blouse.

Later, Sarah suggested that Martin return to his own bedroom for the night. She was afraid that Jonathan would suspect that there had been someone with her. But Martin lingered in the doorway, obviously reluctant to go.

"Is he thinking about staying here after his book is finished?"

"I don't know. Now, will you please leave?"

Martin lingered in the doorway, obviously reluctant to go.

"I wish he'd never come here in the first place," he insisted.

"Hindsight is a wonderful thing to have, Martin. Now, good night." She shut the door, leaving Martin in the hall. He had no choice but to turn and walk toward his own room. His thoughts were still on Sarah's involvement with the interloper, and so he didn't notice the figure standing in the shadows near the staircase.

Jonathan pressed himself against the wall, hoping that the darkness in the hall would hide him from Martin. To his relief, Martin did not even look his way. He held his breath until he heard the click of Martin's bedroom door closing shut and then he heaved a long sigh and pondered the strange scene he had just witnessed.

Sarah had told him not to come to her room, but he had hoped that she might relent if he waited. He had only pretended to go to his room. It had not occurred to him that there might be someone else there, or that the someone else might be the dour Martin.

As he walked softly back to his room, a shroud of mystery engulfed him. So many things did not make sense. Questions he had asked himself before but could not find answers to returned. He had tried so many times to question Sarah, but he seemed to lose his nerve every time he was with her. He would look into her soft blue eyes and lose himself.

But who could he ask? Martin was barely civil to him these days, and he had frightened Jessica Bankroft so badly she had refused to speak to him alone since that episode in the kitchen. Devon was in no condition to speak about anything and old Jason Gibbons seemed to have dropped out of sight. Sarah's uncle Luke had supplied all the information he seemed capable of supplying.

Where was he to turn now? And how was he to pose the questions that fought to be asked without sounding like a madman himself?

He was mixed up in something he might never fully understand—a new sensation for him and it bothered him. Or was he afraid that he would discover the truth? Was that what he was running from?

* * *

It was a hot summer afternoon when Sarah came in from working in her rose garden and found Uncle Jeffrey in the living room, talking to a hard-faced young woman. He introduced the woman as Everett's ex-wife.

Sarah had heard about Ruth Jarrod Bankroft but they had never met before. Now she stared at her. The young woman had bleached-blond hair that was dark at the roots. She wore too much make-up and her voice was loud and tough. Cheap and common were the words that seemed appropriate to use in describing her appearance. Sarah was surprised that her dearly departed brother would have married such a girl, but everyone knew the marriage had been short-lived.

"Widow," the woman corrected Uncle Jeffrey. "Even though we were divorced before poor Everett died, I know he would have wanted me taken care of."

"He made no provisions for you in his will," Uncle Jeffery assured her.

"Oh, I see," she said, without surprise. She leaned back comfortably on the red velvet couch. "Well perhaps, Mr. Bankroft, you could see your way clear to providing some financial assistance."

"Financial assistance comes from a bank," David snapped. "This is not a bank."

"I understand that, but I was married to the owner of this place. I just thought—"

"Thought that you would come here and ask for money," Uncle Jeffrey said gravely. "That is a totally tasteless act."

"I beg your pardon."

"Ruth—"

"Mrs. Bankroft."

"Very well, Mrs. Bankroft," Jeffrey agreed, but he was not intimidated. "I'm afraid you've come to the wrong place, and to the wrong people. I think you had better go."

"I deserve that money. I was married to Everett and I fully intend to try to get what is mine."

"You go right ahead if you think it will do any good."

Ruth Bankroft stormed out of the great house, slamming the door behind her.

"Can she really take Cherron from us?" Sarah asked her uncle.

"No," he assured her. "Although I don't think she's the most pleasant enemy to have, legally she doesn't have a leg to stand on."

"Of course, we don't know what a court will decide," David added sarcastically.

Sarah knew that, no matter what Uncle Jeffrey said, Ruth Bankroft was a woman who got what she wanted. Now she wanted Cherron. It was as simple as that.

She brooded about it for several days; then she discussed it with Martin. He agreed that they had to do something, and he agreed that her plan was the best.

They waited until Martin's father left town for a lawyer's conference in Tallahassee. Then Sarah called Ruth Bankroft at the Arcadia Hotel and told her.

"I shouldn't be talking to you," Ruth said when she realized who was calling. "My lawyer said there should be no contact between us."

"I understand how you feel," Sarah said sympathetically. "I feel just terrible that we can't get to know each other, you being family and all."

"That's very nice of you," Ruth acknowledged.

"I happen to know that my uncle Jeffrey is going to be out of the house for a day, and it would give me the perfect opportunity to show you around Cherron. I'd like very much to give you the grand tour."

"That's really very sweet of you, after all the things I said."

"Not at all. As a matter of fact, perhaps I could work something out with Uncle Jeffrey. If Martin and I spoke to him, maybe he could do something for you after all."

"You think he'd give me money?"

Sarah winced at the woman's greed, but she pressed on.

"Even more," she assured her. "Perhaps he would let you come live at Cherron. Won't you please come?"

"I'd like to, very much."

"Oh, that's wonderful," Sarah said over the phone. "And you won't even have to drive. Martin can come and pick you up."

Ruth Jarrod Bankroft hung up the phone and smiled. She was pleased by Sarah's call and even more pleased that Martin Bankroft would be her chauffeur, He was a hunk, that was for sure. Tall, dark, and handsome, just the way she liked them. On the quiet side, but then still water ran deep. She wondered just for a minute if it might be incest to fuck your ex-husband's cousin. She didn't normally like to get involved with anything kinky, although for a guy who looked like Martin she might make an exception.

She decided to wear her polka-dot dress, the one that showed off her tits. She had a great body; why hide it?

To tell the truth, she found most of the house a little boring when Sarah showed her around. After she'd seen one room filled with antiques, she felt she'd seen them all. But she could tell the Bankrofts had big bucks, and there was no reason for them not to share them with her.

They must have walked through twenty rooms, she thought, not counting the walk around the stables and the curing barns and the ten minutes she wasted admiring Sarah Bankroft's rose garden. At this rate, by the time Sarah left her alone with Martin she'd be too tired to make a move.

Sarah and Martin stopped at the back of the great staircase.

Thank goodness, over at last.

"Is that it?" she said, a touch too eagerly, she realized.

"No, the tour isn't over yet," Sarah said, and her voice sounded different, harder, tougher.

Suddenly Ruth was frightened. The lawyer was right. She should never have come out here alone.

"I've had enough," she said nervously. "I want to leave now."

She turned away from Sarah, but Martin was behind her, blocking her way. He grabbed her arm, scratching it slightly so that it bled.

"I don't want to see any more," she protested.

"Of course you do," Sarah purred. "Don't you?"

"Yes, Yes." Ruth found herself agreeing in spite of herself. She followed Sarah and Martin down the stone steps to a large beautifully furnished room. Sarah pointed to a darkened room beyond.

"Go in there," she ordered.

"May—may I have a candle?" Ruth pleaded.

"No, of course not."

Timidly Ruth Bankroft walked into the pitch-dark room. She walked tentatively, groping with her hands, searching for something to hold onto; but the room seemed to be unfurnished. Her heart was pounding wildly and, in a panic, she turned to run, but Martin and Sarah were standing in the doorway, watching her. She turned and began walking again.

Maybe they were playing a game with her. That was it. This was some kind of child's test to show that she was not afraid of things that lurk in the dark. When she passed they would all be friends. They were only teasing her. Then she tripped and, with horror, she felt herself lose balance and fall, fall, down. She screamed.

Martin and Sarah carried their candles into the small room. Poor Ruth had been correct. There was no furniture, but being correct did her no good now as she fought for her life. They watched as she screamed and struggled in the dim light. Her blood occasionally splashed up onto Martin and Sarah. Once she managed to raise an arm and grope blindly in the air, but most of the flesh had already been stripped away. She looked at her naked arm bone and screamed in terror; then her cries began to fade.

Martin turned away, unable to face the horror of it all, but Sarah continued to stare, her eyes glittering and sparkling with that unearthly glow long after Ruth Jarrod Bankroft and been reduced to a pile of clean white bones and a few polka-dot rags.

"I guess our little friends don't like polka dots," Sarah said wistfully, turning away.

"Well, we try to keep them happy," Martin said.

* * *

Martin and Sarah were inspecting the fields. The dogs walked behind them as Sarah fanned herself to relieve the heat. It was time to top the tobacco plants, to cut off the bright pink buds before they had a chance to bloom into flowers. It made for a better and tastier leaf, but it always made Sarah sad to think of the flowers that never got to blossom.

"It's hard to believe that it's June already," she sighed. "Soon it'll be time for harvest."

"Not soon enough," Martin muttered. "Some things go on too long around here."

She knew what he was talking about, and it wasn't the tobacco crop. He resented the attention that Jonathan Evans had been paying her. It was funny that, with all her suitors, the only one who seemed to bother Martin was this writer. But that was what she had always loved about Martin. He was sensitive to her every feeling, and now he seemed to sense that her feelings for Jonathan were different than they had ever been for anyone else, even him.

"He's been asking you to leave Cherron. hasn't he?"

"You know he has, Martin," she admitted. "And you know that I wouldn't consider it for a minute."

Trying to hide his anger, he began to break off some buds from the tobacco plants as they passed. She watched him and shook her head sadly.

"Martin, darling, why is it we spend so much of our time together talking about him? Can't we just enjoy each other, the way did before he came?"

But before he could answer, they were approached by Jeremiah, who had a list of the areas to be pruned next.

* * *

Sarah found her new friend Adela standing outside her wretched shack. The old woman's fat gray cat, Elvira, was beside her, and Adela was stirring something in the black iron pot that hung over an open fire. A large white heron was wading in the stagnant stream nearby, and the bird's crisp elegance contrasted sharply with the old crone's filthy rags and wild hair.

"Sorry to hear about your brother fallin' off the cliff," she cackled, but she didn't sound sorry at all.

Sarah wondered if the old woman knew what she had done. She decided to tell her about the things she had learned about her new power, but Adela was not impressed.

"Girl, I don't know what you're gettin' at," she snapped when Sarah told her about her new idea.

"Don't you see, Adela? When I first came to the swamp, I thought you were a witch, but you're not."

"I never told you I was a witch," the old woman sniffed.

"I know, Adela," Sarah assured her. "But I wasn't sure. I've been doing a lot of reading now, and you know what I've got?"

"Sure, I do. You got the power. I taught you how to use it."

The chubby little girl shook her head.

"What I've got has always been inside of me, Adela. I would have discovered it sooner or later. It's all in the book."

"Damn book learnin'," Adela said, angrily stirring her pot. "I told you it weren't any good. I told you, girl, I gave you that power, me, and me alone."

"The book calls it telekinesis, Adela," the girl went on, unfazed. "You have it to a certain degree, but I have more." You know, I can focus my energy on anyone or anything now."

"Stop talking that way," the old woman shrieked. "I gave you those powers and I can take them away."

"Go ahead and try, Adela," the girl said and smiled.

The old woman shook her head.

"Try," Sarah insisted.

Adela didn't like the idea of being challenged, especially by the little child she had taught. Why, if she hadn't shown the kid how to unlock those doors in her mind, she'd still be the brunt of all those other stuck-up Bankrofts. Instead of being grateful, she came back here and started telling her that it wasn't her power at all, but something called teleki—something. She had to be taught a lesson.

She narrowed her eyes and stared at the little girl, concentrating all her energy on the child.

Sarah could feel Adela's mind attempting to touch hers. It felt as if a great, heavy blanket had been thrown over her, smothering her. She threw it off and laughed.

"You're not trying, Adela," she taunted. "Try harder."

Adela concentrated harder. Her wrinkled face grew taut and she began to tremble with the effort.

The girl just stood there, smiling.

"See? I told you so."

"Didn't you feel anything?" Adela asked, puzzled.

"Sure, I felt it. I felt your mind trying to touch me, but you failed. You're just not as strong as I am."

"I think you'd best go home now, child. I need to rest."

"I'll see you next week, Adela."

As the girl passed out of the swamp, Adela watched fearfully. She had the strange feeling that she had lit a small match that was going to blaze into a raging forest fire. And there was nothing she could do to stop it now.

As Sarah made her way across the field, she saw Martin and called out to him.

"Where are you going?" he said, obviously pleased to see his little cousin. He noticed she looked flushed and triumphant, as though she had just won a game.

"I'm walking back to the house," she said. "Will you join me?"

As they waded through the field of wild irises, cornflowers, and roses, Martin began to pick flowers. Soon his arms were filled with them. He bent low and handed them to her.

"I want to fill your life with flowers, mademoiselle," he said, laughing.

Suddenly, the sky seemed to darken and there was a loud rumble of thunder. Martin looked up anxiously at the gray clouds.

"Is it going to rain?" she asked.

"Yes, but just follow me."

He gripped her arm tightly and they started to run across the field towards an old barn that should have been torn down years ago. Rain began pouring and Sarah was soaked. She struggled to keep up with her tall cousin.

"Martin," she panted. "I can't make it."

As she spoke, a bolt of lightning split the sky. The rain began to come down harder than ever. She realized it was the beginning of a hurricane.

"I'll carry you," Martin said without hesitation. And, in spite of her protests, he picked her up in his arms and ran with her the last few yards to the abandoned barn.

Once they were inside they were in total

darkness, but at least it was dry. Martin fumbled for matches, lit one and managed to find a rusty lantern that still held some kerosene. As he lit it, a soft glow spread over the room.

The barn was more like a large shed. It was used mainly to store the gardening tools and camping equipment which were strewn about.

"I don't know how long this will last," he muttered. "But at least we can see ourselves now."

They stared at each other. Her cotton dress was completely soaked so that he could see through it. It clung to her body like a second skin, and for the first time he was aware of the fullness of her developing breasts and the roundness of her hips.

"You'd better get out of those clothes," he muttered, as he took off his own soaking chino pants and work shirt.

"I don't know, Martin," she said shyly.

"Suit yourself, but at least this way they might be dry by the time we get out of here." He was already wringing out his clothes and she could see the water pouring out. There must have been at least a gallon gushing to the earth floor of the barn.

"All right," she said.

Slowly she began to unbotton the top of her dress. It was not only soaking wet but also ice cold, and it would be a relief to get out of it. Martin had turned his back and was rummaging through the camping equipment. She watched him, still thinking about her quarrel with Adela. She was getting stronger every day. Her power was now greater than the old woman's, she had proved it. She had gotten rid of her brother Michael who had tormented her and made her life miserable. No one would ever stand in her way again.

Martin was still moving about near the camping supplies. How handsome he is, she thought. Maybe someday she could have a man as handsome as he was, someone who was as kind and good as Martin. Martin, Martin, Martin. She concentrated on his name in her mind.

"Did you call me, Sarah?" he said, looking up.

"No." She realized that he had felt it, the power of her mind.

He looked at her, standing in front of him in the odd, flickering light of the kerosene lantern. He moved toward her. Now he was conscious of his own nakedness and he felt a sudden strong desire for her.

But she's only a kid, he told himself. *She's my little cousin.*

She smiled at him as if she understood what he was thinking about.

He told himself that was impossible, that she was too innocent. He looked into her blue eyes and he noticed that the light of the kerosene lamp gave them an odd, magnetic glow.

"Sarah," he whispered hoarsely. "Sit down."

He sat beside her on a pile of straw.

"Do you understand what men and women do when they start to grow up?" he said gently.

She smiled. "You mean like what Mama and Papa do at night?"

"You know about that?" He was surprised.

"I hear them sometimes."

"But do you know what they're doing?" He put his strong arm around her shoulder as he looked into her innocent eyes.

"I think so, Martin." she said.

With her new power, she realized that he was far more nervous than she. "Don't worry, Martin," she assured him. "I have to learn sometime. It's better to learn with you. I can't think of anyone else I'd rather learn from than you."

He leaned over and kissed her gently. To his surprise she responded warmly, pulling him closer to her. She brushed his black hair off his face and looked into his sad brown eyes.

"I've always loved you, Martin," she whispered.

The rain was still pounding loudly outside and occasionally a hurricane-force wind would rattle some of the loose boards on the barn. But the two exiles of Cherron were in a world of their own.

Later, as they lay together in the straw, Martin held her in his arms. He was thinking about what he had just done, alternating between his deep love for his little cousin and his shame at seducing her.

"Don't be ashamed," she assured him, sounding as if she was reading his mind again. "I wanted you as much as you wanted me."

"Still, we're cousins, Sarah."

"And we love each other, and that's all that matters."

She was relieved that he seemed satisfied for a while. She wondered what Adela would think of her latest conquest. She took Martin's strong hand and held it affectionately.

"What were you doing by the swamp today,

Sarah?" he whispered.

"I was visiting Adela," she said. She had already confided in him about her friendship with the odd old woman and he accepted it. He accepted anything that made her happy.

"How is she?"

"Not so good. I told her that I understand what my power is now."

"You mean the things she taught you?"

"They were only the beginning, Martin. I've been reading about my power in one of Nanna's books. It's called *Telekinesis*."

"Sounds very mysterious."

"It is. Not many people have it. I guess that's why so few people believe in it."

"I believe in it," He had seen Sarah demonstrate it on animals and farm tools.

She kissed him on the cheek.

"You know, I've been thinking, Martin. If I can move objects and change things around, why can't I try to change the way I look? If I concentrated on myself very hard, maybe I could make myself pretty."

"I like you just the way you are, Sarah."

"You'll like me even better, Martin, I promise."

She lay there, comfortable in her lover's arms, planning their new life together.

In the months that followed, only Martin Bankroft seemed to notice the changes that were beginning to come over Miss Sarah. Her parents were indifferent to her and the rest of the family still thought of her as ugly.

She began to spend many hours a day in front of her vanity mirror, her eyes glittering as she willed her appearance to change.

She started with her stringy, mousy hair, commanding it to grow long and silky. It began to lighten in color from mousy dishwater blond to rich, creamy gold.

Encouraged by this, she started to work on her face. The acne and the blotches began to fade and her skin took on the soft, velvety whiteness of a camellia. Her small, dull-blue eyes grew slightly larger and deeper in color. Her face itself, like the rest of her body, slimmed down, revealing a beautiful bone structure. Her thin, colorless lips became full and sensual.

One afternoon her visiting aunt Jessica cornered her in the upstairs hall. She took Sarah's face in her hands and peered at her with interest.

"Why, Sarah, I believe you're becoming quite pretty," she said, obviously surprised. "Perhaps you're a Bankroft after all."

If Aunt Jessica only knew that it wasn't the Bankroft blood, but rather the power of her own mind, that was making the change.

For the next several months she worked on her chubby awkward body. Her thick legs grew long and delicate. Her square red hands softened and became graceful and elegant. Encouraged, she started to paint her new, long nails with rose-pink polish.

Her breasts, once so small as to seem nonexistent, grew full and ripe. Her waist tapered and her hips became round. Every morning she would examine herself in the mirror to record her progress. Yes, the change was miraculous, and she had done it all herself.

It took her over a year to accomplish her goal, but the improvement was staggering to everyone, even Adela, who seemed quite surprised that she could pull it off.

Her ability to do this to her own body gave her an incredible, heady feeling. For the first time she felt that she had power over her destiny.

* * *

Chapter Nine

Jessica Morrow was already in the kitchen when Jonathan came downstairs for breakfast. She offered to make him breakfast and he asked for coffee and toast.

He had still not figured this strange woman out. She was a cultivated woman and he could see that she had once been a beautiful one. She had lived all over the world, yet she seemed to plan on spending the rest of her days living at Cherron, keeping house for her niece. It wouldn't have bothered him if he believed that she was doing it out of love, but it was clear to him that Jessica and Devon Morrow resented every minute they spent at Cherron. It saddened his heart to think of Miss Sarah surrounded by greedy relatives who showed her no love.

He watched her as she set down the plate of buttered toast and began to pour the coffee. He decided to try one more time to bring her out.

"Miss Jessica," he started. "Have you ever heard of any grave robbers around here?"

"Grave robbers?"

It was Sarah's voice and he looked up to see her standing in the doorway. She was wearing a crisp red-and-white gingham shift and was carrying an armful of fresh roses.

"Now, what's this about grave robbers?" she repeated.

"Oh, just a rumor I heard," Jonathan said sheepishly. "I thought it might add some local color to the story." He was a little ashamed to tell her that the accusations of old Jason Gibbons were still on his mind.

As Jessica poured his coffee, he noticed that her hands were shaking. She spilled a little on the table and quickly began to wipe it up with a napkin.

"Are you all right?" he asked her.

"Yes, fine, thank you."

He didn't believe her, but he didn't want to make her any more upset than she was. He watched as Sarah stood at the kitchen sink, filling a vase with fresh water for the roses.

"There, isn't that much better?" she said brightly, as she placed the flowers on the table.

"You really are quite a gardener, Miss Sarah," he assured her.

"Well, I'll leave you two alone to talk," she said, going out as quickly as she had come in.

The fresh-cut yellow roses had a heady fragrance, and Jonathan breathed deeply of it before trying to talk to Jessica Morrow again.

"Miss Sarah is quite the gardener, isn't she?" he remarked. "Do you garden yourself?"

Even that innocent remark seemed to upset the woman.

"Oh, no. Miss Sarah put in that rose garden and she tends to it herself. It's like her second home. She's won a lot of prizes, you know."

The woman rattled on like a wind-up toy that had been programmed to say key phrases without thinking.

"You know, Miss Jessica," he said, patiently. "I worry about Miss Sarah."

A guarded look came into the woman's eyes.

"As her aunt, and her only living female relative, I thought maybe you could to talk to her, woman to woman."

Jessica Morrow still didn't seem to understand what he was talking about. She stared at him blankly.

"It's about the basement."

The color drained from her face and she continued to stare at him. She was gripping the side of the chair as if she expected to fly off of it and her knuckles had gone white. She seemed stunned by the question.

"The basement?" Her voice sounded choked.

"Yes, the basement. I understand that Miss Sarah keeps a lot of her family's things down there in a kind of museum."

Jessica seemed to relax slightly and a trace of her old hauteur returned.

"I don't think you should concern yourself with that," she sniffed. "No one goes down there except

Martin and Sarah. No one else is allowed."

"I just think she should forget the past."

"You should forget about it," Jessica said sharply. "I'm sorry, Mr. Evans, but the cellar is Miss Sarah's business and you're interfering." She began to clear away the breakfast dishes, but the glass she was holding slipped out of her hand and landed on the floor. Trying to pick it up, she cut her hand.

"Are you all right, Miss Jessica?" he asked, jumping up from his chair. He could see her hand was bleeding.

"I'm fine," she insisted, running cold water on the wound and then wrapping a paper towel around it.

"Forgive me, Mr. Evans, but I have some work to do upstairs. I'll clean that up later."

He was surprised at her reaction. Everytime he mentioned that basement room it seemed to upset her. Perhaps it was time for him to have a look at the room himself.

He tried the hall door, which was unlocked, and then he descended the cold, stone stairs in the dark. At the foot of the stairs was a wooden door. He twisted the brass knob several times but it refused to yield. To his surprise it was locked. No one had said anything about any valuables being in there. Why did they want it locked? Why wouldn't Sarah want anyone else to go in? Somehow this made him more worried about Sarah than ever.

Jonathan was waiting for Dr. Luke to finish with his last patient of the day. When he opened the door to the office he recognized the woman in there as Regina Quillam. He was surprised at the change in her. She was still dressed in a loud print dress, white hat and gloves. And she sure hadn't lost any weight, but she looked terrible. Her skin was red and peeling and the woman was scratching vigorously, obviously embarrassed, but unable to control herself.

She smiled wanly at him and hurried out of the office.

"Poor Mrs. Quillam," Dr. Luke muttered as he led Jonathan inside. "I just had to give her some bad news."

"Oh?"

"Yes, I'm afraid that awful itch that's been bothering her must be an allergy to her roses. Nothing else seems to explain it. It came on very sudden. Now she can't stop scratching."

"But she's been growing roses for years."

"That's the way it happens sometimes, Jonathan. You can live with something for years, then all of a sudden, pow! you're allergic. The system builds up to a certain level of intolerance."

"It must be quite a blow."

"Yes, but I told her she had to burn up every last rose bush on her property or she was going to peel herself to death."

In spite of himself, Jonathan smiled. While he didn't enjoy another person's misery he knew that Sarah would be pleased to know that her rival in the war of roses was vanquished.

"Now you told me on the phone that you're worried about Sarah," the doctor began.

"That's right. I talked to Mrs. Morrow about it,

but she doesn't seem to be able to do anything. I was hoping you could."

He sat in the worn leather armchair in front of the doctor's desk. Dr. Luke leaned back in his armchair and seemed to be thinking. Jonathan wasn't a patient, after all, and it was nice to relax while he talked to him. He even lit a cigar and offered one to Jonathan.

"Thanks. Do the leaves come from Cherron?"

"You bet they do, son. The best in the world."

"Do you know about the basement room at Cherron, Dr. Luke?"

The doctor seemed to be trying to imagine the layout of Cherron in his mind. Yes, he remembered the basement room. It was below the great staircase. He remembered that Miss Sarah used to play down there when she was a little girl. It was one of the few places where she was free from the teasing of the other children.

"Yes," he agreed. "I think they keep some old furniture and things down there now."

"Are you aware that Miss Sarah is down there at least once a day?"

The old man looked surprised at that. He hadn't realized Sarah spent time in the basement, but at the same time he didn't think it was any of Jonathan's business. After all, he was only a guest.

"I appreciate your concern for my niece, Jonathan," he said, chewing on the cigar. "But Cherron is Miss Sarah's home, and I think she's entitled to sit in any room she wants."

"It's just that I think she spends too much time brooding about the past, about the loss of her people. She seems to have a lot of conflict between her anger towards them and her guilt that they all died so young."

Although he did not approve of amateur psychologists, Luke Bankroft had to admit that the young man had a point. He promised to talk to Sarah about the folly of brooding too much about the unchangeable past.

"What else have you been learning about our part of the world?" he asked.

"Well, Jason Gibbons mentioned something about grave robbers."

"Jonathan," the old man roared. "You can't be serious! The poor old fool is crazy. Everyone in Arcadia knows that."

Somewhat chastened by his meeting with Dr. Luke, Jonathan returned to Cherron prepared to try to talk to Martin again. He found him out by the curing barns, directing some of the Cherron workers to prepare the barn for the first crop of leaves. They would be bringing them in soon.

He glared at Jonathan as he saw him approach, but Jonathan chose to ignore it. The fellow had been avoiding him for days. In fact, now that he thought about it, the only person at Cherron who didn't seem to avoid him was Sarah. She seemed to be the only one who encouraged him to stay. Nevertheless, he had made up his mind to get through to Martin Bankroft.

"How are things?" he said casually.

Martin had been giving instructions to a young black man in work clothes. He turned to face

216

Jonathan.

"Fine."

"I wonder if you know how I can get into the basement?"

"That's no concern of yours, Evans," Martin said sharply.

"I just thought that viewing the heirlooms of the Bankroft family would help me to describe them better, get a better sense of how they lived. I understand from your uncle Luke that some of the best stuff is down there."

"I told you to stop interfering, Evans."

"Why are you so angry with me, Martin?"

Martin abandoned any pretense of working and glared angrily at Jonathan.

"You're intruding in our lives and in things that don't concern you. You're poking into matters that are none of your business." His voice was so loud that some of the men stopped what they were doing and stared. They rarely saw the quiet Martin Bankroft show any emotion at all. The two labradors began to bark loudly at Jonathan, but he ignored them.

"In case you've forgotten, Martin, I do have Miss Sarah's permission to learn all I can about the family."

"That doesn't give you any right to intrude on our privacy."

Jonathan stared at his rival. He didn't think he would ever understand this cold, bitter man who seemed to have only one interest in his life; his neurotic attachment to his lovely cousin.

"How am I intruding?"

"What do you call what you pulled the other night?" Martin snapped. "Knocking on her door like that, treating her like she was some kind of—" He realized what he had said.

It was too late to take back the words. Jonathan had not quite grasped what they meant.

"How did you know I knocked on Sarah's door?"

"I heard a noise in the hall and went to investigate," he lied.

"Still playing protector?" Jonathan smiled. "Your cousin doesn't need protection from me."

"Doesn't she?" Martin said bitterly. "You try to get in her bedroom at night and you say she doesn't need protection? I know what you're after and you can't have her. She'll never leave Cherron and she'll never leave me."

Jonathan wanted to be sympathetic towards the overprotective cousin, if only for Sarah's sake, but Martin had to learn that she was a woman now, not a little girl he had to watch over all the time.

"Miss Sarah doesn't need you hovering over her like a mother hen," he said patiently. "She's a grown woman and what we have together is none of your business."

"Everything that happens in Cherron is my business, especially anything that concerns Miss Sarah."

"I know you're worried I'll pull something like Roy McEndrews did, but my God, man, I love her."

Martin stared at him. "I love her too."

"I know that, but she's your cousin and I'm the man in her life now." The dogs' barking chorus grew louder.

Martin smiled. "And you expect her to run away with you?"

"No, I don't expect that any more. I know how she feels about this place. She takes her responsibilities to the people who work here very seriously."

"Responsibility?" Martin said bitterly. "Is that what you think I am to her, a responsibility? You know nothing about Miss Sarah, do you?" Martin said sadly. "She stays here because she wants to, not because she has to."

Suddenly, Sarah was standing between them. The dogs stopped their barking and gazed at her meekly.

"What is going on with you two?" Sarah asked sternly. "You, of all people, Martin, should know better than to argue in front of the workers."

Jonathan looked around. He realized that all work had stopped as the men in the curing barns watched him and Martin battling.

"All right, fellas, back to work," Miss Sarah ordered.

The men quickly picked up their leaves and threads and got back to work. Only an occasional buzz among them gave evidence of the impression the quarrel had made on them all.

"Tell him to stop snooping, Sarah. Tell him to finish his damn book and leave us alone," Martin yelled as they walked back to the house.

As a peace-making gesture, Sarah insisted that Martin take her right arm and Jonathan her left, but it didn't seem to help. They were still trading barbs as they walked up the white marble steps of the verandah.

"Stop it, both of you," she finally ordered. "Now who started this? What were you arguing about?"

"All I did was ask Martin for the key to the basement room. I thought if I could see some of the things down there it might help me to understand the Bankrofts better."

"Try minding your own business," Martin yelled, as he stormed inside the house.

Sarah sat down on a step between two of the great white columns. Jonathan took a seat beside her.

"I didn't mean to upset him," he apologized.

"Then why did you?" she snapped. "You know the basement room is not for outside eyes."

"Is that what I am, Sarah? An outsider?"

"Don't change the subject, Jonathan. I don't mind your asking questions about my family, but I won't satisfy your morbid curiosity."

"Sarah, I'm terribly sorry. I had no idea it meant that much to you."

"What else were you arguing about? Me?"

"Yes," he admitted. "Sarah, he's so possessive of you. I think he actually believes he owns you."

She turned to look at him, her blue eyes shining with anger.

"Now you listen to me," she said deliberately. "Martin has always been here for me. If he seems possessive it's because we've shared so much. We've shared things you wouldn't understand."

"You're pretty possessive of him, too, aren't you?" Jonathan managed a smile.

"That's because he fought for me when we were

children. For that I will always be on his side."

She realized sadly that Jonathan would never understand what Martin and she had been through. She remembered the many lonely nights when she used to pray for someone to talk to after her grandmother died, someone just to be with, to listen to her without putting her down all the time. With all her power, she still could never convey that kind of pain to him.

Even without asking she knew that Jonathan had grown up in a loving home. No one had ever humiliated him. She, on the other hand, could remember crying so hard at night that her whole bed shook. She had spent many nights then wondering if she would ever have anyone.

Not only had Martin talked to her, but he genuinely cared for her. She wouldn't forget that, not ever.

"I look at my things in the basement room to remind me of what it was like, Jonathan. Don't you see? I don't ever want to forget what Martin did for me. Get rid of them? Never. When I start to feel myself losing the past, I look at them and I remember all over again how kind Martin was to me. Perhaps you have friends enough to throw away. I don't. Not for you, not for anyone."

"Would you like me to apologize to Martin?"

"No, not if you don't mean it," she said bitterly. "He doesn't need empty gestures of friendship."

"Don't be mad at me, Sarah," he said gently. "My only excuse is that I love you."

"And no one else is supposed to feel that way about me because you entered my life? Suddenly you're supposed to be the only one in my world simply because you love me. Well, Martin loves me too and I'll never turn my back on him."

"I have to learn how to share you with people. I will learn, if you give me the chance."

"Let's forget about it for now," she said, standing up and brushing off her skirt. "I have to change for dinner. Uncle Luke's coming tonight. I hope this will be the last fight between you and Martin."

After she was gone, Jonathan sat alone on the veranda. He breathed deeply of the mingled scents of the magnolias and the jasmine, he watched the birds play on the lawn, and he listened to the songs of the workers in the distant fields. He knew now that he could not challenge her fierce devotion to her cousin. Perhaps he understood a little better, what brought the two cousins to their dependence on each other. He would force himself to accept it for the time being, or Sarah would never be his.

Jessica Morrow had a small kitchen garden behind the house. There she grew herbs and tomatoes for her cooking. She was working there, on her hands and knees, when Jonathan found her. She was wearing a faded housedress and a sad-looking kerchief was wrapped around her head. Devon, as usual, was beside her, handing her the tools. He stared up at Jonathan blankly.

"You and your niece are both excellent gardeners, I notice," he said casually. "Those roses of hers are incredible. How does she get them to grow like that?"

"I don't care for the roses, Mr. Evans. Sarah does that." She never looked up but rather concentrated on her weeding.

He ignored her implied dismissal. He had made up his mind he was going to break through to this woman.

"I heard that you had some problem with your eyes. I hope they're not giving you any more trouble."

"They're better, thank you," she muttered, still not looking up. She was hoping that if she was rude enough the reporter would leave her and Devon alone.

That was all she wanted now, to be left alone. She was uncomfortable with his constant questions, with the way he persisted in asking about the basement. Of course she realized it was strange that there was a lock on the door! After all, whatever was down there had belonged to her family as well. She was a Bankroft too. But it was Sarah's house now. And she had no right to see whatever was there.

She and Devon were lucky to have a home at all. Yes, sometimes she wondered about Sarah; but then she would start to get those pains in her eyes again, or she would remember the way Robert had looked when they pulled him out of the flaming wreckage of his plane, and she would be unable to continue thinking about Sarah.

She could feel the pain starting again now. If only the man would leave. She was sure it would stop if only he would leave.

"Have you ever met the woman called Adela?"

he asked.

"Never heard of her!" she snapped. She began to weed furiously. Devon just stared blankly.

"I understand that she used to live in the swamp on the Cherron land, and that she was a childhood friend of Miss Sarah."

"Miss Sarah never mentioned her to me," she said.

She could feel the pains starting. She stood up to get away from the persistent young man, but, as she did, her knees buckled. She almost fell to the ground, but Jonathan grabbed her by the arms.

"Are you all right?" he asked with concern.

"I have to go," she insisted.

"Please, Mrs. Morrow, I know that you're hiding something; and that something could help Miss Sarah."

"Leave me alone, can't you?" she pleaded. "I don't know anything. Please, let me go."

He held on to her arm.

"Why are you so afraid, Jessica?"

"She's just a sweet young woman, that's all she is," Jessica screamed. It sounded as if she were yelling the words at someone else, not at him. Then she turned and ran into the house. Slowly, like a boy in a trance, Devon Morrow rose and followed his mother.

Jonathan watched the pitiful mother and son as they went inside. There's a reason, he thought. There's got to be some reason why they are so afraid to talk to me.

But the only reason he could think of was that Jessica Morrow was terrified of her niece.

The evening was chilly and Martin lit a fire in the fireplace in the living room where they were having their after-dinner coffee. As usual, Jessica and her odd son had excused themselves early and gone to bed, leaving Dr. Luke alone with Sarah, Martin and Jonathan. Dinner had finished without an incident, although they were all aware that the tension between the two young men was thick enough to be cut with a knife.

Jonathan watched as Sarah poured the coffee. He admired her graceful hands. It was hard to believe that she worked so hard in the garden and still managed to keep such graceful hands. She had changed into a long, dark-violet skirt and a white blouse, and her long blond hair hung loosely around her shoulders.

"Uncle Luke, you look so tired," she said with concern.

"It's been quite a day." He told them about Mrs. Quillam's strange new allergy to roses.

"How sad for her," Sarah said quietly. "Perhaps I should send her some photographs of mine. At least she won't get all itchy from them."

Sarah had suggested a picnic alone, just the two of them, and so they had taken the horses Jason and Isis up to Benson's Cliff. They sat now under the shelter of a broad hickory tree and stared at the forest and the swamp beyond. Sarah was wearing a blue cotton dress that emphasized the blue in her eyes. With her magnolia-white skin and yellow hair she looked to Jonathan like a young Aphrodite.

A wonderful, strange feeling seemed to come over him. It was odd. When he was alone he had such great determination to discover the inner secrets of the Bankroft family, but whenever he was near Sarah he lost that determination. He was falling in love with her, he realized, and losing his reporter's objectivity. He couldn't ask difficult questions. He couldn't bring himself to distress her any more than he already had.

She smiled at him. "Why are you looking at me that way?"

"I was just thinking how nice it would be if we could just sit here always."

"Yes," she sighed. "Yes, that would be lovely."

"I got a letter from my folks this morning, Sarah. My brother's getting married at the end of the summer."

"That's nice."

"Would you like to come to the wedding with me? It would give you a chance to see New York."

"Will your book be finished by then?"

The truth was that his book was almost finished now. He was reluctant to tell her that because it meant he would no longer have any excuse to stay on. And suddenly, he couldn't bear the thought of leaving.

"Not yet," he lied. "But it won't be long."

"I thought you were in a hurry to get back to your exciting city," she teased.

"Maybe I'm not in such a hurry anymore. But I would like you to come back with me. You could meet my parents. I've already written to them about you, Sarah."

"I'm flattered," she said, blushing slightly. "You're very close to your parents, aren't you?"

"Yes, I suppose I am." He didn't often think about them, actually. Perhaps until he met Sarah and the rest of the Bankrofts, he had taken his happy family for granted.

She smiled sadly. "I wish it had been that way with my parents. I believe that if I had been a kitten my mother would have drowned me."

"Sarah!" he exclaimed. "I can't believe they'd have ever thought of going that far!"

"No?" she sounded bitter. "They were planning to send me away to a boarding school just a few weeks before they died. They didn't want me here to embarrass them because I wasn't as pretty or as bright as the others."

It hurt him to see how deeply the old wounds from her childhood still affected her. She had to learn to forget the past. He had to help her. He told her that as they sat there on the picnic blanket, watching the bright red sunset over Cherron.

* * *

Her parents were dressing for a party and the door to their bedroom was ajar. Sarah listened in the darkness of the hallway as they discussed her future.

"The season will start soon, Dan," her mother was saying. "What are we going to do with her?"

Her mother was sitting at her mirrored vanity coaxing curls into her upswept beehive hairstyle.

She was dressed in a gown of emerald-green satin and, as usual, she looked beautiful. Her mother always looked beautiful.

"I've been giving it a lot of thought, Martha," Sarah's father assured her. "I think it's best if we send her away."

He was a tall, broad-shouldered man who resembled Clark Gable. The tuxedo he was wearing couldn't hide his powerful build. He grinned at his wife as he spoke.

"Where? Who'd take her?" Martha Bankroft said. Sarah could tell that she liked the idea.

"My sister Jessica recommended a school in the south of England: Miss Coburn's. They answered my inquiry and said that they'd be happy to have Sarah. She can stay there until she's eighteen."

"Three years!"

"I know, it seems like such a short time. But who knows? Perhaps by then she won't want to come back."

Sarah's heart was beating wildly. She was terrified that someone would walk by and find her crouched at her parents' door, but she was riveted by what they were saying. They were planning to send her away for three years with no warning at all.

"Sometimes I wonder how we ever produced such an ugly child," her mother was saying. "All the others are so beautiful."

"Sometimes I wonder if you weren't fooling around with the gardener," he teased. "I know good and well I couldn't have fathered her."

"That's what your sister Jessica said, too," Martha Bankroft laughed. "Oh, it'll be a relief not to have to make excuses when Sarah embarrasses us."

"It'll be better for the other children as well. I want them to grow up around beautiful people. And beauty begins at home."

Sarah slipped back into the shadows and ran to her room. She could hardly believe how much her parents wanted to be rid of her. She felt so alone, so helpless. Then she realized that she wasn't helpless at all.

She remembered the look on her brother Michael's face as he went over that cliff. Too bad that Michael couldn't come back and tell the others how to behave, she mused. She would have to do it herself.

She found Martin in his room, and she told him what she had overheard.

"You're too good for them, Sarah," he said angrily. "But you can't leave now. If you go away we won't see each other for years." He held her in his arms the way he had that afternoon they hid from the hurricane in the old barn. He remembered how she had confided in him about her newfound power.

"Sarah, can you do anything about it?"

She still had not told him about Michael, but she knew that he would never object to anything she did to protect herself. And she needed to protect herself now. She decided to give her parents one more chance.

"I'll talk to them in the morning. I'll tell them I won't go."

"And if they say they'll make you?" Martin

asked.

"I'll think of something."

They lay there in the darkness of his room, clinging to each other. It was almost as if they were daring Sarah's parents to discover them.

Chapter Ten

A night's sleep had not changed Sarah's mind. If her parents insisted on sending her to England she would carry out her plan.

She found them having breakfast in the dining room. Her mother was wearing a red satin robe and her father had on a blue Oriental kimono. They both looked a little hung over.

It was eleven o'clock and all the other children had gone into Arcadia for the day, all except Martin who was supervising the workers in the field. He was the only one of them who seemed interested in the tobacco fields, the source of all of Cherron's wealth. It was another thing the two of them shared.

Sarah had dressed in a white cotton pinafore. She sat down on one of the chairs and stared across the dining room table at her parents. She looked like a cat in the jungle watching its prey, ready to spring, so quiet no one knows it's there.

"Sarah, we're glad you're still here," her mother said with false brightness. "There's a matter your father and I would like to discuss with you."

"Really? What is it?"

"Aunt Jessica has been telling us about a very good girl's-boarding-school in England."

"I don't want to go away to school," she cut her mother short.

"You know your grades haven't been very good," her father added. "Your tutors say they have trouble getting through to you."

"I try my best."

"This school would be an excellent opportunity for you, academically and socially," her mother joined in.

"But I don't want to leave," Sarah insisted. "Cherron is my home."

"The trouble with you is that you don't appreciate what you have," her father said.

"And what do I have?"

"What do you have? What do you have?" her father shouted. "Why, you ingrate! You have this beautiful house, food, clothing, and a name you should try to bring pride to, not shame."

"We're only doing this for your own good," her mother added.

"You're doing it because you hate me."

"That's enough," her father said. "We'll discuss it after breakfast. Why don't you see how Clemmie is doing? Tell her we'll eat now."

It was useless to argue with them, she realized. They held all the cards. The only thing she had was her special power.

She stood at the kitchen door watching Clemmie, the stout, black Bankroft-family cook, pick out certain mushrooms for their breakfast omelets. She stared at several rather large ones and infused the poison of her hate into the plump white mushrooms. Her eyes glittered and the strange glow came into the whites of her eyes. But if Clemmie noticed she just assumed that the sunlight was hitting Miss Sarah's eyes in a strange way.

It took but a moment, and it was done. Sarah guided the hand of poor Clemmie, who, with only the slightest hesitation, selected the mushrooms. Sarah watched as she sliced them and then began to prepare the eggs. Satisfied, Sarah returned to the table.

Sarah poured coffee for herself and her parents. Then she began to chew on a piece of buttered toast as Clemmie served the omelets to her mother and father.

"Aren't you eating?" her mother asked.

"Just toast," she said. "I'm not hungry."

"You better start thinking about what you want to take with you to school," her father said as he began to consume his mushroom omelet.

"That's right. I know you'll change your mind a hundred times before you leave," her mother added.

"Yes, Mother, whatever you say."

She watched every forkful of food that entered their mouths. She imagined the journey down her father's throat, into his stomach, and finally into his bloodstream. She thought about the tasty yellow omelet sliding down her mother's long white neck. Her father liked to say that his wife had the prettiest neck in Arcadia County.

She wondered how long it would take.

Finally, after what seemed like hours, a pained expression came over her father's face.

"Dan, what's wrong?" Her mother screamed, jumping up and rushing to her husband's side.

He pushed himself away from the table and was sitting in the chair, doubled over, clutching his stomach.

"I don't feel very well," he said weakly.

"Do you want me to call a doctor?" she said. "Dan? do you want me—" Suddenly she stopped. She began to feel the same sharp pain in her stomach, like something ravenous was trying to eat its way out of her body. Cold sweat broke out all over her body.

"Sarah," she said to her daughter. "Call Uncle Luke."

The girl just stood there, staring. Her eyes glowed oddly, as though the whites of her eyes had been charged with electricity.

"Did you hear your mother, Sarah? Call Uncle Luke."

The girl refused to move.

"Sarah," her father moaned from the floor. "Do as you're told." His tongue was swelling and it was becoming difficult for him to speak.

"I'll never need to do as you say ever again, dear Father," she said sweetly.

"Clemmie!" he called out, but Sarah raised her hand and the kitchen door closed tightly. Clemmie could hear nothing.

"She can't help you, Father. Not even Uncle Luke can help you and Mother now."

Her handsome father's face was distorted by swelling. His eyes bulged to twice their normal size and the swelling in his lips and tongue made it difficult for him to make more than an animal-like sound.

"Oh God, the pain," he moaned. "I can't stand the pain." Martha Bankroft held her dying husband in her arms.

"Take a lesson from your daughter," Sarah told them both. "I've lived with pain all my life and I've managed."

"What have you done to us?" her mother cried. Her lovely long white neck was mottled purple now, and blood was beginning to pour from her swollen mouth.

"You should never have tried to send me away," she said.

Martha Bankroft stared at her monstrous daughter. It was the eyes that fascinated her. They were glowing like two blue coals, two horrible, burning coals. In her painful delirium she decided that, if only she could get those eyes, she could save her husband and herself. She struggled to her feet, gripping the white damask table cloth; but she pulled too hard and she slipped down again, bringing the dishes and silverware clattering down on top of her.

Fortunately, the coffee on the sideboard was untouched. Sarah poured herself a cup.

"I'd offer the two of you some coffee," she said

politely, "but I don't think you could stand anything in your throats just now. They do burn, don't they?"

"You did something to our breakfast, didn't you?"

"Yes, Father, in a way. I simply had Clemmie pick poison mushrooms. You've been gorging yourselves to death."

"Clemmie would never hurt us," her mother moaned.

"You still don't understand, do you? I made her do it. You'd be surprised what I can do."

Her pitiful parents clung to each other on the floor. They seem to realize that they had no hope.

"You'll never get away with this," her father said.

"But, Father, I already have. Did you really think that smart, strong Michael just fell off Benson's Cliff?"

"You pushed him!" her mother cried. Then she began to vomit all over her red satin robe.

"Careful, Mother," she said. I know how important it is to you that we Bankrofts keep up appearances. I wouldn't want the coroner to see you in a soiled dressing gown."

Her mother did not hear her. She had already succumbed. Her father could no longer manage even a guttural sound. He simply stared at her with a mixture of hatred and revulsion in his distorted features. Then he trembled violently, and he too was gone.

Sarah sighed, finished her coffee, and walked into the kitchen.

"Oh, Clemmie," she cried, willing tears to come to her eyes. "Something's happened to my parents. Call Uncle Luke."

There was nothing else she could have done, they all assured her. She stood watching the bodies taken out the front door of Cherron on a stretcher. By that time her brothers and her sister had returned from town. Monica fainted immediately at the news, and Everett and David spent their time trying to console her. They hardly noticed Sarah.

But Martin did. He followed her out of the house and onto the clearing on the lawn next to the great house. He caught up with her there.

"Well, Martin, it's done."

"Yes. And you'll never have to leave Cherron."

"Or you," she added. "Tell me, Martin, don't you think this would be an excellent place for a rose garden?"

* * *

It was time to start packing up the picnic things and head back to Cherron. Jonathan watched Sarah as she gathered up the empty containers.

"What were you thinking just then?" he asked.

"The day my parents died."

"Sarah—"

"I know. I can't change the past. What's gone is gone."

"No more sad songs?"

"No. No more." She smiled at him.

He took her by her slender wrists and drew her

closer to him. She did not struggle as he held her in his strong arms.

"When I hold you like this, Sarah," he whispered. "I want to chase away all the bad memories for you."

"I told you, Jonathan, we need those bad memories so we can appreciate the good things."

"You're a philosopher," he teased.

"A philosopher is just a person who can't change the bad times and knows it."

"See what I mean?"

They both laughed and then he kissed her, gently at first, then with more force. To his surprise she responded to him. Encouraged, he caressed her breasts and gently pulled her back down on to the blanket.

"Please, Sarah," he whispered. "I want you."

Suddenly they heard the sound of a horse approaching and, as they fumbled with their clothes, Sarah looked up to see Martin staring angrily down at the two of them.

"What are you doing here?" she asked him.

"Jeremiah tells me that the field hands are not picking the ripe leaves fast enough."

"And you rode all the way up here to tell me that?" she said.

"I thought it was important." He glanced angrily at Jonathan who tried to avoid his eyes.

"I can understand that you don't want to discuss business in front of me," Jonathan said. "I'll just head back and leave you two alone."

"Thank you, Jonathan," Sarah said as he climbed up on the Morgan. "I won't be long."

When he was gone she turned angrily to her cousin.

"What's wrong with you, Martin? Do you have to watch my every move?"

"I can't help it," he said. "I just don't want to lose you."

"You'll never lose me. But if you keep watching our every move he's going to know about us."

"Maybe then he'd leave us alone."

"Sure," she said sarcastically. "Or maybe he'd be the best man at our wedding. Wake up, Martin. If anyone else finds out about us they'll do the same thing David and your father did. They'll try to put us away.

"Oh, Martin, don't you see? You and I can't go on this way forever. I must marry sooner or later. I need a child to carry on Cherron."

"I can give you children."

"That's out of the question and you know it," she snapped. An affair with her cousin was one thing; bearing his children was another.

"You know he spoke about learning to share me, Martin. You should learn that."

"I have shared you with others. He's different." Martin looked grim. "With him I could lose you altogether."

She placed her head on his shoulder so he could not see her tears. She had done this to herself. With her powers and her love affair with Martin she had brought herself to a point where she was within reach of everything she ever wanted. And yet she felt that her happiness was threatened now.

"Oh, Martin, you'll never lose me. I've told you

239

that. Don't you believe me?"

The anguish in his eyes said more than any words.

The next morning Jonathan reviewed his notes in the library, but he found it difficult to concentrate. There were so many nagging questions about the Bankrofts that he had been unable to answer. Too many things didn't make sense.

For all practical purposes his book was finished. No one else need ever know about his questions: about why Jessica Bankroft Morrow and her son were so terrified that they could barely speak; about the crazy old man who had insisted on making wild accusations and then disappeared. No one but he seemed to care that the old derelict had simply vanished. And he still had not managed to find the old woman Adela, either.

He worried about the effect of all this on Sarah. She was so beautiful. She was a beautiful, rich young woman and she was wasting herself down here hiding on her plantation in the middle of a bunch of parasitic, eccentric relatives. She cared about him, too. He could tell. He was sure that if Martin hadn't surprised them up at Benson's Cliff she would have yielded to him. She had wanted him at that moment just as much as he wanted her.

Yes, he told himself. For Sarah's welfare and for his own peace of mind he had to talk to Martin Bankroft again.

He found Martin out in the fields, supervising the men who were beginning to harvest the tobacco leaves. He watched with interest as they picked those leaves that had ripened from dark green to a lighter shade, and, with the aid of a needle, strung them together.

"I never realized they were so big," he remarked to Martin.

"Yes, they get as big as three-feet," Martin answered.

"What happens next?"

"We'll hang them in the curing barns," he said, indicating the tall square buildings that stood between the great house and the planting fields. "They'll dry in there before we pack them up in hogsheads for the auction."

Martin seemed to relax when he talked about the crop.

"When is the auction?"

"In the fall, but I guess you'll be gone by then."

Jonathan knew very well that Martin would like him to be gone by tomorrow, but it was not his decision.

"I have a problem, Martin. The Bankrofts are such an interesting family I keep finding more people I want to learn about," he said, grinning affably. "Like your parents."

Martin looked at him with a cold stare. "What do you want to know?"

"Whatever there is to tell. I know your mother left Cherron when you were only ten."

"Yes," he said bitterly. "She didn't meet the Bankroft standards either. But she wasn't as strong as Sarah is. Her only choice was to run away."

"And your father?"

"He died last year. Heart attack."

Jonathan noticed that Martin showed very little

regret over the recent death of his father. Perhaps that was what he and Sarah shared, a common hatred for cold and unfeeling parents. He decided to pursue another subject.

"I imagine running a plantation like Cherron takes up a good deal of your time," he said casually.

"It does."

"I mean, you must have to deal with business problems in the evening as well as during the day."

"Occasionally."

"Was last night one of those occasions?"

"Last night?" Martin seemed unaffected by the question.

"I accidentally saw you coming out of Sarah's room late last night. Were you discussing business with her?"

"If that's what you can live with," Martin said, avoiding his gaze.

"What does that mean? Were you discussing business or not?" Jonathan fought to control his temper.

Martin merely glared at him. "I'm perfectly willing to answer any questions you may have if they concern your book, Evans, but that happens to have nothing to do with it. Is there anything else you'd like to know?"

"Not right now," Jonathan admitted.

"Then you'll excuse me, won't you?" Martin stalked off into the barn, but he had won this round and Jonathan knew it.

"Again?" Sarah said from behind him.

He turned to look at her. She was smiling and

her blue eyes glittered in the sunlight.

"I guess I'm no diplomat," he shrugged. "It seems we hardly have to talk to argue."

"So I've noticed," Sarah said grimly. "Excuse me. I think I'd better go calm him down." She left Jonathan to admire the roses alone and went off to be with her cousin.

She found him in the barn. "Martin, what's wrong?" she asked.

He looked at her, his eyes serious. "He saw me coming out of your room last night."

She gasped, but ignored the pounding of her heart. "What did you tell him?"

"Nothing. He asked me if we were talking business," he sneered with contempt.

"And you said absolutely nothing."

"No."

"You could have told him he was right."

"Yes, I could have."

"Now he has his suspicions and you have what you wanted."

"He won't put it together; he's too square."

"He's not stupid, Martin. He's a sophisticated man."

"If he's so damned sophisticated it won't matter to him, will it?"

If only she could believe that, she thought.

*   *   *

"Sit down, both of you," Jeffrey Bankroft insisted. He had called them both into the library. They knew that something was wrong. His face was grim.

243

"What's all this about, Uncle Jeffrey?" Sarah asked.

"I was going through your brother David's effects yesterday and I found a journal that he kept. There are several entries that disturb me."

He took a thick black book from inside his desk and laid it on top. Neither Sarah nor Martin recognized it, but they both had a pretty good idea what the entries were about. They looked at each other but said nothing.

"It says here that David found the two of you in a — compromising situation. Is that true?"

"Yes." Martin answered without hesitation.

He was not prepared for such honesty. He had expected them to be ashamed and contrite. At least they could have the decency to deny it.

"You mean to say that the two of you — you've been —'," he sputtered helplessly. "The two of you have been —"

"That's right, Father," Martin said calmly. Occasionally he would look to Sarah as if for encouragement and support.

A look of total disgust suffused the older man's face. "How could you? You're both Bankrofts. How could you do such a thing?"

"We love each other."

"You offer no excuses?" he shook his head in disbelief.

"No," Sarah said firmly.

"How long has this been going on?" he asked.

"Ten years," she said.

"My God." He had no idea that they had managed to conceal their wickedness from so many for so long. "I can't believe it."

"Well, we just told you it was so," Sarah snapped.

The older man shook his head. In his thirty-five years of practicing law he had never seen a more repellent twosome than his own son and his niece.

"I can't believe you're being so nonchalant about this," he said. "You do realize the seriousness of the situation?"

"We neither feel guilt nor shame," she said defiantly.

"Don't you understand, Father?" Martin protested. "We love each other."

"Don't give me that," Jeffrey Bankroft snapped. "You realize I'll have to do something about this?"

"What do you have in mind?" Sarah asked disinterestedly. She was staring out the window at her rose garden; its lovely blooms were a lot more pleasant to look at than her angry self-righteous Uncle Jeffrey.

"I want you to think about what you've done, the shame of it all, and what it will do to the Bankroft family name.

"If the two of you are willing to recognize the loathsomeness of your conduct and to apologize to me for your behavior, I will forget the matter. But you must also promise never to touch each other again. Otherwise, I'll have to take other measures," he said firmly. "And believe me, I'm not anxious to bring any more dishonor to the Bankroft family name. Although I suppose that means nothing to you."

He left them alone in the library to think about

what he had said. He promised to be back in an hour.

They didn't need an hour; they knew exactly how they felt. Nothing had changed.

"Don't you wish you were a rose, Martin," Sarah said. She was still staring out the window. "They have no families, no taboos against doing as they please. All they have to do is be beautiful and smell sweet."

"Please, Sarah," Martin pleaded. "We have to think of something before my father comes back."

"We've gone through too much together, Martin," she assured him. "I won't allow anyone to separate us now."

"But what can we do?"

"Remember what I told you about my power? Remember what I did to Dr. Sheffield?"

"Please, Sarah," he said. "I don't want that to happen to my father. I just want him to die."

"Then he'll die," she said. "I would never do anything like that to your father without discussing it with you first."

"You have my permission," he said. "Do whatever it takes."

Jeffrey Bankroft shook his head in disbelief when he returned to find that nothing had changed. They still refused to admit that they had done anything wrong.

He had assumed that, when confronted, the two would beg for forgiveness; but they acted so calm, that he didn't know what to make of it. He had thought he knew Martin better than that.

"Your coldness frightens me, son," he said at

last. "I think the two of you are ill; but if I were to send for a psychiatrist, as David intended, I'm afraid that it would leak out somehow. I'll not have the Bankroft name tarnished because of this destructive situation."

Simultaneously, Martin and Sarah recalled seeing the remains of Dr. Sheffield at the bottom of the piranha pool. Then they realized that, as far as Jeffrey Bankroft knew, David had never contacted the doctor.

Jeffrey took a deep, troubled breath. In just a few hours he seemed to have aged ten years.

"I've decided to send both of you away from here," he said. "I don't want you continuing your abominable relationship here."

They looked at each other again. Their worst fears had been realized. Jeffrey planned to split them up and send them both away from Cherron.

"Martin, you have good business sense. I'm sending you to New York. An associate of mine will look out for you. You can go to work for him." He turned to his niece. "Sarah, you're to go off on a trip through Europe. I haven't told Jessica anything about your disgusting behavior, but she will accompany you."

"Do you honestly believe that by splitting us up you will erase our feelings for each other?"

"I can't erase what's already taken place here, but I can keep you from ever seeing each other again."

"Father, has it ever occurred to you that Sarah and I are adults? We can't be simply sent away, dismissed like children. Suppose we refuse to leave?"

"In that case, I have no alternative but to have you both committed."

"I see," Martin said sadly. "That's your final word on the subject?"

"Yes, it is. Do you understand?"

"Yes," Sarah said. She was staring at his chest. In her mind's eye she saw a large hand, its palm pressing down on her uncle's black heart, harder and harder, exerting great pressure.

Jeffrey Bankroft suddenly felt an excruciating pain in his chest. He screamed.

"Do you feel pain, Uncle Jeffrey?" Sarah asked; but she continued to stare at his chest. There was an odd glow in her eyes and they glittered and sparkled with an unnatural force. In spite of his pain, Jeffrey Bankroft stared at his niece's eyes in fascination.

"I think it's my heart," he muttered, clutching his side. He tried to stand up.

"You can't get up, Uncle Jeffrey. You can't move your legs."

It was true. He tried to force his legs to lift him but they would not obey.

"You see Uncle Jeffrey," the girl said. "You're helpless. There were many times when Martin and I felt helpless, too. It's not a pleasant feeling, is it?"

"What are you doing to me?" he cried, still transfixed by those glittering, glowing eyes.

"You'd be surprised at the things I can do. Why, I could have even changed your mind about sending Martin and me away. But it's so much neater this way. You won't be here to interfere with us."

But Jeffrey Bankroft was nobody's fool. He knew

that he still had a weapon. He just had to figure out how to use it. Unfortunately, he once again underestimated his niece.

"What's that, Uncle Jeffrey?" she smiled. "The diary? Don't you realize that I can read your thoughts?"

He realized what was happening now and he struggled to keep her out of his mind, but he was no match for her superior strength. He watch in horror as the key to his desk floated out of his pocket and hung in mid-air.

She laughed as she moved the key playfully in the air. Martin merely smiled. He knew that this was one of Sarah's simplest tricks, one of the first things she had learned when she was still testing her strength.

"Take the key, Martin," she ordered.

He caught it and went to the desk, rifling the drawers, looking frantically for David Bankroft's journal.

Sarah was angry at her uncle for trying to fool her. She began to exert even more pressure on his chest. He began to gasp and his face and hands started to turn blue. His pathetic heart was no longer pumping enough blood to satisfy his body.

"Do you feel the pain, Uncle Jeffrey? It's growing more intense by the second, isn't it?"

"I've got it," Martin announced with satisfaction. He held the thick black book in his hand.

"Throw it in the fireplace," she said. "I never want to see it again."

He tossed it into the fire and watched curiously as the pages turned first yellow, then orange. Finally they were reduced to gray ashes.

Jeffrey cried out in agony as he saw his last hope extinguished.

"Please, I won't send you away, I promise. I'll never tell anyone what went on between you."

"We can't take that chance, Father," Martin said. "It must be dealt with; you told us that yourself." He turned to his mistress. "Do it, Sarah. Finish it, please."

In his pain and panic Jeffrey Bankroft had lost all control of himself completely. The stench of excrement and the horror of approaching death combined to make the atmosphere in the room unbearable.

Martin stepped forward for one last look at his father. He looked at the man with hatred burning in his eyes.

"You made my mother run away, and you made my life miserable. I've hated you deep inside of me for years. Now you're being punished for it, for hurting my mother and for hurting me." He spit down at the miserable figure. "Finish it, Sarah. I'm tired of waiting."

The blinding light that came from Sarah's eyes seemed to double in power. "Goodbye, Uncle Jeffrey," she whispered.

He cried one last time in intense pain, then he died. His eyes remained open, staring in horror as he saw death approach him.

"Shall I close his eyes?" Sarah asked her cousin.

"Leave them like that. He couldn't see in life, perhaps he can see more clearly in death," Martin said.

He took her in his arms, looking into her eyes. The unearthly power there had subsided and all that he saw were the blue eyes of the woman he loved more than life itself. Now Cherron was theirs and no one would ever separate them. They would be together forever.

Chapter Eleven

The idea had occurred to Jonathan during the long, lonely night. He realized that if this Adela woman he had heard about was still living in the swamp, perhaps he could find her and talk to her. The prospect of entering the swamp again did not exactly appeal to him, but he had no place else to turn and no one left to interview.

He was not surprised that Sarah disapproved of his plan when he told where he was going. He had found her in the rose garden where she was still filling a large basket with flowers, and he continued to talk to her as she walked among her prize-winning bushes.

"What do you want to find Adela for?" she asked him.

"Just to talk to her."

"About what?"

"The Bankrofts."

"I don't know what a crazy old woman would know about my family."

"Well, she's been here a long time; she must have seen their behavior. She probably formed an opinion about them. It would be interesting to see the Bankrofts through her eyes. Sometimes an outsider can tell more about a family than its members. I just thought—"

Sarah had been concentrating on picking the best flowers, filling her basket with yellow, scarlet and purple blossoms, but she could not take his question much longer.

"You want to talk to that old crone about what Jason Gibbons said about me, don't you?" she snapped.

"Well, I—"

"You don't have to lie about it."

"I'm not lying," he protested. Now he'd really gone and done it. He'd hurt Sarah's feelings. Why couldn't she understand that he was trying to help her, to free her from her past?

"You're beginning to believe all that crazy talk," she pouted.

"No, I'm not; I swear it. It's just that some very strange things have happened here since I came, what with Jason Gibbons disappearing and Jessica having those strange attacks on her eyes. And you said yourself that you and Adela were friends."

"I said we spoke a few times," she said as she started walking again.

"All right. But she used to hang around here all the time. I just wanted to ask her some questions."

"What kind of questions? Whether she's a witch

and can cast a spell on people?"

"No, of course not."

"You thought you'd just go behind my back and talk to a stranger instead of me."

Jonathan was beginning to regret the whole thing.

"I honestly don't believe she's a witch, and I don't believe a thing that Jason Gibbons said either."

"But you're looking for her in the swamp?"

"I just want to see her."

"You're very persistent."

"You already know that about me." He grinned.

At least he agreed that she could come and be his guide to the swamp. He felt that it was the only way that she would let him go, and she was, after all, his hostess.

She led the way with little effort and the swamp seemed like a different place with her at his side. It had taken on a strange new aura. Fog swirled thickly around them so that he could barely see, although he noticed that Sarah seemed to have no trouble. The birds neither chirped nor sang; the swamp animals made no sounds. It seemed as if all the living inhabitants of the swamp were following their progress with great interest. Even the wind was still.

It gave him an eerie feeling, and he suddenly felt a chill up and down his spine as he followed Sarah deeper into the swamp. He felt like an interloper in this world of darkness.

"Do you know where you're going?" he asked, although she certainly walked as if she did.

"There's only one clearing that I know of," she said. "If Adela is still here she'll be living there."

Her steps were even and steady, and it seemed to him that she must have been this deep in the swamp more than a few times to know it so well. As he stepped gingerly on the soft, spongy ground, ever on the alert for snakes and alligators, he felt as if he were going deeper into a foreign land, one from which he might not return.

It seemed like an hour before they finally came upon the clearing. The wretched shack was a tired, sagging mass of rotting wood and tar paper. It seemed to hang its head in shame at its deplorable condition.

"This must be it," he said.

"It doesn't look as if anyone's lived in it for quite a long time, Jonathan."

"Hello?" he called out. "Anyone here?" Adela? Hello, anybody?"

There was no answer. He walked over to the remains of a camp fire. A sad little iron pot sat in the middle of a pile of ashes. It looked as though no fire had burned there for quite some time.

"I didn't think she'd still be here," Sarah said.

He pulled the handle on the wooden door to the shack and it fell off its rusted hinges and into his hands. He picked up the splintered pieces and threw them aside with disgust. Inside, the cabin was even darker. He looked around at Adela's pitiful possessions with a mixture of sadness and curiosity.

He had lit the nub of a yellow candle but there still wasn't much light to see by—not that there was much to see.

"God, it stinks in here," he complained. A heavy, musty odor permeated the cabin. "The smell makes me nauseous. How could anyone live here?"

Together, they surveyed the room. The rusty cot where Adela had slept had collapsed with age. The mattress reeked and, as Jonathan pulled down the moth-eaten blanket, he saw that it was infested with bed bugs. He threw the blanket down and shivered in disgust.

The stuffing of the old couch was pulled out and part of it had been carried off, probably by some animal or bird building a nest. Ants crawled around the old, battered pots in which Adela had made her evening meals.

"I told you no one was here," Sarah said. "Come on, let's get out of this place. The smell is giving me a headache."

"Not yet. I want to look around."

He started to search, for what he did not know. He opened the drawers in the bureau and swiped at the spiders who had been making their home there. He found some bent spoons that had tarnished badly and some old pieces of strange metals.

"What are you looking for, Jonathan?"

"I don't know, something to tell me what the old woman was about."

He opened and closed drawers until something in one of them caught his eye. Pushing away the dust, he reached in to pull out an old, faded photograph.

"Why, it's a picture of you, Sarah!"

"Me?" she said with surprise. She looked at it with interest. Yes, it was a photograph of her as a little girl. It must have been taken when she and Adela were just getting to know each other.

"I wonder what she was doing with a photograph of you." He smiled at the idea. "Did you know some primitive tribes believed that someone who holds the photograph of another holds his soul?"

Sarah ignored the implication.

"Jonathan, you're looking for a woman who lived on other people's garbage!" she protested. "She probably found my picture and didn't even realize who I was."

He eyed her suspiciously for a moment. He could tell that she was upset about the photograph and that she was not comfortable in the old woman's untidy shack. It had been selfish of him to insist on staying there.

"I guess there's nothing more to see here; we can go," he said. But suddenly a clap of thunder broke the silence of the swamp. It was one of those sudden, violent storms that come out of nowhere.

"We'd better not try to get back. It's too dangerous walking through the swamp in an electrical storm. Too many trees," she warned him.

They gingerly seated themselves on old Adela's wrecked couch to wait out the storm.

* * *

It was dusk and Sarah had decided to surprise her friend. She found Adela bent over her kettle chattering to her cat. It wasn't until she was at the edge of the clearing that she could make out what the old woman was saying.

"Oh, my Lord," she groaned as she stirred her dinner and talked to her fat gray companion. "You know, Elvira, it won't be too long now. That girl's got the power all right, and what a power. Yes sir, it's in her. And one day real soon she's going to give us our revenge on them high falutin' Bankrofts."

The only light in the swamp was the pale yellow of Adela's campfire. Sarah crouched in the darkness and listened.

"Tell me to get off their land, will they?" the old crone babbled on. "Orderin' me off like I was a peasant and they was the royal family. You'd think with all the money and land them people got they'd allow an old, sickly woman to squat on a tiny piece of property. How much room do you and I take up? Too much for them, apparently. But they'll get theirs, somethin' they never expected either, and it'll come from one of their own. Ain't that a kick in the head, Elvira? From one of their own."

Pain filled Sarah's heart. All Adela had been doing was using her, pretending to be her friend, pretending she wanted to help her.

Blithely unaware of Sarah's presence, the old woman continued to stir her old iron pot and to chatter to the purring Elvira.

"And when she has complete control of their minds, then I'll take control of hers," she said gleefully. "I'll make her let us live up there in that fancy house. Think of it, Elvira, you and me livin'

258

like a couple of queens up there. And they'll have nothing to say about it. Imagine, sleepin' up there in them soft feather-beds, eatin' all that good food."

The pain in Sarah's heart had vanished and anger rose in her. Her eyes began to shine with intense hatred as she stepped out into the clearing.

They stood there facing each other. The sunlight above was shut out by the tall cypress trees and the thick Spanish moss. The only light came from the blaze of Adela's campfire. Sarah stood in the light of the fire waiting for Adela to look up from her chattering and recognize her.

"Girl, what are you doin' here?" the old woman said when she saw Sarah standing there. "You ain't supposed to be here today." She still had no idea that Sarah had heard every awful word she said.

Sarah tried to control her rage as she spoke.

"If I hadn't come, Adela, I'd never have known of your treachery," she answered.

"Known what?" Adela tried to pretend indifference, but her hand began to stir faster.

"Don't play innocent with me, Adela. I heard what you said. You used me! You never wanted to be my friend; you merely wanted to get even with the Bankrofts for throwing you off our land."

"Now, girl, listen to me," the old woman protested. "Let Adela explain to you." She was obviously scared now that the truth had been revealed.

"I heard your explanation already," Sarah said angrily. "I don't need to hear anything more. And to think I trusted you, Adela, I believed in you.

"Let Adela help you, let her help you defend yourself against those kids," she mimicked the old woman.

"Let's calm down now, girl," the old woman cautioned. "All right, so I wanted to live at Cherron. I wanted to get even with them. So did you."

Sarah shook her head angrily. The old woman still didn't understand why she was so furious.

"Why didn't you just tell me that was what you wanted all along? Didn't you think I'd have let you live there just for being my friend?"

The swamp clearing had become very quiet, except for the occasional splash of an alligator in the pond nearby. Sarah had the sensation that they were being watched, by a thousand tiny swamp creatures. She reminded herself that this was Adela's territory and that Adela knew every plant, tree, and animal in the swamp. Still, with her newfound strength she was confident that she was the stronger of the two.

She glared at Adela and her eyes began to glow with hatred.

"We can talk about this," the woman assured her. "Now that we understand each other we can work it out."

"There will be no more talking. You betrayed me." The girl stood and stared at her. "You must be punished for making a fool out of me."

Adela smiled nervously and put down her spoon. Even Elvira seemed to sense that something was wrong; the little cat began to hiss and spit at Sarah.

"Do you really think your powers are stronger

than mine?" the old woman said.

"I know they are."

"I have powers you ain't seen yet, girl."

"I'll surpass them with my own."

"Girl, I don't want to fight you, because if I do I'll destroy you."

Sarah would hear no more. In her anger and disgust with her former friend she made a gesture of dismissal with her hand. The force she summoned up surprised even Sarah, for with that one gesture she threw Adela off balance and knocked her to the ground.

Shocked and angry at herself for being taken unaware, the old woman got back on her feet.

"A feeble attempt," she chided the girl.

Next she summoned up her own power and Sarah was pushed back slightly, as if by a strong wind; but she held her ground, smiling at the old woman. Irritated, Adela raised her eyes to the darkened sky and then looked back at Sarah, staring at her intensely.

Sarah could feel the old woman, could feel the pressure of Adela's mind on her own, but she resisted.

"You're not strong enough, Adela," she taunted the old crone. "I've gone far beyond you."

Suddenly, Adela was picked up by the wind and smashed up against the thick trunk of a tree. She lay there, stunned.

Sarah began to laugh, and her eyes almost blinded the old woman with their intensity.

Slowly, it began to dawn on Adela that she was in a battle to the death. She could still not accept that her student had become stronger than she was, but she realized that it would take every ounce of her strength to beat the girl down. She reached into the darkest recesses of her mind and called forth her power.

Sarah was thrown ten-feet backwards, to the edge of the clearing. Stunned, she shook her head and rose quickly. But Adela had the advantage and she begun to hurl iron pots, sticks, and pieces of tableware at the girl. They sailed through the air towards Sarah, and the girl raised her hands to cover her face from the attack.

Encouraged, Adela moved closer to the girl, her eyes gleaming with that familiar white beam of light. Sarah struggled, but an invisible force, Adela's force, smashed her head against the trunk of a tree. Her eyes blurred and her senses whirled. She looked down to see blood all over her dress, and she touched her face. She was bleeding from the nose.

"I told you I can bury you," the old crone spat out. All pretense of friendship had vanished.

The anger in Sarah rose to the boiling point, but she forced herself to stay calm. It was true that so far the old woman had the advantage, but she was convinced that she held the greater power. It was only that she had never used it on a real rival before. All the others had no idea what she was doing until it was too late. With Adela she had met a real challenge.

"Have you had enough, girl?" the old woman asked as she stood over her.

"Please, don't hurt me any more," Sarah

moaned. "Please don't."

"You behave yourself, girl, and I won't." Adela felt complacent and pleased with herself, so she was unprepared for the enormous force of energy that Sarah hurled at her.

The girl's mouth opened and emitted a horrible hissing sound. The force sent Adela five yards backwards and she crashed violently into the cabin door, knocking it partly off its hinges.

Sarah rose to her full height, stretching her arms straight up to the sky. Suddenly a violent streak of lightning split the sky and thunder roared. They were deluged with sheets of rain.

"You see, Adela," she said quietly. "I can summon powers you never dreamed of." She pointed a finger at Elvira and a golden lightning bolt shot from her hand directly to the little cat. It screamed and jumped into the air, but too late. At once the little animal began running madly about the clearing, its gray fur a mass of flames.

"Stop it. Stop," Adela screamed, but Sarah only laughed. Soon there was nothing left of Adela's pet but a pile of gray ash. Adela bent down next to it and started to cry. Finally she managed to compose herself and she rose and stared at Sarah with hatred.

She realized now that she had created a monster in this girl. She would have to destroy her. She walked towards Sarah, but as she moved closer she began to feel a strangling sensation. She couldn't breathe. She tried to inhale, to draw in air, but none would come. She could see Sarah smiling at her as she struggled and gasped.

Then, unexpectedly, the girl released her lungs and she could breathe again. She started to swallow great gulps of air. Then she began to feel her eyes water. She raised her hands to wipe away the tears. When she lowered them again she saw that they were red. She was bleeding! Blood was pouring from her eyes. All she could see was blood.

"I can't see," she moaned. "God, oh God, I'm blind. No more, please, for God's sake, no more."

But Sarah's rage was still not satisfied. She began to concentrate on Adela's campfire which was still blazing. The black iron cauldron went flying on its side and a great mass of boiling hot stew splashed all over the old woman, soaking her in the red-hot liquid. It was getting quite dark now and, as the coals of the fire began to sail through the air, raining on the old woman, they looked like gigantic fireflies.

"No, no," the old woman moaned as she was pelted with the red hot coals. She decided to put everything she had into one last gesture. In spite of her bleeding eyes, her aching, burning body, she focused her concentration on the soft, spongy earth of the swamp. She looked down at the grass and concentrated on it with all her might. She realized that this was her last chance.

Without warning, the ground of the clearing seemed to come alive. The earth gave up its creatures as snakes, moles, turtles, rats, and all the vermin of the swamp heeded the call of their mistresss. Sarah was in the center of the clearing, near the remains of the camp fire, and she watched in horror as these lowly creatures, completely under Adela's power, moved toward her in one awful wave. For a minute she froze. But only for a minute.

She still knew that hers was the superior power, and, to prove it, she looked towards the sky once more. This time, the shower she called forth was far from the innocent, life-giving showers familiar to Cherron. For this was an acid rain and, as it rained down on Adela's soldiers, it turned them to a mass of slimy jelly that quickly covered the clearing and gradually began to sink back into the spongy earth.

Sarah watched in delight as the old woman stood rooted to the ground and the shower splashed over her, gradually erasing her features, disintegrating her rags, until all that was recognizable of the woman were her shining eyes. Soon these too disintegrated, and the woman dissolved into a puddle of silvery jelly that gradually disappeared back into the swamp.

Only Sarah had been untouched by the acid rain and she still looked as pristine as she had when she entered the swamp. She smiled, muttered something to herself about "the last betrayal," and turned and left the swamp

* * *

"I wonder where she went?" Jonathan said as they walked out of the swamp and back to Cherron.

"Who knows?"

"Any idea how long she was living there?"

"Not a clue." Sarah gave the impression that she was completely uninterested in the vanished old crone.

"Did you know her last name?"

"She said she didn't have one."

"No last name?"

"Not one she could remember, anyway."

Jonathan shook his head.

"That's sad."

"Why?" Sarah asked. They had reached the verandah of Cherron and they sat beside each other on the marble steps.

"She was a lonely old vagabond with no name and no place to go," he said sadly.

"She must have enjoyed that kind of life, she choses to live it."

Jonathan was disappointed to hear Sarah talk so coldly. He began to wonder if her sensitivity only extended to the Bankrofts. Then he recalled the library she had built in the town, and her kindnesses to people like Roy McEndrew and Regina Quillam.

"No one chooses that kind of life, Sarah," he insisted. "It's thrust upon them. How could anyone like living in that garbage dump? Besides, it's not living; it's just existing, and badly."

"I guess you're right," she said.

"Did she ever tell you anything about her life? I mean, where she came from, or if she ever married, or had any children, or anyone who cared about her?"

"She never spoke about anything in her past."

"Did you ever ask her?"

"If she wanted me to know she would have told me, Jonathan. I just didn't feel it was my place to pry."

"Like I'm doing?" He smiled sheepishly.

"I didn't mean it that way." She smiled back. "You must remember I was just a child. I wasn't brought up to ask such personal questions. It would have been impertinent."

He still could not stop thinking about the old shack.

"It's funny, isn't it? From the look of it she's been gone a long time, maybe years. And now the old guy's vanished, too."

"You mean Jason Gibbons?"

"Yes. It's as if the two of them knew something, something that someone didn't want them babbling about."

"Only a fool would believe anything either one of them said," Sarah snapped.

Jonathan realized that he was upsetting her. He told her he was sorry; it was just his reportorial instincts getting in the way again.

"That's all right, I understand," she said. "I have to be going anyway; it's time to get back to work."

"You work too hard," he told her.

"It has to be done. I want to keep the business solvent. How would I pay for the upkeep of Cherron? And I'd never want to let my workers go. Some of them have been with the Bankrofts all their lives."

He watched her as she headed for the curing barns, a small feminine figure who seemed quite capable of directing an army of field hands while remaining every bit a woman.

He noticed a small squirrel digging around in her rose garden. This must be her latest rescue attempt, he realized, and walked over to take a look.

The little animal ran away when it saw him approach, which meant, he assumed, that it was fully healed. Another conquest of Miss Sarah's. He looked down at the hole where the little animal had been digging.

Something white and shiny glimmered in the sunlight, and he picked it up.

He turned it over in his fingers, studying it carefully. It seemed strange and yet familiar, this piece of hard white material about two inches long. It looked like—no, he told himself, it couldn't be. But it did look an awful lot like a finger bone. More likely an animal, he told himself. Yes, that would be Miss Sarah's way. She must have buried some favorite pet among the rosebushes. Absentmindedly, he put the bone fragment in his pocket and went back into the house.

He found Jessica Morrow and her son playing a game of cards in the living room. Jessica greeted him but Devon just gazed at him blankly.

"Miss Sarah has quite a way with animals, doesn't she?" he remarked.

"Yes," the woman agreed.

"It must hurt her badly when she loses one of them."

The woman looked at him a little nervously. "She never loses any of them," she said.

"Never?" he sounded surprised. "She must have

268

lost one sometime."

"I don't think so, Mr. Evans. Animals don't die on Miss Sarah, only people."

"Well, now, that's strange," he said. "Because I think I found an animal bone out by the garden. Take a look at this."

He held the shiny white relic in his palm and forced the woman to look at it. To his surprise the woman began to reel and her son started to jump up and down, moaning. It was the first time he had seen the boy so animated, but it was a pitiful sight.

"No, no, no," the boy whined, as his mother fell to the floor in a faint.

"Mrs. Morrow? Mrs. Morrow? Are you all right?" he said as he knelt down beside her. She was out cold, but she seemed to be breathing regularly.

"What in God's name is happening here?" Martin shouted as he entered the room. Sarah was right behind him and she glared at Jonathan.

"What have you done to Aunt Jessica?" she demanded.

"I was just asking her a question," he insisted. "I never meant to frighten her so badly."

Martin had brought a glass of water and he held it to the woman's lips. Her face had gone white and she sipped the glass with great effort.

"What kind of question would cause her to faint?" Martin asked. He was clearly enraged.

"I asked her about this." Jonathan showed them the piece of bone. Martin sucked in his breath, Devon's whining grew louder, but Sarah remained unruffled.

"It's a bone chip," she said, fingering it. "That's all. Where did you find it?"

"By the rose garden. It must have been buried in the earth and a squirrel digging there uncovered it."

"Well, that explains it," she smiled. "It's from an old cat that belonged to my sister Monica. When it died I buried her in the garden. She loved my roses."

"But your aunt told me you never lost an animal," Jonathan said.

She laughed at the idea. "Even I am not that good a nurse, Aunt Jessica. Everything dies at the proper time. You just forgot that, didn't you, Aunt Jessica?"

"Yes," the woman agreed. Jonathan noticed that she was still shaking badly.

"Devon, will you quiet down?" Sarah said, turning to her young cousin. "If you can't control yourself I'll have to do something."

The whining ceased and the old blank-faced Devon Morrow returned. He sat staring into space as his mother was led upstairs by Martin Bankroft on one arm and Jonathan on the other.

"No," Jessica screamed from the foot of the great staircase. "Keep him away from me." She refused to let Jonathan touch her.

"I think it's best if I manage alone," Martin said, as he led the woman away.

Embarrassed at the way the older woman had turned on him, Jonathan returned to the living room. Sarah was obviously still angry with him.

"I think your questioning has become destructive

and vicious, Jonathan," she said angrily. "And I won't tolerate it much longer."

Jonathan sat at the game table and began to fiddle with the checkers that Jessica and her son had abandoned.

"All I did was ask her about the bone. Why should the sight of an old cat's bone send her into such a state?"

"Maybe it was your tone, Jonathan. You obviously did something to terrify her."

"I don't think that I'm what's terrifying her."

"Oh?" she said with interest. "What do you suppose it is, then?"

"I don't know," he shouted. "But something has your aunt frightened out of her mind. If we don't do something she'll probably end up like that crazy Jason Gibbons, wandering around Cherron, jumping every time she hears a sound."

"I would appreciate it if you would leave her alone," she said firmly.

"But all I did was—"

She cut him off. "For God's sake, Jonathan! Have some compassion. My aunt is ill. There will be no more questions. And please put that thing back wherever you found it.

"It's very strange, though," he muttered.

Sarah realized that the questions would continue. She began to call upon her power to reach out and touch his mind. She felt contact. He continued to speak but she did not hear his voice; she was watching his face, his warm sea-green eyes. He was so sweet and strong; she loved him so much. She drew the power back.

Damn, why couldn't she bring herself to reach his mind? It would be so easy and it would be over in a matter of moments. She just couldn't bring herself to do it.

"Did you hear me?"

"What? I'm sorry," she said wistfully. "What did you say?"

"Your thoughts were a million miles away."

"I know. What were you saying?"

"Nothing important." He smiled.

She watched him. He had begun something he would not be able to finish. Martin was right; she had to put her personal feelings aside in order to protect what they had. She forced her mind to touch his thoughts.

You will stop all the questioning, she ordered. *You will forget about Jason Gibbons.*

Jonathan wiped his forehead and twisted uncomfortably in his seat. He looked so innocent, so helpless. He would have no way of fighting back. Her heart went out to him. She pulled her power back again. It was useless. She withdrew the force completely. She would have to find another way; this one would not do.

Jonathan could see that his relationship with Sarah was deteriorating rapidly and it frightened him. The idea of losing Sarah or even upsetting her suddenly was more than he could bear.

"Excuse me now, Jonathan, I'm going up to check on my aunt." She left the room as Martin Bankroft entered. The cousin sat in a chair opposite Jonathan and stared at him with a mixture of triumph and contempt. He, at least, was pleased to hear Jonathan and Sarah quarrelling.

Jonathan stared glumly back at the sullen Martin. It was gradually beginning to dawn on him that unraveling the mysteries of Cherron would alter his relationship with Miss Sarah, and probably not for the better.

Jessica Morrow was lying in bed when her niece came into the room. The heavy draperies had been drawn and the room was dark. Martin had lit a fire and it was crackling in the white marble fireplace. Jessica was surrounded by the mementos of a happier time. The furniture was mostly antiques she had inherited from her husband's family. In addition there were paintings, figurines, and bibelots that she and Robert Morrow had collected in their trips around the world.

On the table beside her bed there lay a worn Bible and two photographs in gold filigree frames. One was of the dark, smiling man who had been Robert Morrow, and the other was of a laughing child, running after a ball. It was hard to imagine that her listless son Devon had once been that laughing child.

Sarah entered quietly so that Jessica didn't hear her at first. She stood at the foot of the bed and Jessica could barely make her out in the dim light.

"You must learn a little self-control, Aunt Jessica," she cautioned.

"But he—he had that thing. He demanded I tell him what it was."

"Well, you saw how easy it was to handle him. Now stop making yourself sick over it."

Jessica pulled up the faded red quilt. It was almost as if she hoped it would shield her from her niece. "I didn't mean to faint," she pleaded. She could tell that her niece was angry.

Sarah's eyes were glittering in the darkness, emitting that strange unearthly glow. She was staring at the flames in the fireplace and Jessica looked at them to see what her niece saw in them.

In the midst of the flames she could see her beloved Robert the way he had looked when they took him out of his burning plane. She saw her handsome husband, screaming in agony as the flames ate him alive. It seemed to Jessica as though he was calling out to her now, begging her to rescue him.

"I understand, Aunt Jessica," Sarah said kindly. "Mr. Evans took you by surprise. You must learn to handle these things. I think you've already been saying too much to him and I don't want you to say anymore. Do you understand?"

"Yes," she said and the vision in the flames began to fade.

"Absolutely nothing," Sarah cautioned.

"I understand."

Sarah slipped out of her aunt's room, leaving the woman alone with her memories.

Martin came to her room that night, but she could see that he was still upset about Jonathan. They made love, but it was as if they were both distracted, Martin by his anger and jealousy and Sarah by she knew not what.

There was no doubt about it, Jonathan Evans

was becoming a real problem. She wondered why. She had never before hesitated to use her power against anyone who threatened their happiness. Could it be that she felt differently about Jonathan?

She thought about the way he had held her that afternoon of their picnic on Benson's Cliff, the way she had gazed into his sea-green eyes. Yes, there was no doubt in her mind that if Martin had not happened along when he did she would have let Jonathan make love to her. And she would have enjoyed every minute of it.

But she couldn't let this situation continue.

"Why don't you just stop him?" Martin demanded. "You have the power to get into his mind and tell him to knock it off."

"No," she said flatly.

"Why not? It won't hurt him. I don't understand this attitude of yours, Sarah."

As they lay there in her canopied bed, feeling the warmth of each other's bodies, Sarah tried to make sense of it herself.

"I just want him to stop on his own," she said.

"Oh, that's just fine, Sarah. You mean you want him to be so much in love with you that nothing that's happened here would matter to him?"

"That's right," she admitted.

"You're relying solely on his love for you to make him stop?"

"What if I am?"

"It won't work," he said. "Look, Sarah, it's gone too far already. Jonathan Evans is not going to buy any more of the stories we've been feeding him. A

275

steady diet of lies only brings more questions from someone like that. Do you really think he believes that a little old cat bone would make Aunt Jessica faint?"

"Maybe."

She began to caress him again, hoping to distract him, but Martin seemed to be obsessed with Jonathan Evans.

"Be realistic, Sarah, he's getting too close. What if he starts asking other people questions?"

"I'll handle them."

"What the hell are you going to do? Follow him around for the rest of his life controlling the minds of every human being he speaks to? Even you can't do that!"

"I'll figure something out."

"You'd better do it quickly. We don't know if he's written any of this in his book."

"He wouldn't do that. He has nothing substantial to go on."

"Not yet. But he has his suspicions and they're enough to ruin us."

"All right, all right," she said impatiently. "I'll think about it.

"You'd better do more than think about it, Sarah, before it's too late."

As much as she hated the thought, Sarah had to admit that her cousin-lover was right. Something had to be done to halt Jonathan's relentless progress. But what was the answer?

Sarah still couldn't sleep and she decided to slip downstairs for a brandy. Maybe that would help.

She put on a sheer blue robe and slippers and quietly slipped out of the room so as not to wake the sleeping Martin.

She was startled to find Jonathan sitting alone in the darkened living room, staring at the remains of the fire.

"You couldn't sleep either?" she asked him.

"I guess the events of this afternoon upset me."

She poured two glasses of brandy and handed him one.

"I'm sorry I was so angry with you, Jonathan," she said.

"That's all right." He swirled the brandy around in the glass. "I've been sitting here still trying to understand something."

She sighed. "More questions."

"I just can't understand why the bone of a dead cat would cause your aunt to panic so. Why did it upset her so much to see it?"

She shook her head and made an exasperated expression.

"Jonathan, Jonathan. It's easy to see that you grew up in New York," she said.

"What's that supposed to mean?"

"Just that you don't recognize a real old-fashioned Southern belle when you see one. My Aunt Jessica's spent her life having fainting spells and becoming hysterical. It's her way of getting attention."

"I'm sorry the whole thing happened," he said.

"That's what comes of prying so deeply into people's lives. You have to learn that you can carry it too far. There are some things that should stay buried, no pun intended, I assure you."

"It's very strange, though," he muttered while he stared into the fire, and she realized that he was still thinking about the many unresolved questions in the Bankroft family history.

She stared at him, her eyes glittering with a surge of power and concentration. She began to call up the power to reach out and touch his mind. She could feel herself make contact as he continued to speak, but she could no longer hear his voice. She was concentrating on his face. It was so sweet and strong and she loved him so much.

She drew the power back. The light subsided from her eyes.

"Did you hear me, Sarah?"

"What? I'm sorry, Jonathan. What did you say?"

"Your thoughts were a million miles away," he laughed.

"I know. What were you saying?"

"Just complaining," he said. "I thought I felt a sharp pain in the back of my head, but it faded quickly."

He had felt her touch, she realized, watching him sip his brandy. Martin was right. She must put her personal feelings aside. Once again she forced herself to touch his thoughts.

You will stop all the questioning, she ordered. *You will forget about Jason Gibbons.*

She watched as Jonathan began to wipe his forehead and twist uncomfortably in his seat. He looked so innocent, so helpless. He would have no way of fighting back once she released the full impact of her power. She pulled back again. It was useless.

She would have to find another way.

Arcadia was a quiet town and the Arcadia jail was a small two-room affair on Main Street. It had a barred room in back for drunks, vagrants and big-mouths who irritated Sheriff Larry Byner, whose office was in the front.

Lawrence Byner, Jr., was a huge man, about six feet four, and at least two hundred and seventy pounds of muscle. He looked more like a football player than a lawman. He sat at a golden-oak rolltop desk, and he spun around when he heard Jonathan come in.

"I heard there was a writer staying out at Cherron," he said when Jonathan introduced himself. "How do you do?"

"I'm well, thank you," Jonathan answered. The sheriff had a powerful grip but a surprisingly soft voice and gentle manner.

"Is there anything I can do for you, Mr. Evans?"

"Well, as you know, I'm writing a history of the Bankroft family."

"Yes, I heard. Quite a story there for a writer."

"So I'm finding out. I'd like to ask you a few questions about them."

"Certainly."

"How long have you known Miss Sarah and her family?"

"Well, I was born here, so I've known Miss Sarah all my life, and the rest of the family too."

"I see. They weren't very popular with the people of Arcadia, were they?"

"Because of their attitude, no," the sheriff said reluctantly. "Of course, many people here worked for them, either in the fields, or as household servants. For years Cherron was the main employer around here. The Bankrofts thought they owned everyone."

"I see," Jonathan said, making a few notes. "And Sarah?"

"Miss Sarah was always different. She loved the people here. She was always one of us. Sometimes you even forgot she was a Bankroft."

"Because of her kindness?"

"Yes. I think she wanted to forget she was one of them herself." He began to recite the litany of Miss Sarah's accomplishments, recalling her generosity, her gift of the library, the way she treated Cherron employees. Jonathan had heard it all before.

"You have some local characters here too, I notice," Jonathan added.

Sheriff Byner smiled. "Oh yes, but we keep them under control."

"I was thinking especially about Jason Gibbons."

The Sheriff looked puzzled. "Haven't seen old Jason around in a while, come to think of it."

"Neither have I," Jonathan admitted. "But last time we talked he kept harping about having seen grave robbers. I was wondering if you knew anything about such an episode?"

The sheriff leaned back in his swivel chair and gestured expansively. "Ol' Jason is crazy, Mr. Evans. Don't you go believing anything he tells you."

"Would you know if anyone tried to rob the

Bankroft family graveyard?"

"I would for sure. Miss Sarah or Martin would inform me immediately if anything like that happened," the sheriff assured him. "You can't believe anything that Jason Gibbons has to say anyway. He's been rattling on for years. People in Arcadia just ignore him. His brain's messed up."

"Will anyone look for him?" Jonathan wondered.

"I doubt it, Mr. Evans. He's been living in those swamps for a long time. I expect he knows them pretty well by now."

After some more small talk about the Arcadia crime rate and the sheriff's policies on law enforcement, Jonathan made his exit, still unsatisfied. He seemed to be the only one who took Jason Gibbons seriously. Still, as a reporter, he was pretty skillful at telling when people were lying, or even just deceiving themselves. And he was pretty sure that Jason Gibbons had been telling the truth. And sometimes he had the uneasy feeling that the people at Cherron, even Miss Sarah, were hiding something.

Regina Quillam was staring at herself unhappily in the mirror. All the shades on her windows were drawn now and she rarely left her cottage. The last time she had been outside was to supervise the workmen who had come to burn her rosebushes. That old fool Luke Bankroft had assured her that it was an allergy to roses that was making her skin itch so unbearably, and so she had destroyed them all. Now she didn't even have the comfort of watching them from her window.

She had tried bandaging her hands to keep from scratching, but it was no use. The itch was unbearable. Now most of the top layer of skin had been rubbed off her body and her skin looked pink and scaly. In some places she had scratched almost to the bone, but still the itching continued.

As she looked at herself in the mirror she started to weep. Her face was red and raw and ugly scabs had formed. They never lasted long enough to heal, though, because she had to scratch them away. Most of her white, blue-rinsed hair had fallen out and her scalp was pink and scaly.

She tried to recall when she had first started feeling the awful burning itch. As near as she could remember it had been that afternoon when she ran into Sarah Bankroft in the Palmetto Leaf Cafe. The stuck-up little thing had been so full of herself because she was with a writer who was going to write about the Bankrofts.

Regina couldn't resist teasing her about her roses and insisting that this fall she was going to beat her at the rose fair. And she would have, too, if she hadn't come down with this awful curse, She'd gotten to the girl, too. She remembered how Miss Sarah had looked at her.

It had been a look of total hatred, but it was also more than that. Her eyes had taken on a strange color, a glow, really, a shining. It was as though some surge of power, almost like a bolt of lightning, was being summoned up from within.

That was it, Regina Quillam realized. It was at that moment that she had first begun to feel that awful tingling feeling. She was sure that there was some connection between her unknown disease and the way Miss Sarah had looked at her. But suddenly she couldn't seem to concentrate anymore. All she could do was claw at her skin and weep.

Sarah and Martin were quarrelling in her bedroom again. It seemed to her lately that they quarreled more than they made love. She was standing at the French windows looking out at her rose garden and Martin was behind her on the canopied bed.

"You've done nothing to stop him, Sarah," Martin shouted.

"How do you know?"

"Because he's still asking his questions, still sticking his nose in where it doesn't belong."

"Please, Martin. He won't get any more information out of Aunt Jessica. I ordered her not to talk to him again.

"It's not Aunt Jessica he's talking to now, it's Larry Byner."

She never thought he would go to the sheriff. "He's gone that far?"

"Gibbons told him he saw grave robbers. He asked the sheriff about it. The sheriff just laughed at him, of course."

Sarah looked relieved

"If only he hadn't pried so deeply," she sighed.

"Get your head out of the clouds, Sarah. We have an explosive situation on our hands," Martin insisted. "You've got to find out what's on his mind."

"I'll take care of it."

"That's what you said before, Sarah. You have to take care of it before he takes care of us."

Martin was right. She had to take immediate action. She had to find out why Jonathan was so obsessed with the Bankroft graves.

Martin put his hand on her shoulder in a comforting gesture.

"If it means that much to you, Sarah, and I know that it does, you won't have to hurt him. Just erase the questions from his mind."

Sarah shook her head sadly. "I thought he loved me enough to put an end to this himself, to accept, the way you did."

"You never needed to use your power on me, Sarah, I would have accepted anything you did."

She threw her arms around her cousin and held him tightly. He smoothed her blond hair and tried his best to comfort her and give her strength for the time ahead.

"He's created waves that could drown us, Martin. You were right; it would have been better if he had never come here."

"Aren't you afraid he'll see us?"

"There was a small seed of doubt; I saw it coming; it was there in a dark corner of his mind. What does it matter if he did see us? It would be only one more thing I'll have to wipe clean from his mind."

"And that's my fault," Martin said sadly.

"No," she insisted. "I should have listened to you in the first place. You never wanted him here. I thought it was simple jealousy, but you sensed something tragic would happen. I should have known you were right about him. No outsider should ever have been welcomed into our world so intimately."

"My darling Sarah, I can feel your heart beating so fast. I can feel all that pain."

"If only I had treated him like all the other men. One night, may be two, then on his way."

"There's no need to torture yourself about it now. You know what has to be done to insure our survival."

"Why did I try to pretend it didn't exist? I've never been fortunate like other people. My problems never seem to disappear."

"I'll be with you. I'll always be with you here at Cherron, remember?"

"I remember."

"Let's go downstairs and feed them. You can breathe free for a while."

Jonathan realized that there was still one Bankroft he had not questioned, Jessica Morrow's strange son, Devon. In spite of the boy's zombie-like behavior, Jonathan was convinced that he understood everything that was going on. He simply had made a decision somewhere in his life to remove himself from all emotional involvement. He seemed to float about Cherron like a silent witness.

He found Devon sweeping out the stable.

"How are you, Devon?"

"Fine, Mr. Jonathan." As usual, the boy's voice was flat and unemotional.

"We haven't had a chance to talk much since I've been here."

"Yes, Mr. Jonathan." The boy never looked up, he just continued concentrating on his sweeping.

"Do you like it here at Cherron?"

"Yes, Mr. Jonathan."

"But a boy like you, must want to get out into the world, to make new friends. Don't you?"

"No, Mr. Jonathan."

"I'm sorry about what happened to your mother the other day," he said.

"It's all right, Mr. Jonathan."

"She seems like a very sensitive lady."

"Yes."

These monosyllablic answers were giving Jonathan a headache, and he was frustrated that his reportorial skills seemed to have so little impact on the boy. He decided to try another tack.

"I understand that when your father came to Cherron he took a great interest in the tobacco business."

The boy looked up briefly from his sweeping. At last Jonathan was getting a reaction. He pressed on.

"I was very sorry to hear about his accident," he added. "You must have missed him very much."

"I did." The boy stopped sweeping and looked off into space. He could still see the flames and hear his father's screams of pain as they pulled him from the wreckage of his plane.

"Well, have you two been having a nice talk?" It was Sarah. She was standing in the doorway of the stable. It was odd, Jonathan realized, how Sarah turned up so often, so unexpectedly, and always just when he thought he might be on the verge of learning something. He dismissed the thought as quickly as it had surfaced.

"Excuse me, I have to finish my work," Devon said as he left the two of them alone.

Sarah watched him walk away and shook her head sadly. "He's not an easy person to talk to since the accident."

"It's like to talking to a postcard," Jonathan observed.

"Being a writer, that must drive you crazy."

"He's really troubled, Sarah. Have you tried to get him help?"

"Uncle Luke thought that, after the shock of his father's death wore off, Devon would return to normal. Unfortunately, it's been six years and he hasn't come out of it. We sent him away once, but it did little good. He feels secure here."

"Even though this is the place where he saw his father die?"

"It's also the only real home he's ever known," she said, taking Jonathan by the arm. "Come, I'll take you back to the house and give you a hard-working writer's lunch."

As they walked across the lawn of Cherron from the stable to the great house, they walked over the very area where Robert Morrow's plane had come down. Sarah did not point out the landmark.

* * *

"I don't want to play with you," the dark little boy said as he threw his croquet mallet down on the ground. Sarah and Devon were playing on the lawn of Cherron, in the shade of the pecan grove.

"I want to play with Monica," he insisted. "She's the pretty one."

"I told you, Devon," Sarah repeated to her cousin. "Monica is going to a party."

Everyone at Cherron was going to the party except for Devon, because he was too young, and Sarah, because she was too plain.

"Mother says you're not even Uncle Dan's daughter. You're not pretty enough to be a Bankroft," he yelled.

"I told you to stop it, Devon. I'm warning you."

"What's going on here?" Aunt Jessica said. She was already dressed for the party in a lime-green silk dress. Her long black hair was pulled up in a dramatic chignon. She looked like the sophisticated, worldly woman that she was.

"I was just telling him to stop calling me names. He says I'm not even a Bankroft."

Jessica Morrow sniffed. "That's probably true. You certainly don't look like one."

"I'm warning you, Aunt Jessica; don't ever say such things to me again or you and Devon will be very sorry."

She stared at her aunt angrily and her eyes started to shine with hatred.

"Are you threatening us?" Jessica asked.

"Maybe."

"I don't think your uncles and your brother David would be pleased to hear that," Jessica said sharply. "Your behavior is disgraceful."

"My behavior!" Sarah cried. "What about yours? How can you let your son call me names?"

"We have every right to say what we please and don't you ever forget that." Jessica was holding her son affectionately by the shoulders and they both faced Sarah.

"I'll punish you, I swear I will."

The mother and son just laughed, laughed until they heard the roar of the small, single-engine plane as it flew overhead. It was Robert Morrow's plane, and he executed a beautiful swoop in the air to show off for his wife and son.

"He's such a brilliant pilot," Jessica said with pride.

A pink magnolia blossom had fallen to the ground. Sarah picked it up and held it in her hand. She couldn't understand how her aunt and her cousin could be so cruel. What was it about the Bankrofts, she wondered, that made them so intolerant of anyone who was different?

"Well, are you going to stop teasing me?" she repeated.

"Certainly not," Jessica said, still laughing.

"Yeah," Devon added. "And I'll tell my father. He'll fix you."

"No, I'll fix him," she said firmly. Her eyes had begun to glitter as she concentrated on summoning up her strength. "Do you know what I'm going to do, you two? I'm going to make Uncle Robert's plane blow up. Would you like to watch?"

"Are you insane, child?" Jessica said.

"No, Aunt Jessica. You can watch me do it."

They looked on in amusement at first as the girl stared up at the small plane circling in the sky above them. Sarah narrowed her eyes and they began to shine and glow. The whites took on an unearthly color that neither Jessica nor Devon would ever forget.

Sarah could see inside the cockpit. She saw handsome, dashing Robert Morrow at the controls. How he loved his plane! He really thought he was in total command!

Next, she concentrated on the engine. She tried creating a hole inside it. Fuel began to leak out. She could see it seeping towards the red hot engine. A tiny spark collided with the black oil. That was all.

Jessica and Devon's amusement turned to horror as they saw the plane burst into flames in the sky. There wasn't even the sound of an explosion, only the sudden flash of bright orange light, like a setting sun; only the sun was crashing, crashing to the earth.

It landed on the lawn of Cherron, only a few yards from them, but they couldn't get near it because of the intensity of the heat. They could only watch and listen to Robert Morrow's agonized cries.

"Father, father, father. Oh, God," Devon moaned. His mother stood stark still as if she were trying to convince herself that this was a terrible dream.

"I warned you two," Sarah said calmly. "Now you can see what I can do. But you'll never be able to tell anyone else, will you?"

Her eyes were still glowing like they too were afire, but with a harsh cobalt light. Both Devon and Jessica felt the same painful tingling sensation in their brains.

"You'll both do exactly as I say, won't you?" she said.

Devon sobbed as he fell to his knees. Jessica knelt beside him, holding him, trying to comfort her orphaned son. She looked up at Sarah with anguish in her eyes.

"Yes, Sarah," she said. "Yes, we will do as you say."

From that time on they belonged to her.

*   *   *

Sarah found Jonathan at work in the library. He was seated at the long mahogany table and surrounded by piles of notebooks and papers. He looked up with surprise when she walked in.

"I came to see how your work is coming." She smiled as she stood in the doorway. She was wearing a simple white eyelet dress and her long blond hair was tied with a blue ribbon.

"It's coming along very well." He hesitated to tell her the truth: that his work on the Bankroft family was complete and he was merely looking for excuses to hang on. "I've just completed another chapter."

Sarah knew better.

She stared at Jonathan, her eyes glowing with the force of her power. For the first time she was delving into his mind, examining his thoughts. Until now she had tried to manipulate and control him with friendly words and a pretty smile. But Martin was right: it had gone far enough and she had to know what Jonathan was really up to.

Jonathan felt only a pleasant sensation, a kind of mental fogginess. He was unaware that Sarah had overpowered his own mind and that she was methodically examining his very core.

As she walked down the long corridors of the mind of Jonathan Evans, Sarah Bankroft saw many things. He was in love, very deeply in love. This she read in his mind. She glided past to the doubts and questions until she found what was causing them. There it was. Like a small, poisonous nematode at the root of a tobacco plant, the words of Jason Gibbons had fixed themselves in Jonathan's mind. And there was something else, a tiny suspicion about her relationship with Martin. He had seen Martin leaving her room early in the morning!

She realized that it would only be a matter of time before Jonathan put everything together. All the elements were already there in his brain, waiting to be assembled into the awful truth.

She had to talk to Martin.

Slowly, gently, she retreated from Jonathan's brain. He felt the fogginess lift and he assumed that he had been daydreaming.

"Oh, I'm sorry, Sarah," he apologized. "Were you saying something?"

"Only that I see I'd better leave you to your work."

She slipped back out of the room.

Sarah found Martin in the basement room. She was beginning to realize that, with Jonathan Evans in the house, this was the only room where they were truly alone and safe.

"What did you find out from Jonathan?" Martin asked eagerly.

"He lied to me." She sounded a little hurt. "He says that he still has to work on his book, but, when I examined his mind, I found that the book has been finished for more than a week."

"I'm not surprised," Martin said cynically.

"As for the rest, so far he's refused to clarify the disjointed thoughts he has about Jason Gibbons and the graves." She smiled and her eyes flickered with the power for just a minute. "He loves me, Martin."

"For how long?"

Martin was right. It was only a matter of time before Jonathan put everything together, and, when he did, he would change his mind about her. Martin was different. Although he had never mastered the power himself, he had accepted anything she did. She threw her arms around him in a burst of affection and held him tightly.

"He's created waves that could drown us, Martin. You were right from the beginning. It would have been better if he had never come here."

There's no need to torture yourself about it now, Sarah. You know what has to be done."

Yes, she knew. First, she would have to go to work on Jonathan Evan's mind, cleaning it of all doubts. Second, she must force him to leave Cherron. She had created a world here, a world where she was the ruler, just as Adela was the ruler of the swamp. Nothing could threaten that world.

The rest of the basement room was darkness. The dining table set so elegantly, the Bankroft family heirlooms, the great paintings of the Bankroft men and women, all lay cloaked in darkness. Suddenly, not for the first time, Sarah felt an enormous wave of bitterness and hatred for her family well up within her.

"You, you're the cause of this," she lashed out at the darkened room. "If it hadn't been for your brutality I wouldn't be dealing with this kind of situation now."

There was no answer from the rest of the room.

"Sarah," Martin said gently. "Come away. Don't trouble yourself."

Tears came to her dark blue eyes. "No. They forced me into a corner. All of them, evil people, evil, miserable people."

In a fury she ran to the table and, picking up a Limoges dish, she threw it up against the stone basement wall. It shattered, sending pieces flying across the room.

"Sarah, please. It'll be over soon and the hurt will go away."

"The hurt never leaves," she said bitterly. "It's inside of me, growing like a cancer. No matter how much I cut out, there's always something else they do to bring it back."

"We were the ones who allowed Evans to stay."

She picked up a razor-sharp carving knife from the table and caressed the blade with her hand.

"I just wish I could take this knife and cut out all the bitterness so that it would never return."

"Put that thing down, Sarah. You make me nervous."

"I swore they'd never win again," she murmured,

still holding the knife.

"And they haven't," Martin told her. "You triumphed over all of them. We just made an error in judgment and now we're going to correct it. Come on, leave them be."

He took her arm and led her to the door. But there was someone standing in the doorway.

"Jonathan!" Sarah gasped. How much had he seen? How much had he heard?

"What the hell are you doing down here?" Martin demanded.

"The cellar door was unlocked," Jonathan said easily, looking past Martin and Sarah and into the room they were about to leave.

A look of agonized fear flashed across his handsome face.

The large room had been furnished with the same exquisite taste as the rest of the great house. Only the stone walls reminded him that he was in the basement. There was a comfortable-looking pink settee and several Chippendale occasional chairs. There were bowls and vases of freshly cut roses everywhere. But this was not where the horror lay.

He stared at the long mahogany dining table, set for dinner with the finest Limoges service and the most beautiful silver tableware. Here, too, the table was decorated with the pride of Miss Sarah's rose garden.

But it was not the sumptuous dinner table that shocked Jonathan Evans; it was Miss Sarah's dinner guests. Every chair at the table was filled. For one merciful moment Jonathan actually managed to believe that they were filled with wax dolls, lifelike dolls. But, curiosity once again got the better of him. He struck a match and lit the huge silver candalabra at each end of the table. Then he looked again.

They were not dolls at all. They were people. Or at least they had once been people.

Now they were simply mummified, lifeless corpses. He stared in horror at their faces. He thought he recognized most of them.

The old white-haired man at the head of the table must be Grandfather, and Nanna must be the tiny white-haired woman at the other end. It was easy to see that, in spite of this travesty, Sarah still felt something for the old woman, for she was dressed beautifully in an old-fashioned black silk dress and her make-up was delicate.

Not so the other woman at the table. He felt a sickening wave of nausea at the sight of Martha Conroy Bankroft. Her black hair had faded in death, but her make-up was garishly bright and she smiled out blankly with a huge, bright, red-lipstick smile.

"Let me introduce you to Mother," Sarah said, standing behind the dessicated corpse.

Jonathan recoiled in horror.

"What's wrong? Don't you like my family?" Sarah asked.

"Sarah!" he gasped. "I had no idea!" He was still struggling to somehow justify this madness.

Unruffled, Sarah continued her introductions.

"I'm sure you recognized Grandfather and Nanna. I do hope he likes the way I dressed him, in his favorite cutaway. He so wanted everything to be perfect."

Jonathan stared at her as she made her way around the dining table, touching each corpse gently as if it were still alive.

"Here's Michael," she said indicating a battered young man with the same blank look, his skin dried like leather. Every bone in his body had been broken in the fall. To seat him at the table she tied him tightly to the Chippendale chair.

Curious, Jonathan touched the boy's hand, but some of the skin crumbled off like old, dried paper. He shrank back.

"Michael was the first," she explained casually. "Thank goodness Arcadia soon got a more skillful embalmer."

There were three other men. She introduced them as her father, her brother Everett and her uncle Jeffrey. Then they came to the last two seats at the table.

Up until now Jonathan had truly felt that somehow he would be able to justify this in his mind. Sarah watched in amusement. She could see that poor Jonathan was struggling to sort all the awful elements he had just absorbed into some kind of rational explanation that would exonerate her.

He almost thought he had it. He had decided that Sarah and Martin had created a pathetic little museum because, in spite of everything, they wanted their family around them. Now he understood what Jason Gibbons had been talking about. Of course the two had been robbing graves, but now he understood why.

"It's like a monument," Martin said quickly. "Famous people are always being immortalized in statues or paintings. We wanted to do something like that for the Bankrofts."

"You should never have let her do it, Martin," Jonathan said brusquely. "Why let her torment herself with all this?"

"It was my decision," Sarah said. Her eyes were glittering.

Martin came to examine the last two chairs at the dining table. At one was a monstrous-looking figure dressed in a man's dinner jacket. His face was unlike anything human; all his features seemed to be covered with a mass of dark-red scar tissue. Empty eye sockets gazed out blindly at the table.

"Uncle Robert, meet Jonathan Evans," Sarah said. "He's writing a book about the Bankrofts, and Aunt Jessica and Devon have been a great help to him."

He couldn't mistake the cruelty in her tone. With mounting fear he realized that this was not the Sarah Bankroft he thought he knew.

At last he came to the final chair.

On first glance he had thought it was empty because there was no one—or maybe nothing would be a better term—at eye level. But then he looked on the seat of the chair. It was the mummified arm of a human being, a muscular arm with a signet ring on the mummified hand, a man's arm.

"I'm afraid that's all that was left of poor Everett after the 'gator got him," she sighed.

Jonathan felt the room spinning around him. He was sure he was going to be sick. He could feel the cold sweat all over his body and his hand was trembling, but he struggled to control himself. Even he could not accept this particular horror.

"Sarah, how could you?" was all that he could bring himself to say.

She shrugged. Martin moved protectively to her side.

"Surely you wouldn't expect me to bury him with the others? Everett was a Bankroft; he couldn't bear it."

"Others?" Jonathan's voice was so tight with fear that he could barely get the words out. "There have been others?"

"Of course," Martin snapped.

Jonathan shook his head. He was beginning to believe that he was having some sort of freaky nightmare and that soon he would awaken. Everything would be back to normal. Miss Sarah would once again be an innocent girl who was falling in love with him, and this basement room wouldn't even exist. You could control your dreams, he knew, and he decided to try it. Yes, he would simply walk out of the dream room. He started to move toward the door.

Sarah looked at him directly, her eyes shining brightly. He had never noticed before how the whites of her eyes glowed. Suddenly a great surge of power forced him back. He flipped in the air and landed on the pink velvet settee.

Stunned, he looked up at Sarah and Martin.

"What was that? What happened?"

Martin smirked. "That was her power."

"What power?" He could feel his body tense. Even his teeth were clenched.

"Telekinesis," Sarah explained, smiling. Her eyes were glowing brighter than ever. "It was old Adela who taught me how to use it. I can control people and objects just by concentrating on them."

"Adela? Where is she now?"

"Oh, she's gone. She tried to control me, tried to take over Cherron. Can you imagine? She failed, as you can plainly see."

"Where is her body?"

"Sunk back into the swamp where it belonged. I certainly couldn't have given her a place here, could I? I told you what snobs the Bankrofts were."

Jonathan was still struggling to make sense of it all. One thing was sure now. This was no dream.

"You said something about others, Sarah. What others?"

Sarah and Martin exchanged glances. They were always sneaking those looks, Jonathan realized. He'd noticed it since he'd arrived at Cherron.

Like a drowning man, Jonathan Evans clutched at the last straw, the last faint hope that Miss Sarah was the woman he wanted to believe she was.

He stood up in a fury and glared at Martin Bankroft.

"It's you, isn't it?" he shouted. "You put her up to this madness. She's completely under your thumb."

Sarah clutched Martin's arm.

"No," she screamed. "Everything we did, we did

together."

"Together?" Jonathan considered this. "You mean—No, I don't want to hear this. I can't believe it."

"Believe what?" Martin said triumphantly. "The truth is that we're lovers. We've been lovers for years."

Now he knew it was all true. These two were capable of anything.

"That bone I found in the rose garden," he said. "It was a human bone, wasn't it?"

"Yes, Jonathan. I'm afraid it was. Since my family won't entertain any of our other guests, Martin and I had to get rid of them another way."

"How did you do it?"

"Come, we'll show you."

They led him to the other end of the basement room and showed him the large green-malachite pool. He leaned over and saw the fish and recognized them immediately.

"Piranhas?"

"Yes," she smiled. "Dear Uncle Robert gave us some when we were children and I managed to keep two of them alive. Fortunately, we had a male and a female. They're quite an affectionate pair, I should say. They've produced over fifty more in the last ten years. Pick the bones clean and you get the makings of an excellent bone meal. Makes the roses bloom well, don't you think?"

"Who?" Jonathan asked sadly.

"A psychiatrist my uncle Jeffrey brought out here, my avaracious sister-in-law, and some others you wouldn't care about."

"Sarah can get anyone to do anything," Martin said proudly. "She's got the power."

Jonathan turned to Sarah. "You've used this power on me, haven't you, Sarah? To make me fall so hopelessly in love with you?"

"No, no, Jonathan," she insisted. "I never used it on you. I wouldn't."

"The other night, when we were sharing the brandy, I felt something; something touched me. You were trying to get into my mind then, weren't you?"

"Yes, I considered it," she admitted. "But I didn't want to do that to you. What you feel for me is real. I swear it."

He still could not make up his mind. Was she a monster with an inhuman power or was she a sad, lost little girl? It didn't matter, he realized with horror. Because either way he loved her.

"Darling, you need all the help I can get for you. And Martin, too," he added hastily.

"What kind of help?" Martin asked.

"A doctor, for God's sake. Don't you think one is called for? Can't you see that? You've both committed murder."

"That can never be proven, actually," Sarah reminded him.

"And if it were, Sarah and I would both go to prison," Martin added. He seemed to have sensed Jonathan's weak spot.

Jonathan realized they were right. He couldn't bare the thought of Sarah locked in a dark prison cell. He would lose her forever. no one else would ever understand. Somehow, he had to protect her secret.

"Does anyone else know what's in here?" he asked.

"No one."

"Then we have to destroy it, and now."

"How?" Martin asked.

Jonathan thought for a moment. "We'll fill it with concrete. We can bury it and them at the same time."

"Even our fish?" Sarah said wistfully.

"Everything. Everything has to go. We can make a fresh start."

"Do you know how much concrete it would take to fill this up?" Martin said. "Tons."

"Then we'll use as much as it takes. We can't leave it like this."

"But, Jonathan," Sarah protested.

"I don't want to hear any arguments." He was now taking complete control of the situation. Someone had to. "We'll bury everything under tons of concrete; then we'll wall up the door. No one will ever know this room ever existed. They'll never get wise to this part of it."

"And what part will they know about?" Sarah asked. Her eyes glittered and she had a fixed smile on her face.

"Darling, I love you. I can't live without you. But you need professional care; both of you do. I'll get you a doctor. He'll help you so that you won't need Martin anymore."

"Not need Martin?" She screamed and clutched her cousin. A silence descended on the room and the three of them stared at each other. The only sound was the occasional splashing of the piranhas in their pool.

"You don't seem to understand, Jonathan. I'll always need Martin. He's part of me. I could no more imagine life without Martin than life without you."

"Sarah, this affair can't go on."

"He's trying to tear us apart, Sarah," Martin pleaded. "Don't let him do it."

"I'll get a doctor for you, Sarah. Darling, I'll wait for you, and when you're better we'll go to New York and never come back here. I don't ever want to see this place again."

Jonathan began to move towards the stone staircase.

"Sarah, don't let him leave here with our secret," Martin begged. "He'll destroy everything."

"It's for your own good," Jonathan insisted. "I'll go to Dr. Luke; I'll try my best to explain it to him. I'm sure he'll know a good psychiatrist. And he'll be discreet."

"You haven't been listening to me," Sarah said quietly, her eyes bright with an unearthly glow.

"You can't tell Uncle Luke," Martin insisted. "Think of Sarah."

"I am thinking of her. That's more than you've done."

This seemed to enrage Sarah. "Don't you ever say that to him," she shouted. "He's been protecting me all my life."

"How? By sleeping with you?"

"I wanted him. I loved him and I still do."

"That's why you need help, and I'm going to get it for you."

Jonathan started to run toward the steps.

"Sarah," Martin implored.

Her eyes started to shine more brightly than ever. She saw it all now. He had no intentions of getting any concrete. He was going to tell Uncle Luke; he was going to have her and Martin separated and sent away. She'd never see Martin again; she'd never see Cherron.

In her anger she summoned up all her strength and reached out.

Jonathan had run halfway up the stairs when he felt the thrust of a great invisible hand pushing, pushing him down the stairs. He resisted, lowering his body and attempting to charge at the invisible force with the strength of his shoulders, but it was no use. He slipped, or was pushed, and rolled down the hard, cold stone steps, coming to a stop at the foot of the stairs. Sarah and Martin were standing over him.

"You can't leave here, Jonathan," Sarah said. "No one must ever know what goes on in this house. Ever."

He struggled to his feet. "You used your power on me, didn't you? After you said you wouldn't."

"You lied to me."

He saw the glow in her eyes now, the awful unearthly shine.

In her rage she began to make the Limoges plates float into the air and smash against the stone walls. Jonathan watched in fascination and horror as she managed to destroy the entire tableau in a matter of minutes. Bodies flew around the room, colliding with each other, but they were so dried that the lifeless hair and skin would fly into the air as they disintegrated on impact. The air was full of the sound of shattering china and crystal and the crunching of dry bones.

She really did have the power, he realized.

She turned around to look at him. "So now you believe me, don't you. You see what I can do?"

She was furious because she had read his mind and she knew that, up until now, he had not believed in her special powers.

The girl's eyes glowed brighter than ever and to Jonathan they looked like the eyes of some awful night-monster. The beautiful Miss Sarah had completely changed into this terrifying figure with the power of death in her eyes.

That was it, the eyes. If he only could control her eyes he would be free. He moved towards her, but Martin grabbed him by the arms. He struggled to break free while she laughed. She was surrounded now by the wreckage of the mummified bodies and the elegant ruins of the room.

The fire still crackled in the fireplace. Jonathan saw the fireplace poker. If only he could reach it. If only he could break away from Martin for just a minute, while his mind was still his own.

"Fire! Is that what you want?" she laughed. She had read his thoughts. "Here's a fire."

Laughing, she stared at the rug at his feet. It burst into flames. But his own clothes did not burn.

"They won't burn because I don't want them to burn," she explained. "In spite of everything, I don't want to hurt you, but you're forcing me to."

The fire from the rug was beginning to spread to the rest of the room. The dried clothing of the mummies was highly flammable, and the room began to fill with thick black smoke.

Miss Sarah had gone too far.

She didn't realize what was happening at first, only that her eyes were tearing from the smoke. She was having trouble focusing because of the tears. She raised a hand to try to brush away the tears.

"Sarah, are you all right?" Martin asked, releasing Jonathan and moving towards his cousin.

Jonathan realized immediately what was happening. It was her eyes. If she couldn't see because of the smoke and the tearing, she would be helpless. He simply stood there, watching, as the strength, the glow, ebbed away from the whites of her eyes.

But he couldn't stand there forever; the room was thick with black smoke. He was beginning to cough. They were doomed, all three of them, if they didn't make a run for it soon. They were trapped in a boiling inferno that had taken on a strange, mystic atmosphere. Everything was weaving around slowly, swirling and moving before his very eyes as the heat rose up to engulf them. He struggled against the feeling. He had to get out of there.

He looked around. Sarah and Martin had completely disappeared into the thick black smoke.

"Sarah!" he yelled. "Where are you? I can't see you!"

"Help, somebody, help," she moaned. She too, realized what had happened.

"Take my hand, take my hand," someone called out in the midst of the inferno. A disembodied hand appeared in the dark smoke. Her eyes burned and watered and she wondered, just for a second, if this was what hell was like.

"Martin," she called. "Jonathan." She began to cough uncontrollably. She couldn't see either of the men as she called out their names. She was helpless. For the first time since she was a little girl she was helpless.

She felt the panic rise within her; her heart was beating wildly. She was losing consciousness. Still holding tightly onto the stranger's hand, she collapsed onto the floor.

"Ashes to ashes, dust to dust. From that which we have been made, so we return. Let us pray."

The assembled mourners lowered their heads.

"A young and tender life has been lost, O Lord, and I commend this soul into God's firm hand. May it rest in peace."

The graveside service was concluded and the mourners slowly made their way from the Bankroft cemetery. Old Jeremiah, dressed in a dark suit out of respect for the occasion, shook his head sadly and threw a red rose into the open grave. Regina Quillam, heavily veiled, stood by with the sad-looking McEndrews. There were many people from the town there, the women dabbing at their misty eyes, the men shaking their heads in disbelief. Soon they were all gone.

It was a nice day for a funeral, though. The sun shone brightly, and Cherron, in spite of the damage from the fire, had rarely looked better. Miss Sarah's beloved rose garden was in full bloom and the magnolias and jasmine scented the air of the little family cemetery.

Luke Bankroft shook the Reverend Marbury's hand and thanked him for the service.

"Such a tragic thing to happen," the reverend said sadly.

"I can hardly believe it myself," the old man muttered. "Sometimes, reverend, I think there's a curse on the Bankrofts. I really do."

"It's God's will, Luke. You must go on from here."

"But so many tragedies in one family."

"Try to pull yourself together, Luke."

They both headed back to town in thoughtful silence.

Most of the damage from the fire had been confined to the basement and the great staircase above it. Now the house was alive with repairmen hurrying about like ants.

Jessica Morrow and her son sat in the kitchen, staring at each other across the table. They could hear the painters and carpenters laughing with each other, and occasionally one would pass through the kitchen, smile, nod, perhaps ask for a glass of water, and be gone. Sometimes a worker might even give a second thought to the sad-looking mother and son who just sat there, gazing at each other blankly. But that would be all.

Upstairs, in this particular bedroom, there was no sign of the havoc wrought by the fire. The canopied bed was covered with a white lace spread, and sunlight streamed through the open French windows. A small mockingbird came to rest on the balcony and serenaded the occupants with its imitation of a bluebird's song.

Miss Sarah entered with a breakfast tray. She was still dressed for the funeral, but black was a becoming color for her: it set off her flawless, magnolia-like complexion, her blond hair, and her bright blue eyes. She put down the tray and began to fluff the pillows for her patient.

"It's been quite a day," Jonathan said as he propped himself up in the bed. "Was it bad?"

"I've seen worse. But it was not as bad as last night," she said. "It's just that I hate funerals."

Jonathan patted the bed beside him and Sarah sat down.

"You think he's happy now?"

"Yes, I hope so. He deserves happiness."

"Poor Martin. You know, I miss him already? And when I think of how hard you cried when you woke up in the hospital and they told you he was dead. . . ."

"It's all right," she insisted. "I kept my promise to him. He's still here at Cherron and he's still with me."

"It should have been I who died."

"Shhh. Don't talk foolishly." She buttered an English muffin and handed it to him.

"I promise you, Sarah, I'll make it up to you."

"I know you will. Lord, it was so hot out there today."

"Sarah, you won't ever make me leave you, will you?" Since the fire, the idea of being separated from her frightened him. He couldn't bear to think about it. "I want to stay with you always."

"And you will, darling."

She poured them each a cup of coffee, and handed Jonathan his. As he sipped it he thought again about last night.

"Have you thought about what we're going to do to your aunt Jessica and Devon?"

For the first time this morning her eyes flashed angrily.

"Imagine those two standing out there on the front lawn, listening to our screams, and not lifting a hand to help us. They didn't even call the fire department. They wanted us to die."

"I know," he said gently.

"No one should have perished in that fire. Martin could have been saved if they had helped."

"They're totally responsible," he agreed.

She looked out at the green lawn and watched the singing bird. How lovely it was, she thought, Cherron was truly an Eden. It was a shame that she had to share it with two people who hated her, who seemed to want her dead.

"What will we do, Sarah? Will you use your power to punish them?"

"I have to think about it. They deserve something very special for what they did, something very special, indeed."

"I can't wait to help you."

"If it hadn't been for Jeremiah, you and I would be dead too. Imagine him pulling us out like that. If he hadn't come when he did, the whole house might have burned down."

"We should reward him for that."

"Yes, a special reward. I'll have to think about that as well."

"We were very lucky that everything burned up so quickly. They could never tell anything from those ashes."

"No," she agreed. "And thank goodness we managed to save the fish."

"Have you fed them yet?"

"No, I'll wait until the workmen leave. As far as they're concerned, they're just ordinary gray fish."

"I love you so much, Sarah. Promise I'll always be here at Cherron with you."

She was staring at the small bowl of roses on the breakfast tray.

"Regina Quillam spoke to me at the services this morning, Jonathan."

"I couldn't bear the thought of leaving you, ever."

"She said she had something she wanted to talk to me about."

"I want to be here in this bed with you forever."

"And you will, darling," she said, leaning over to kiss him. "But there will always be people who are jealous of our happiness; I realize that now. And we will have to deal with them when they come along."

"I wish Martin were here with us," he went on sadly. "I know now that I could have shared you with him because it's what you wanted. I'm sorry to have caused so much trouble over something so trivial."

"Regina said she knew something strange was going on here."

"It was foolish of me to be so angry at him for loving you as much as I do."

"I think I'll invite Regina Quillam for tea. She's always wanted to see the inside of Cherron and I'll give her a chance. Perhaps I'll call her today."

"After all, it's impossible for any man not to love you."

"She had a nasty look in her eyes. And she looks just terrible with that awful, peeling skin. She's all covered in veils now, but I could still see, of course. Somehow, I think she blames me for her troubles."

"Anyone would love you, anyone at all."

"Yes, I'll invite her here as soon as the repairmen are finished. I'll give her a complete tour of everything in the house. I'll even show her our pets."

Jonathan smiled and nodded his head in agreement.

"She wouldn't dare come between us, would she, Sarah?"

"No, darling. No one will ever come between us."

He held her in his arms. He belonged to her now, body and soul.

SOMETHING FOR EVERYONE—
BEST SELLERS FROM ZEBRA!

FRIENDS   **(645, $2.25)**
by Elieba Levine
Edith and Sarah had been friends for thirty years, sharing all their secrets and fantasies. No one ever thought that a bond as close as theirs could be broken . . . but now underneath the friendship and love is jealousy, anger, and hate.

EPIDEMIC!   **(644, $2.50)**
by Larry R. Leichter, M.D.
From coast to coast, beach to beach, the killer virus spread. Diagnosed as a strain of meningitis, it did not respond to treatment—and no one could stop it from becoming the world's most terrifying epidemic!

ALL THE WAY   **(571, $2.25)**
by Felice Buckvar
After over twenty years of devotion to another man, Phyllis finds herself helplessly in love, once again, with that same tall, handsome high school sweetheart who had loved her . . . ALL THE WAY.

RHINELANDER PAVILLION   **(572, $2.50)**
by Barbara Harrison
Rhinelander Pavillion was a big city hospital pulsating with the constant struggles of life and death. Its dedicated staff of overworked professionals were caught up in the unsteady charts of their own passions and desires—yet they all needed medicine to survive.

Available wherever paperbacks are sold, or order direct from the Publisher. Send cover price plus 50¢ per copy for mailing and handling to Zebra Books, 21 East 40th Street, New York, N.Y. 10016. DO NOT SEND CASH!

FICTION FOR TODAY'S WOMAN

THE FOREVER PASSION   **(563, $2.50)**
by Karen A. Bale
A passionate, compelling story of how a young woman, made
hostage by a band of Comanche warriors, becomes captivated by
Nakon—the tribe's leader.

THE RIVER OF FORTUNE: THE PASSION   **(561, $2.50)**
by Arthur Moore
When the beautiful Andrea Berlanger and her beloved Logan leave
their homes to begin a new life together, they discover the true
meaning of love, life and desire on a Mississippi Riverboat and the
great . . . RIVER OF FORTUNE.

BELLA   **(498, $2.50)**
by William Black
A heart-warming family saga of an immigrant woman who comes
to America at the turn of the century and fights her way to the top of
the fashion world.

BELLA'S BLESSINGS   **(562, $2.50)**
by William Black
From the Roaring Twenties to the dark Depression years. Three
generations of an unforgettable family—their passions, triumphs
and tragedies.

MIRABEAU PLANTATION   **(596, $2.50)**
by Marcia Meredith
Crystal must rescue her plantation from its handsome holder even
at the expense of losing his love. A sweeping plantation novel about
love, war, and a passion that would never die.

---

*Available wherever paperbacks are sold, or direct from the
Publisher. Send cover price plus 50¢ per copy for mailing and
handling to Zebra Books, 21 East 40th Street, New York, N.Y.
10016. DO NOT SEND CASH!*

BESTSELLERS FOR TODAY'S WOMAN

THE VOW (653, $2.50)
by Maria B. Fogelin
On the verge of marriage, a young woman is tragically blinded and mangled in a car accident. Struggling against tremendous odds to survive, she finds the courage to live, but will she ever find the courage to love?

FRIENDS (645, $2.25)
by Elieba Levine
Edith and Sarah had been friends for thirty years, sharing all their secrets and fantasies. No one ever thought that a bond as close as theirs could be broken . . . but now underneath the friendship and love is jealousy, anger, and hate.

CHARGE NURSE (663, $2.50)
by Patricia Rae
Kay Strom was Charge Nurse in the Intensive Care Unit and was trained to deal with the incredible pressures of life-and-death situations. But the one thing she couldn't handle was her passionate emotions . . . when she found herself falling in love with two different men!

RHINELANDER PAVILLION (572, $2.50)
by Barbara Harrison
Rhinelander Pavillion was a big city hospital pulsating with the constant struggles of life and death. Its dedicated staff of overworked professionals were caught up in the unsteady charts of their own passions and desires—yet they all needed medicine to survive.

Available wherever paperbacks are sold, or order direct from the Publisher. Send cover price plus 50¢ per copy for mailing and handling to Zebra Books, 21 East 40th Street, New York, N.Y. 10016. DO NOT SEND CASH!